THE CHOCOLATIER OF HIDEAWAY BAY

Hideaway Bay Book 6

MICHELE BROUDER

Editing by Jessica Peirce

Book Cover Design by Rebecca Ruger

PART ONE

Valerie

CHAPTER ONE

Valerie

May 5th

V ALERIE FISHER SMILED AT her former colleagues gathered around the table at her favorite restaurant in downtown Denver, Colorado. Even though she'd been downsized from her job months earlier, her coworkers had called her and insisted on taking her out for her birthday.

She'd initially dragged her feet about joining them. With twenty-five years of service at her government job, she'd been able to retire early, but she'd been inert since then. Florence, however, had wheedled and cajoled and refused to take no for an answer, despite all the different excuses Val had rattled off.

There was amiable chatter amongst the group, the sound of Annmarie's chortle reaching all the way down to Val's end of the table. Jonathon was entertaining those around him with some story about buying eggplant at the local farmer's market. At Val's feet sat a variety of gift bags and small boxes. She smiled, thinking how lucky she'd been to work with such a great group of people. Their thoughtfulness had touched her. It was nice to be remembered. She was glad she'd accepted their invitation.

"Any special plans for your birthday, Val?" Florence asked.

"Next year's the big one!" Jonathon said, his eyes widening in reference to Val turning fifty in another year.

"I don't know," Val said with a smile. "I'm sure Jeff has something planned."

"That's so romantic," Annmarie crooned, clasping her hands in front of her chest. "To still be surprised after so many years of marriage."

Val plastered on a smile and thought, *If you only knew.*

Pretty soon, chairs were pushed back, scraping the floor as everyone stood to leave, their lunch hour over.

"You're so lucky you don't have to go back to the pit," Jonathon said, rolling his eyes.

Yes, that's me. Lucky.

He helped her carry out her gifts to her car in the parking lot next to the restaurant, and she tucked them safely into the back seat.

She hugged everyone goodbye, thanking them, her eyes filling with tears.

"I really miss you guys!" she said.

"Enough to come back to work?" Florence asked with a teasing grin.

Val cracked a laugh. "Not that much."

She waved them all off as they made their way to their cars. Hers was the last one out of the lot, following behind them single file. They all turned left and headed back toward the federal building where they worked, while Val turned right, heading in the direction of home. As she drove, she wondered if Jeff really did have anything planned for her birthday, but somehow, she doubted it.

May 7th

Valerie stood facing the kitchen table, illuminated by the soft glow of the lit birthday candles. Jeff hadn't fussed too much. Four pink candles stood evenly around the top of the cake, their flames high.

Forty-nine.

When had that happened? And fifty next year?

An unfamiliar churning gripped her stomach and as much as she loved birthday cake, she wasn't sure if she could get it down.

Beside her, Jeff sang "Happy Birthday" off-key.

They were having cake early and then dinner would be later in the day. Jeff had asked if they could do the cake before the start of the afternoon baseball game. Apparently, it was just another day for her husband.

She stared at the candles, the wax beginning to creep down the sides of them and dot the frosting with little pink specks. Jeff finished the first song and launched into "How Old Are You?"—again off-key, in his own arrangement of high notes and low notes, ending each line with a double clap of his hands. Behind the cake stood a vase of gas station flowers he had picked up earlier, a mixture of carnations and daisies and one lone red rose.

He tries, she told herself.

The singing stopped and Jeff clapped his hands again. "Make a wish!" he encouraged. "Go on."

She looked at him and hesitated before closing her eyes and blowing the candles out in one breath.

She did not make a wish.

Quietly, she cut the cake, using the serrated knife to slice through the dense layers.

She'd just plopped the first slice onto a small plate when her phone rang. She set the knife down and picked up her phone, an automatic smile emerging on her face.

Jeremy, her oldest.

"Hi, honey," Valerie said as she answered.

"Happy Birthday, Mom!" he said. The background noise sounded like a crowd of people.

"Where are you?" she asked.

"We're out watching the baseball game," he shouted over the crowd. *Like father like son.*

"Oh . . ." Valerie said, her voice trailing off.

Out of the corner of her eye, she caught Jeff gesturing to her, holding up the plate of cake and pointing to the family room. She thinned her lips. *Couldn't he wait until I got off the phone? And the first piece traditionally goes to the birthday person.* But she nodded anyway. What did it matter?

"What did you do for your birthday?" Jeremy asked. Their oldest had moved to the East Coast after college four years earlier, working as a chemical engineer.

"Nothing special," she said. She wanted to add "Just another day," but didn't want pity. She looked around the empty kitchen. The countertops were clutter free and the floor shone after the mopping she'd given it yesterday. That was a treat for herself: a clean house. She'd spent all day Saturday working on it.

"I got you a gift, but it'll be late," Jeremy said.

Was it that hard to get someone a gift on time for their birthday? "No problem," she said, but her response was lost as he spoke to someone in the background.

"Have you heard from Renee?" he asked, referring to his younger sister.

Valerie nodded and smiled. "She called first thing this morning." Renee, an artist, lived in France, not far from where Val's grandmother was born.

Jeremy sighed, exasperation evident. "Her and her need to be first."

Valerie could practically hear him grinding his teeth. "I don't know. I think it's kind of nice."

When he didn't say anything, she added, "Maybe you're upset that she beat you to it."

"As if," he scoffed.

That hurt. But she didn't know why. She glanced at the beautiful overlarge floral bouquet her daughter had had delivered yesterday. It took up a large part of the countertop. Renee had spent a lot of money. Maybe men were different from women when it came to remembering birthdays and giving presents. And maybe she was too sensitive.

"Have you decided whether you're coming home at all this summer?" she asked Jeremy, hopeful. He'd mentioned it when he came to visit at Christmas. She'd been looking forward to seeing him.

"Um . . ." Jeremy hesitated.

"Uh-oh," Valerie said.

"Actually, a group of us were thinking of going to Costa Rica for a few weeks," he said hurriedly. There was an uptick in volume behind him, the shouts becoming a roar.

Before she could respond, Jeremy said, "Look, Mom, I've got to go. Have a great birthday!"

"Thanks, honey—"

But he was gone.

Val stared at the screen and sighed. She stood for a moment, thinking, looking around the kitchen and at her birthday cake in the middle of the table. She placed the plastic dome over the cake, snapping the edges into place, then gathered her purse, jacket, and keys and popped her head into the doorway of the family room.

"I'm going out for a bit," she said.

Jeff didn't turn around. Didn't look up. Didn't even ask where she was going. He raised his hand and said over his shoulder, "Okay." On the coffee table in front of him sat his mostly empty plate, only crumbs and a scrape of frosting left behind.

Who doesn't finish frosting?

The day was bright and warm for May. Val pulled her car through the wrought iron gate of the Mount Calvary cemetery five miles from her home, decreased her speed, and looked around the place. The dense green grass was short, looking as if it had recently been cut. She drove slowly past the mausoleum off to her left. Further on, a woman knelt on kneepads and clipped the grass around an inlaid headstone with a pair of garden shears. An elderly man carried a bouquet of roses to the grave he visited, his gait slow and lumbering. As she pulled the car over to the verge of the grass to park, she spotted the fresh burial mound of a recent arrival. By the looks of the mass of flowers covering the grave that were starting to go off, she concluded the person had been buried within the last few days.

She peered around and tucked her purse beneath the seat and out of view, then stepped out of the car and strolled through the rows between the tombstones and headstones, the grass soggy from recent rainfall. She knew every inscription on every grave on her route to her parents' final resting place.

There they were up ahead: *Jean-Paul Brandt. Marjorie Brandt.* Her parents' headstones were simple: rectangular salmon-colored granite with the names etched in black. They were a little off-center. Her father had predeceased her mother by fifteen years from early onset Alzheimer's, and time had slightly tilted his headstone. She stood for a few minutes at their graves. Despite frequent visits, she did not feel their presence there, as hard as she tried. What she felt was their absence.

"I miss you, Mom and Dad," she whispered as she swiped away a tear. She stuffed her hands in her pockets and walked on. The graves belonging to her paternal grandparents were a few rows back.

The most important people from her past, her parents and grandparents, were gone and were from a time when she'd had plans for her life. Now here she was, on the cusp of fifty with no dreams realized. Marriage and motherhood had been the most important things to her but in that priority, she'd sacrificed her sense of self. Not that she regretted it. If she had to do it all over again, she would probably make the same choices. But now that her kids were grown and gone and she was retired, she felt as if her life had no meaning.

The headstone at her grandparents' grave was an elaborate affair with a weeping angel. She smiled at it. Her grandfather had had it commissioned after her grandmother's death. Where he'd gotten the money, she never knew. He'd always been a dreamer. A bit unorthodox, but she couldn't help but smile at the memories of him.

She bent down and traced her fingers along her grandmother's name: *Delphine Giroud Brandt.* Of the four, her grandmother had been the first one to go. Val had been twenty-one and away at college when her father called her in her dorm room.

Abruptly, she stood, deciding she didn't want to think about that day. How everything had changed suddenly. How her compass had been lost. To this day, she couldn't think about chocolate without thinking about her grandmother. Her grandmother had been a chocolatier and although she hadn't had a shop of her own, she'd been successful, running a cottage industry right out of her kitchen. Those had been happy days when she'd stood alongside her grandmother as a child, making truffles and other chocolate candy. And Nana had been so encouraging, always telling her she was the best helper and that someday, she'd be a happy chocolatier too. Interesting choice of words, Val mused. Not the greatest chocolatier or a successful chocolatier, but a happy one.

She wished she'd paid more attention, wished she remembered how to create the delectable confections her grandmother had made. Her memory was vague but there were some things about the creation of chocolate that had stayed with her. But as hard as she'd tried over the years, using her own kitchen as a test kitchen, her attempts felt off.

Her grandmother had moved from her village in France to the United States after World War II when she'd married Val's grandfather. They'd moved around a lot before eventually settling in Colorado. But the one place Nana had spoken of more than any other was a little town called Hideaway Bay in New York. She'd made no secret of the fact that of all the places they'd lived, Hideaway Bay had been her favorite. Not for the first time, Val wondered why.

If only Nana were still here! She had so many questions to ask her.

She swallowed hard, pivoted, and walked quickly back to her car.

She slid in and buckled up and started the engine, letting it idle as she rolled down the window. Leaning back in the seat, she closed her eyes, revisiting old hopes and dreams. Things had not turned out like she'd thought they would. More than half her life was over and aside from raising two good kids, she wasn't happy with it. She'd always thought there'd be more in the way of satisfaction.

After a while, she opened her eyes, threw the car in drive, and headed in the direction of home. But halfway there, she took a detour and stopped at a candy store off the main street of their town, a place noted for their chocolate.

As soon as she opened the door and stepped through, she was assailed with the sweet, heady aroma and her mouth watered. A customer stood at the cash register, checking out and making small talk with the attendant, and another patron browsed a side table loaded with various gift sets.

Valerie couldn't help but smile. This kind of chocolate always reminded her of Nana. She leaned over slightly and peered through the glass case, gaping at the assortment of truffles and soft centers. There were glossy, shiny squares of chocolate with sharp corners, and round pieces with dome-like tops. Perfectly round truffles covered in dustings of cocoa powder or tiny coconut flakes or sprinkles of gold leaf.

"May I help you?" asked a middle-aged woman behind the counter. Her foundation had caked in the creases of her face, and her lipstick bled from the edges of her lips. But Valerie thought she was the luckiest woman on earth to be able to work in a shop like this.

"Yes, I'd like a box of twenty-four please," Val said with a smile.

The woman, whose name tag read "Joanne," took a silver foil box and looked expectantly at Val.

"What will you have?"

Val eyed the almond brittle but decided to get that next time. "I'd like a box of truffles. Can I have four each of the milk chocolate, the whiskey, amaretto, strawberries and cream, and champagne?"

"You sure can," Joanne said. "You need to pick one more flavor."

"Oh, gosh, I do," Val said, scanning the display. She lifted her head and said, "You know what? Surprise me."

The attendant smiled. Val looked away, not wanting to see what she picked. At her age, there were so few surprises left in her life that she had to take them where she found them.

When finished, Joanne placed the cover on the silver foil box and wrapped it in a gauzy pink bow. When Joanne totaled up her order, Val did not flinch at the price for the luxury chocolates. This was her birthday present to herself.

Handing over her debit card, she said casually, "My grandmother used to be a chocolatier."

"Really?" Joanne said, eyebrows raised.

It was all the opening Val needed. "Yes. She was from France. She learned the trade from her mother, who learned it from her own mother before her."

Joanne handed back Val's card and a gift bag containing her box of chocolates. "Years ago, before I opened this place"—here her glance swept around the interior of the shop—"I did a course with a renowned chocolatier over in France, just outside of Paris."

"Really?" A twinge of envy went through Val.

"It was expensive, but it was the best thing I ever did for myself and my business." Joanne tilted her head, narrowed her eyes and said, "Know what I mean?"

"I do, actually."

"And are you a chocolatier, too?" Joanne asked.

Val shook her head. "Sadly not." She sighed. "I wish, though."

"It's never too late," Joanne pronounced.

Val thought it was indeed too late. No longer wishing to pursue the topic, she lifted up the bag and said, "Thank you so much."

"Enjoy."

She wandered around the shop for a few minutes, the bag in her hand, looking at the merchandise, picking things up here and there and studying them.

After a few minutes, she left, ready to go home, suddenly tired.

Jeff was right where she left him, his eyes glued to the television as the game played, his arms folded behind his head.

"You're back already?" he asked without turning around.

"I am," she said.

She stepped into the pantry and pulled out one of the drawers and hid the box of candy in there, folding up the bag neatly and tucking it with the other bags she saved. This hidden chocolate was a guilty pleasure all her own. She didn't know why she hid it; maybe she was being childish in not wanting to share it with Jeff.

As she closed the pantry door behind her, Jeff called out, "What time are you ordering takeout?"

"Do you want me to do it?" she asked, hoping he'd take the hint.

"Yeah, sure. The usual for me," he said.

"Okay." It was a rule that she didn't cook on her birthday; she'd done enough of that in her lifetime. But she'd hoped her husband would be able to pick up the phone himself and order the food. She exhaled deeply.

They ordered from a local Italian restaurant, and it was always the same: chicken alfredo for her and eggplant parmesan for him, with toasted garlic bread topped with melted mozzarella cheese. Not wanting to have to go and collect their order, she paid extra for delivery.

Halfway through their meal, Jeff sat with his head bent, his fork moving back and forth between his plate and his mouth.

Val poured herself more red wine and sipped from her glass.

"Jeff, are you happy?"

He lifted his head with a look of surprise as if he'd forgotten she was there. "Huh?"

"Are you happy?"

"Yeah, sure," he said with a shrug.

"Don't you ever get the feeling we're drifting?" That was how she felt: afloat with no sense of direction.

"I'm perfectly okay with drifting toward the family room each night after work to watch TV," he cracked.

Val emitted a heavy sigh. How on earth did other married couples manage to stay together for so long when one spouse grew and evolved and the other one didn't? It boggled her mind. Was there some sort of uneasy truce in those marriages?

"I mean, are you happy with us? Our marriage?" she pressed.

"Yes," he said, nodding.

It wasn't lost on her that he didn't ask her the same questions in return. *Probably too afraid of my answer.*

She picked up her plate and carried it over to the sink, where she scraped the remnants into the garbage can. Without another word or a look in the direction of her husband, she left the room.

❧

She dreamt of Nana that night.

Her grandmother stood behind a counter in a shop similar to the one Val had visited earlier that day. In the dream, Val watched her moving about in that little puttering shuffle of hers. But she was younger looking than Val remembered. Gone was the gray hair—instead Nana had a glorious crown of auburn, similar to what Val had seen in early photographs. Nana was busy filling the glass cases with chocolates, but Val couldn't see where all the chocolate was coming from. It seemed endless. Nana looked at her and smiled and said, "The time is now, Val."

CHAPTER TWO

"YOU SLEPT WELL LAST night," Jeff said the following morning. It was more a statement than a question.

"Yes."

"That's good."

It was. Since menopause had started, she'd been prone to sleepless nights, lying awake several nights a week for hours at a time. She'd tried both prescription meds and over-the-counter sleep aids, but they left her feeling groggy and hungover. There'd been none of the hot flashes her friends complained about, or the intense anger that had given some of them a feeling of homicidal rage. That was something to be thankful for, she supposed, but it was hard to feel grateful when her sleepless nights left her dragging and drowsy all day.

She scrolled through her phone, reading the latest news. Her coffee had grown cold in front of her.

"Anything I can do?" Jeff asked.

She responded with a tight smile and shook her head.

He appeared to hesitate, thumping his forefinger on the table, stalling as if he wanted to say something.

Val glanced at the clock on the wall, silently hinting that he might be late for work.

"I'll see you at dinner," he said quietly.

There was a quick nod of acknowledgement, and she returned her attention to her phone. The whole day was stretched out before her. But she hadn't a clue as to what she might like to do with it.

Two days after Val's birthday, her younger brother, Chuck, phoned her.

"Happy belated birthday, sis!" His voice was full of excitement despite what she guessed was a serious case of jet lag. In his last text, he'd told her he was going to London and Japan for business and would be gone for her birthday. But enthusiasm was Chuck's default nature. Simply hearing his voice made her smile.

"Hey, Chuck," she said. "How've you been? Are you back home in Florida? How are Dee and the girls?"

"Yep, I'm back. Dee's good. I don't know how the girls are because they're teenagers now and I never know what kind of mood they're going to be in. So I try to keep the questions to a minimum."

She could practically see him smiling on the other end of the line. It took a lot to ruffle Jeff's feathers. "Ah, I remember how that used to be." No sense in admitting to him that she missed those years. Looking back, they didn't seem all that bad. Renee had been moody, and Jeremy had been private and complained that she asked too many questions. She'd go back in a heartbeat.

"How's your gang?" he asked.

"They are all well. Nothing new."

"Good. How's retirement going?"

Val grimaced even though he couldn't see it. With a sigh, she said, "It's going."

"Uh-oh, what are you not saying?"

A smile broke out on her face. "I'm adjusting. Trying to figure out what to do with the rest of my life."

Chuck was quiet for a moment before he spoke. "You know, you've been given a gift. Not many people get a second chance at life at this young an age."

She hadn't thought of it like that. And she certainly didn't want to sound ungrateful. But in all her wildest dreams of retirement, she'd never thought boredom would be her biggest problem.

"How long have you been home now?" he asked. "Two months? Three months?"

"Almost three."

"You know what you need, Val?"

"Please don't tell me I need to get a hobby," she griped. She did not want to fill her time with mindless activity. Next, they'd be dropping her off at an adult daycare center.

Chuck laughed. "No, not at all. You need purpose."

"A purpose," she repeated.

"Everybody does. You need a reason to get out of bed every morning. Something you're passionate about."

"I do?"

"Yes, Val."

"Nana's been on my mind a lot recently," she blurted.

"Really?"

"I dreamt of her the other night. It was so real," Val explained.

"I sure miss her candy! That stuff was decadent!" he said.

"I do too."

"I don't think I've ever tasted chocolate like that again," he said wistfully.

"Me neither." She paused. "Remember how she used to talk about Hideaway Bay?"

He snorted. "When did she ever stop talking about it?"

"I know, right?"

"It must have been some place," he mused. "She talked about it her whole life."

"That she did," Val said. "Did she ever say why they left?"

"Not that I can recall. Besides, I was a kid and only half paying attention. I was more interested in the chocolate."

"Me too."

"It's too bad we don't have her journals. They might have given you some answers," Chuck said.

Val blinked. "What did you say?"

"Her journals. Nana kept journals while she lived in Hideaway Bay."

"She did?" Why was this news to her? Or had her grandmother mentioned it to her and like her brother, she'd been more interested in the chocolate. "How do I not know this?" Her heart was all aflutter.

"She never said anything to you about it?" Surprise laced his voice.

"No, never," she said.

"Yeah, she used to tell me if I ever went to Hideaway Bay to get her stuff."

"Really?"

"She said, and remember this is from my childhood so take from it what you will, that the journals were beneath the floorboards of the living room of the house they used to live in."

"Stop it!" she said excitedly.

"That's what I remember," he said.

"Why didn't she take them with her?" she asked.

"That's a good question. If she left them behind, maybe they left at the last minute or something."

"Maybe." It wasn't outside the realm of possibilities. Their grandparents had led a nomadic existence in the earlier years of their marriage, settling in one place and then picking up and moving on. Valerie had always suspected it had something to do with her grandfather. Nothing she could put her finger on, but it was what her gut told her.

Valerie squinted through the darkness at the luminescent hands on her bedside clock. Two-thirty. Ugh. She'd be dragging all day long. *Cheer up*, she told herself. *It's not like you have anywhere to be tomorrow or anything to do.*

She turned over again, fluffing her pillow, trying in vain to find a comfortable spot. Beside her, Jeff snored lightly. It wasn't enough to keep her awake or even to have disturbed her sleep, but it aggravated her nonetheless.

The trick was not to start thinking about anything, to keep her mind vague so she could drift off, but that was difficult to do.

She replayed Jeff's answers to her questions at breakfast the day before. How could he be happy? She was unhappy and dissatisfied. They barely spoke to one another. Sure, they were civil and courteous, but it was strictly superficial. They no longer did anything together, and forget about sex or any form of intimacy. In the past, their sex life had been good. She'd always thought it was an important aspect of any marriage. But in the past few years, it was like someone had flicked a switch off inside her. The desire was no longer there. And despite the different medications and hormone treatments, she'd never been able to get it back. It was as if it had packed its bags and left. This saddened her, because she missed that aspect of her life.

She and Jeff felt more like roommates than husband and wife. It had been like this for a long time now. The kids had moved out, leaving them alone in the house for the first time in years. And they hadn't handled it well. She'd asked him several times if he'd be interested in marriage counseling, and his response had always been the same: he didn't want to discuss their private business with a complete stranger. When she'd last asked him about going to couples' therapy—back in January—his one-word reply had been "Maybe," and that had left her frustrated and confused.

She rolled over onto her belly, stretching her arms above her beneath the pillow, and tried to think instead about the dream of Nana and to make sense of it. But that only got her thinking about chocolate, and she couldn't settle down. After half an hour she gave up, flipped back the covers, and slid her legs out of the bed, feeling around on the floor for her slippers. Jeff remained undisturbed on his side of the bed.

She padded to the kitchen, wide awake, throwing on the switch and casting the room in light. A cup of tea was called for. While the kettle boiled, she went into the pantry and pulled the box of candy from the bottom drawer.

Cup of tea in hand, she carried the box over to the kitchen table and got comfortable. She removed the gauzy pink ribbon from the box, smiling. She surveyed the contents, unable to re-member which one was which, and picked one randomly and popped it into her mouth, leaving a fine coat of cocoa dusting powder on her fingertips. Closing her eyes, she groaned. She took a sip of the hot tea to melt the truffle on her tongue.

It was wonderful. It wasn't the same as her grandmother's phenomenal chocolate, but it was a close substitute. She helped herself to four more pieces, unable to decide which one was her favorite.

She returned the box to the drawer and before she turned off the pantry light, she spotted the candy-making equipment she'd purchased down through the years. When she'd first purchased the items, they'd occupied space on the lower shelves, front and center. It had been a happy hobby that she enjoyed occasionally, especially when the kids were little and making chocolate for them for various holidays had been her thing. She'd even tried to get them interested in it, but that had failed. They were interested in eating it, but that's where it had ended. But as the years went on, the equipment was parked on higher shelves, out of the way. After Jeremy and Renee left to pursue their own lives, it landed at its final destination: the top shelf, which required a step stool to reach it. A shelf for things rarely or never used.

In the top left-hand corner stood a stack of heavy molds, a couple of palette knives, and a variety of spatulas. There was a candy thermometer still in its packaging, and piping bags and nozzles. Shoved to the back, she knew, were a sturdy balloon whisk, a metal bench scraper, candy dipping forks, and chocolate transfer and texture sheets, among other things. She could still remember the excitement that gripped her when she'd purchased the items, thinking she was following in Nana's footsteps. But she really hadn't. All she'd done was clutter her pantry with things she no longer used.

Overcome with melancholy, she flipped off the light in the pantry and closed the door behind her. She picked up her teacup and carried it to the family room. Usually, she'd put on the television, but she didn't feel like that. The idea of doing some laundry or other housework occurred to her, but she immediately dismissed it.

She picked up the paperback she was currently reading but put it down after reading a page. She leaned against the soft cushions of the sofa and laid her head back, closed her eyes, and let out a yawn.

How she wished her grandmother were here to give her direction, to guide her like she'd done when Val was young. Guidance coupled with unconditional love. It was hard not to miss someone who loved you no matter what, who loved you on the basis of you being you. There were so many questions she wanted to ask Nana about her recipes and life in general. She wished she'd paid more attention when Nana was making chocolate. Wished she had written things down, taken notes.

The conversation with her brother replayed in her mind. The thought that Nana had left journals behind in Hideaway Bay intrigued her. The voice of reason told her that the chance of them still existing was slim given that Nana had lived there over sixty years ago.

She spent the next few hours thinking of her life, examining it and making some decisions. Nothing was going to change if she didn't make some changes herself.

"I don't understand," Jeff said quietly.

He'd finished his dinner and had plopped down on the sofa in the family room and reached for the remote on the coffee table. Val had eaten earlier. She liked to eat her main meal by two in the afternoon. When Jeremy and Renee lived at home, they all ate together at five. She'd insisted on it. And if there were after-school sports or clubs or lessons, dinner was scheduled around those things. But after the kids left, she no longer felt tied to the notion of sitting down together, not even with her husband.

"I want to go away for a while," she repeated.

"It's a busy time at work. I'm not sure I can get away right now, but maybe in a few weeks," he said.

Val pressed her lips together and hesitated before she spoke. "Actually, I'm going away by myself." She stared at her folded hands in her lap. He didn't respond right away, which forced her to look up.

Jeff's expression was a mixture of surprise and confusion. "Why?"

She rolled her head to one side and her gaze traveled around the room. "I want to go to Hideaway Bay."

"Where your grandparents used to live," he said.

"Yes."

"What brought this on?"

"I feel compelled to go check it out and try and figure out why they left, and I'd like to see the house Nana spoke so much about when I was growing up," she said.

"I get the urge to go to Vegas a lot, but I don't run off at the slightest whim," he quipped.

"I didn't expect you to understand," she said evenly.

"I'm just surprised, Val, that's all. Of course you should go. How long will you be gone?" he asked.

"I'm not sure."

They went silent, each contemplating the other. The muscle along Jeff's jaw pulsated.

"Is there someone else?" he asked, his voice quiet.

Valerie blinked. "What? Of course not."

"Are you sure?"

She looked at him pointedly. "I'm sure. I think I'd know if I were having an affair."

He lowered his voice. "Valerie, what is going on with you?"

"I don't know," she said truthfully. "I'm very unhappy with everything."

"Does that include me?"

"Yes," she said.

When he didn't say anything, she continued, "You can't be happy with our marriage as it is."

"No," he said, his voice sounding tired. "But I thought you were having a tough time because the kids were gone and you're going through menopause, and to be honest, I don't know quite what to do about it or how to help you."

"I don't think you can help me."

"Is running away to the other side of the country the solution? Won't you be taking your problems with you?"

"I'm not running away," she said tightly.

"Then what is this?"

"Like I said, I want to learn more about Nana," she said.

"Then why don't you ask your brother or call your relatives in France or join Ancestry dot com?" he pleaded.

"First, my brother is younger than me and probably knows less than I do. Second, we haven't spoken to our relatives in France since Nana died and most of them are probably dead anyway. And third, I'm not looking to research my family tree."

Jeff shook his head and sighed. "And what am I supposed to do while you're in Hideaway Bay?"

"I don't know," she said. "Maybe turn off the television and get a hobby."

She hadn't meant for it to sound so critical.

He glared at her. "Thanks a lot."

"I'm not saying that to be mean," she said softly. "I'm wondering if maybe I'm not the only one who is dissatisfied. Maybe you don't even realize it. Maybe you're depressed."

"I'm none of those things," he snapped.

Valerie threw up her hands. "Okay, okay. Everything is perfect in your life."

"I didn't say that either, Val," he said.

She rubbed her forehead, frowning. A headache loomed on the horizon. How did she explain something to him that she didn't understand herself?

"Maybe I need a change of scenery."

"Can't you see a counselor first before you take off?" he asked.

Val shook her head. "My mind is made up. This is something I have to do now."

He exhaled loudly, clearly not pleased.

"Will I hear from you?" he asked. "Or will you just show up when you feel like it and we'll go back to the way it was?"

"I'll keep in touch."

He shook his head and laughed. Abruptly, he stood and the remote fell to the ground, which he ignored. "You'll keep in touch. That's great. I'm your husband, Val!"

Before she could respond, he walked away but stopped in the doorway of the family room. "Do what you want. Obviously, I have no say in the matter. But when you decide to come back, I can't guarantee that I'll still be here."

He left and exited the house through the garage, slamming the door behind him. The walls of the house shook.

Valerie drew in a deep breath, held it, and released it slowly.

CHAPTER THREE

V AL'S PLAN HAD BEEN to pack up her car and leave the following day. However, true to form, she'd been up most of the night, wandering around her house, unable to sleep. After Jeff got out of bed, she climbed back into it and fell asleep.

When she woke just before noon, the house was quiet. She didn't get up right away, preferring to pull the blanket up over her shoulder and reposition herself. But soon the thought of those lost journals back in Hideaway Bay compelled her to get out of bed. There was a little bit of excitement with the revelation of this clue. Despite the doubts that filled her about the existence of the journals, she decided to be hopeful.

She couldn't leave without saying goodbye to Jeff, even if he wasn't speaking to her, so she pushed off her trip for the following morning. It wouldn't be fair to just take off without saying anything. Granted, it probably wasn't fair that she was taking off and leaving her husband for an indeterminate amount of time in the first place.

Jeff didn't understand and if she was honest with herself, she didn't either. Maybe she didn't fully grasp her reasons, but her gut told her that this was something she must do.

She spent the afternoon getting organized for her journey, doing laundry, packing her suitcase, and gassing up the car. As she did all these things, she made a pot of chicken noodle soup for Jeff and a pan of lasagna which would go in the freezer as soon as it cooled. She hadn't the time to make a batch of sauce but jar sauce from the grocery store would do. In between all this, she called friends and neighbors to let them know she was going out of town. She couldn't remember in the recent past being so busy. There was a definite buzz in the air.

Later that evening, she called Chuck to tell him her plans.

"So you and Jeff are going to Hideaway Bay," he said.

Valerie bit her bottom lip. "Actually, I'm going by myself."

This was met by what she presumed was stunned silence.

"Really?"

She felt compelled to explain. "This is something I have to do for myself."

"And Jeff is okay with it?" Chuck asked. Val could practically see his furrowed brow, which was a rare occurrence for her brother.

"Not really but again, it's something I have to do."

"Sis, is everything all right?"

"Yeah, sure," she said brightly. "Why wouldn't it be?"

"Because you're about to go off traveling by yourself and your husband isn't okay with it."

"We're going through a rough patch," she said.

"I'm sorry to hear that," he sympathized.

"Thanks. I'm sure it will work out," she said with a confidence she didn't feel.

"Marriage isn't easy," he said wisely. "And it certainly isn't for sissies."

Valerie burst out laughing. That was the thing about Chuck, he could always make you laugh when you needed to.

They spoke no more of marriages in trouble, focusing on the present and what their children were doing. As they ended the call, Valerie promised to keep in touch and to let him know what she found in Hideaway Bay.

May 15th

"So you're really going to go through with this?" Jeff asked the following morning when Valerie arrived in the kitchen before he left for work. He was dressed in his usual business casual for his IT job: polo shirt and khaki pants.

"Yes. I didn't want to leave without saying goodbye."

"That's big of you," he said with a huff.

"Look, I don't want to fight with you," she said. "But this is something I need to do for myself."

"There is an 'us' here and a 'we,'" he pointed out. His voice had a sharp edge.

She was inclined to say something along the lines of "You wouldn't be interested in going to Hideaway Bay because you barely leave the family room," but she kept her mouth closed, thinking better of it. *Don't say anything that might lead to a massive fight.*

When he returned his attention to his cereal bowl, she picked up her purse and keys. "Goodbye then. I'll call you tomorrow."

He said nothing, but when she reached the door, he called out, "Wait a minute, Val."

With her hand on the doorknob, she turned and looked over her shoulder.

Jeff stood up and walked over to her.

"Do you know where you're going?"

"Of course I do." She wasn't a complete idiot.

"No, I mean, do you know how to get there?"

"Google Maps," she said.

"Do you have a place to stay?"

"Not yet. I'll wait until I get into Hideaway Bay."

"Is that wise?"

Why did his questioning make her feel like his third child?

She bristled and he threw his hands up. "All right. All right. I only want to make sure you're safe."

"I'll be fine."

"What will I tell the kids?"

"Tell them the truth. And I'll probably talk to them before you do, anyway, so don't worry about it," she advised.

"Look, Val, will you at least keep in touch while you're driving. Whenever you stop at a rest stop or a gas station, just shoot me a text to let me know you're all right." Anxiety clouded his expression.

Val nodded, softening toward him. "I promise, I will."

"Good luck."

She nodded.

There was an awkward moment as they stared at each other. How easy the hugs and kissing used to be. A long time ago.

He reached for her, cupped her elbow with his hand, and leaned over and kissed her on the cheek.

It hurt Valerie that she felt nothing when her husband touched her.

Chapter Four

THE TWO-DAY DRIVE TO Hideaway Bay from Colorado was uneventful. The weather cooperated, and the directions were correct and clear. Valerie couldn't imagine how people ever got along using only paper maps prior to GPS. As promised, she'd texted Jeff every time she stopped, and his reply was always a thumbs up emoji. She'd had a brief conversation with Jeff the previous night after she'd checked into her hotel, and he wasn't as angry as he'd been, but things were still cool between them.

As soon as she crossed the New York–Pennsylvania border, excitement and anticipation coursed through her. She couldn't believe she was almost there. Finally, she'd see the town her grandmother spoke so much about and with so much fondness.

She drove north on the highway, passing little towns. Huge billboards invited her and everyone else on the highway to pull off at the next stop and investigate whatever it was they were touting. Usually an antiques shop, sometimes a restaurant with promises like "good home cooking," and once, a theme park with a splash pad. The mid-May weather was sunny and warm. On her left were glimpses of Lake Erie, and she was curious to see the beach and the water. The closer she got, the more excited she became.

Finally, a sign came into view indicating that the turn for Hideaway Bay was two miles away and on the left.

As she approached the turnoff, she slowed down, noting a fruit-and-vegetable stand at the corner of Erie Street and the highway. Beyond the stand stood a field of fresh green sprouts, and she wondered what sort of crop it might be.

Driving slowly down Erie Street, she craned her neck to look at everything on both sides but forced herself to focus on the road and pay attention to where she was going. She drove over a disused set of railroad tracks and headed toward the end of the street. Directly ahead of her, the lake loomed large, a slightly darker shade of blue than the cloudless sky.

At its end, Erie Street split off in opposite directions. To the left was Main Street and what looked at first glance like a charming town with striped awnings adorning small shops. To the right was Star Shine Drive. Her heartbeat ratcheted up a notch or two. She stared down Star Shine Drive, trying to figure out which house her grandmother had lived in. There was no surviving photo, but she had an address.

A car horn honked behind her. Startled, she threw up her hand in a wave, smiling an apology into the rearview mirror. Quickly she threw on her turn signal and turned right, the lake now on her left. To her right was a row of single-family homes that appeared from their designs to be at least one hundred years old. An old woman sat in a chair on the porch of the first house Val passed, right at the corner of Star Shine Drive and Erie. The woman waved, and Val waved back, admiring the mint-condition vintage yellow Cadillac parked in the driveway.

She drove further, slowing down to almost ten miles an hour. Some of the homes were set way back with long, narrow front lawns, and it looked as if that first house on the corner was the largest one on the street. She slowed further as she approached the second last house at the end of Star Shine Drive. Not wanting to draw attention to herself by parking directly in front of the house, she did a three-point turn at the end of Starshine Drive, turned around and parked the car next to the curb across the street. As the engine idled, she took in the view of the property, her face opening in an expression of surprise and delight.

With its panoramic and unobstructed view of the lake, Valerie could easily see why her grandmother had loved this home. She studied it. It was a three-story house with dormer windows on the smaller top floor, with a wide porch in the front. It had the look of a house that had aged but that had been loved. The shutters looked as if they'd had a recent coat of fresh paint in Kelly green. Wind chimes hung around the perimeter of the porch ceiling, and a colorful flag hung from the pole next to the steps.

Suddenly, the screen door opened and a young woman with an abundance of red curly hair emerged. She was followed by a blonde and a dark brunette. All three women were younger than Valerie.

Not wanting to arouse suspicion, Val did a three-point turn and headed back toward town proper. Driving slowly down Main Street, she took in all the sights, finding the little town and its shops with their brick façades and striped awnings endearing. When she pulled off the end of Main Street, she spotted a green space with a gazebo and found parking on the residential street behind it. Making sure her possessions were out of sight, she locked up her car and headed to the gazebo. It was good to get out of the car and stretch and walk after two full days of driving. The grass was trimmed, and the flowerbeds that surrounded the gazebo had recently been dug and were ready for planting. Empty flowerboxes with fresh compost hung off the gazebo railing.

Val climbed up the wooden steps. It appeared the hexagon-shaped structure had had a recent application of paint. There were benches along the inside walls. Preferring a lake view, she ambled over to one of the back benches and rested there, admiring the golden sandy beach stretching out in both directions.

As she took in the amazing view, she gathered her thoughts. Now that she was here, she felt idiotic marching up the steps of the house on Star Shine Drive and asking that they rip up the floorboards of their living room so she could see if her grandmother's journals were there. They might politely refuse her request or, worst-case scenario, they'd call the police. She swallowed hard. She supposed she could ask some of the older town residents if they remembered her grandmother. But those pickings would be slim. After all, her grandmother had lived there in the '50s. And what was she supposed to do? Knock on every door in Hideaway Bay and see if there was any senior citizen who remembered a Frenchwoman named Delphine Brandt? She wasn't even sure how many years her grandmother had lived there. Her father mentioned living there as a young boy and had good memories, but he'd never gone on about it like Nana had.

Out of the direct sun, the shadows of the gazebo were cool. Goosebumps sprung up on her flesh and she rubbed her arms, wishing she'd brought her hoodie with her. She stood and left the gazebo, taking the sidewalk behind it that skirted a semi-circle of houses. As she walked along the sidewalk, she took in the houses and their signs of imminent summer. Flowerbeds were readied, garden furniture had been brought out and washed down, and lawns were cleaned up of debris from the previous winter and spring. She went over in her mind how she would word her request with the present owners of the house on Star Shine Drive. No matter how she mentally worded it, it sounded odd. How would she feel if a total stranger knocked on her front door and asked her to look beneath the floorboards.

But it was what she came here for, among other things. Somehow, she had to get over her fear and summon up the courage to approach the owner. Sighing, she pivoted and walked in the direction of her car. It was best to just get it over with.

With a sense of purpose, she drove directly to the house on Star Shine Drive.

She parked the car directly in front of the house and deflated when she saw the three women still on the front porch, relaxing on white wicker furniture. She'd hoped to have to face only one person, not three. But she soldiered on.

There were three cars parked in the long driveway, and a vintage cherry-red convertible briefly caught Valerie's eye.

She opted to take the paved brick pathway from the sidewalk to the front porch, rather than the driveway. She was acutely aware of three sets of eyes on her as she approached the women gathered on the porch.

There was a loud woof as a Great Dane jumped to his feet and stood at the top of the porch stairs. Startled, Val stepped back.

"Charlie, go lie down!" said one of the women. But the dog stood there, staring at Val and wagging his tail.

"Ignore him. He's harmless," said the blonde.

"But he's also clumsy," said the redhead with a laugh.

Val did not step up onto the porch stair, choosing to remain on the pathway. She didn't want to appear overly friendly.

She looked up, and all three women stared at her. Despite their various hair colors, each bore a familial resemblance to the others. She wondered if they might be related. Sisters? Cousins?

"Can I help you?" asked the brunette. She stood and stepped over to the porch railing. She was tall with a headful of long, dark, curly hair. By the fine lines around her expressive eyes, Val pegged her to be the oldest of the three.

"Hi, I'm Valerie Fisher, um . . ." She paused as all three women looked at her expectantly. She drew in a deep breath and continued. "My grandparents used to live in this house a long time ago. My grandmother was very happy here in Hideaway Bay. And, well, I was looking for the current owner."

Now all three women came out from the shadows of the porch, and sunlight illuminated their faces. They were definitely related.

"That's amazing!" gushed the redhead.

"Actually, my sisters and I currently own the house," the dark-haired one said with an air of authority, indicating the two women standing next to her.

"Would you care to join us?" asked the blonde.

"Where are our manners?" said the redhead. "I'm Alice Monroe, and these are my older sisters, Isabelle"—here she indicated the dark-haired woman—"and this is Lily."

At their invitation, Valerie joined them on the porch and took the wicker rocker at the side railing. Her heart beat fast, and her mouth was dry.

"Would you like iced tea or lemonade?" Lily asked. In her maxi dress and bolero-style cardigan, she was the most delicate-looking of the three.

"Either would be fine. Thank you."

"I'll get us something to eat," Alice said, slipping into the house behind Lily.

Isabelle looked after her and chuckled. "Alice has been baking this morning, so you're in for a treat." Isabelle sat at the end of the wicker sofa nearest Val. She crossed one toned leg over the other. On her feet were lavender flip-flops, and her toenails were painted a matching color. She wore a gold anklet. Charlie, the Great Dane, collapsed at her feet, exhaled, and closed his eyes.

"That's a big dog," Val remarked.

"He belongs to Lily, but we all love him so he's kind of spoiled," Isabelle said.

Val pegged her to be about fortyish. She was beautiful, with high cheekbones and an athletic body. With her own menopausal weight gain, Val felt a little frumpy next to her.

Lily and Alice emerged from the house, carrying beverages and snacks. Charlie immediately sat up, eyeing the food.

"No, Charlie, nothing for you."

"Aw, give him something, Lily," Isabelle said.

"We've still got some of those bacon-flavored treats in the kitchen cupboard." Alice set a tray bearing little squares of two-layer cheesecake down on the low glass-topped wicker table in their midst and disappeared back into the house. It was cute, the way the three of them fussed over this great big dog.

Alice returned and gave the dog a chew stick. Charlie settled down again at Isabelle's feet and went to work on it.

"Ow, Charlie, you're putting all your weight on my foot," Isabelle said. Carefully, she pulled her foot out from beneath him. "You're such a thug." But there was no irritation in her voice, only amusement.

Lily passed out glasses of iced tea, and Alice handed out small paper plates of cheesecake. Val marveled at their hospitality and wondered if they were always like this. Did they serve refreshments to every stranger that landed on their porch?

"You said your grandparents lived in this house at one time," Isabelle said, slicing off a piece of cheesecake with her fork.

Val nodded and took a sip from her iced tea. "That's right. My grandparents moved here after the Second World War. My grandmother was from France. My grandfather met her there when France was liberated." How well she knew that story. She smiled to herself at the memory of it.

"A war bride," Isabelle said with a smile. "I did an article about British war brides once."

From that comment, Val deduced that she was some kind of writer.

"How long did they live here for?" Lily asked.

"They left either in the late fifties or early sixties. That part is a little vague," Valerie said with a grimace.

"As some family history is," Lily said. The three sisters laughed as if they shared some sort of private joke between them.

"Yes. How long have you lived here?" Val asked.

All three went to say something but closed their mouths.

Isabelle took the lead. "Our grandparents bought this house in 1966. They were from Buffalo and moved out here permanently in the mid-seventies. The three of us were born and raised in Hideaway Bay and when our grandmother died, we inherited the house."

How lucky. "Do you know who owned it before them?"

All three shook their heads.

Lily spoke up. "The only thing I remember is my grandfather saying the house was in a deplorable condition when they bought it and they got it for a song."

"Where are you from?" Alice asked.

"Colorado," Valerie replied.

"You're a long way from home," Isabelle said, finishing her cheesecake and setting the plate down on the table. "What brings you to Hideaway Bay?"

"I was very close to my grandmother, and she spoke so fondly of the town that I often wondered why she left in the first place. I thought I'd check it out and see why." Val looked around. "It's easy to see why she fell in love with it."

"What was her name?" Lily asked.

"Delphine Brandt. She was a chocolatier."

"That doesn't ring any bells," Isabelle said. "Of course, she lived here before my grandparents were here so they might not have known her."

Valerie tried not to be discouraged. She'd expected this. The problem was the passage of time between then and now.

A thought occurred to her. "You said your grandfather said the house was in awful condition when they purchased it. Did they do any renovation?"

All three nodded.

"They rewired and replumbed the entire thing," Isabelle said.

"They refinished all the hardwood floors," Lily added.

Val perked up at the mention of this. "Did they ever mention finding anything when they did their renovations?"

The three sisters shook their heads, their expressions clouded with confusion.

"What, like photos or something?" Alice asked.

Val leaned forward, setting her empty plate down on the table. She looked at the floor and scratched her forehead. "This is going to sound strange, but there was talk that my grandmother left her journals underneath the floor in the living room."

All three regarded her, slack-jawed, and then they all spoke at the same time.

"I've never heard anything about the discovery of journals," said Isabelle.

"Surely they'd be long gone by now," Lily said thoughtfully.

"We can pull up the floor and look for you!" Alice gushed.

Isabelle and Lily immediately turned their heads and looked at their sister.

"Wait a minute, Alice," Isabelle warned.

"We can't go digging up the floor," Lily said.

As Val sat there, the three of them went into a brief sidebar about the possibility of pulling up the living room floor, with one for and two against. Slightly embarrassed to be the cause of friction among the sisters, Val lowered her head and watched the dog go to town on the chew stick.

The chatter amongst the sisters quieted, and Isabelle turned to Val. "As much as we are happy to meet someone who shares our history with the house, and as much as we are sympathetic to your finding some answers about your grandmother, you can certainly understand what a big undertaking it would be to pull up the floor."

Val nodded. "I do. And I certainly wouldn't ask that of you. That would be too big of an undertaking."

Across from her, Alice folded her arms across her chest and said nothing. It was apparent she did not agree with her sisters.

"Can I make a suggestion?" Isabelle said.

"Yes, please do," Val said.

"Why don't you start by talking to some of the older residents and see if they remember your grandparents. They may know why they left."

"I will. Can you give me some names?" Val asked. She hated to rely on their generosity, but she had no choice.

"Sure, first I'd start with Martha Cotter," Isabelle said. "She lives in the house on the corner."

Val remembered the elderly woman waving from the porch.

"She's lived her whole life in Hideaway Bay," Isabelle continued. "She might remember your grandmother."

"Also try Lottie Prescott," Lily suggested. "She's lived here her whole life too."

"It's a shame you didn't show up last year before our former librarian passed away," Alice said. "She would have been an infinite resource."

A day late and all that.

Lily stood. "I'll write down Lottie's address and let her know you might contact her."

"Thank you." Although they couldn't accommodate her by looking beneath the floor, they were as helpful as they could be.

"And don't forget Mr. Lime," Isabelle said. "He runs the five-and-dime on Main Street. And he's almost, if not a hundred years old."

"Is his memory reliable?" Val asked.

Lily snorted. "He's as sharp as a tack. Still runs the store by himself."

Valerie stood from her chair. "Thank you so much for your help and the refreshments."

"No problem, sorry we couldn't lift up the floor though," Lily said.

Val held up her hand. "Don't worry about it. It was an unreasonable request."

"I wouldn't say unreasonable," Isabelle said with a tilt of her head.

They walked her to the steps.

"Good luck in your search," Lily said.

Alice finally spoke. "Would you like to see the inside of the house?"

Val caught the exchanged glance between Isabelle and Lily but chose to ignore it.

"If it wouldn't be too much trouble."

"Of course not."

"I'm heading off to the beach with Charlie," Lily said, and she reached for the leash hanging just inside the front door. "It was nice meeting you, Valerie."

"You, too."

"And I must get over to Joe's," Isabelle said. She shook Val's hand and wished her luck.

Alice opened the screen door and held it for Val. "Come on, I'll give you the tour."

Excited to get a glimpse of the inside of the place Nana had once called home, Val eagerly followed Alice inside.

As she stepped across the threshold, her eyes darted about the place. Her immediate impression was shabby chic. The living room was big, and the woodwork was painted in robin's egg blue. The walls were the color of magnolia. Floor-length drapes hung at the windows, their floral pattern a perfect match to the upholstery on the two overstuffed chairs. A red sofa was pushed up against the interior wall, And although its style was traditional, it looked to be brand new, as if it had been redone to match the historical essence of the house. Bookshelves flanked the fireplace at the far end, their shelves crammed with books.

Her gaze went to the stained hardwood floor. It covered a large area, and she realized it would have been too much to ask them to start lifting floorboards.

The space smelled like lemon and cedar grass.

Alice took her through a hallway, past a dining room on their right with built-in cabinets. A few family photos lined the walls. The narrow hallway opened out into a kitchen at the back of the house. When she stepped into the kitchen with its high ceilings, she smiled and imagined that with those east facing windows, the room was bright and sunny in the mornings. She could tell that the cabinets were original. And although everything else had most likely changed in the ensuing seventy years, she could easily picture a younger version of her grandmother in this room, standing at the stove. She could also picture finished chocolate truffles and other candy laid out on the countertops and tables. It was how she remembered her grandmother in her later years when she used to help her.

Unbidden, tears filled her eyes.

Alice reached out to her, patted her arm, and smiled.

"I can imagine my grandmother very easily in this kitchen," Val said, "making her chocolate candy."

"I wouldn't have minded knowing her myself," Alice said.

Val smiled. The Monroe sisters were lovely, but Alice was particularly sweet.

She stood in the space for a minute, trying to memorize every detail, from the placement of the stove near the back window to the size of the cabinets, the height of the ceiling, and the way the light flooded in through the window.

"Come on, I'll take you upstairs," Alice said with a wave.

Val shook her head. "I appreciate that, Alice, but that won't be necessary." She wasn't inclined to peer into their bedrooms and get glimpses of their private lives. They'd been gracious enough.

"Are you sure? We don't mind," Alice said.

Val wondered if the older sisters would say the same thing, but she only shook her head. "I really appreciate the offer, but the kitchen was the room I wanted to see the most."

"All right," Alice said agreeably.

"I won't take up any more of your time," Val said, and she turned and headed toward the front of the house.

They stepped out onto the porch There was one lone gull circling in the sky over the lake, its cry shrill at times.

"Does the sun set over the lake?" she wondered out loud.

"It does," Alice said.

"That must be an amazing sight."

"It is."

"Thanks again."

"No problem."

As she stepped off the porch, something else occurred to her. "Is there a hotel nearby, or preferably a B & B?"

"If you can believe it, there's no bed-and-breakfast in Hideaway Bay. And this place would be perfect for a B & B," Alice said.

Val agreed with her.

"There are Airbnb's and some summer rental cottages, but they're usually booked way in advance."

"That's my tough luck then."

"But there is a motel out on the main highway," Alice said. "Now it's a bit outdated, but it's clean, and the owner, Viv, is lovely."

"Thank you. What's the name?"

"The Highway Hotel," Alice said and rolled her eyes. "Not very original but if you're only looking for a clean room, it'll do the job."

"Thanks."

"How long are you in town for?"

Val felt foolish not knowing how to answer. After all, she only had three people to go and see, and she might be able to wrap up her search in the next day or two. "I'm not sure yet. My plans aren't definite."

Alice nodded and gave her directions to the hotel, and Val left in search of it and a plan.

CHAPTER FIVE

ALICE HAD BEEN RIGHT.

The Highway Hotel was dated but to give it credit, it was exceptionally clean. Its exterior was the color of sand, and its orange doors faced the parking lot. Val liked the illuminated vintage sign out front. The words *The Highway Hotel* appeared in a fancy dark-red scroll against a white background.

It was run by a woman who wore her hair short and appeared to be a no-nonsense person. Small gold hoop earrings dotted her lobes.

The woman, who introduced herself as Viv, handed Val a receipt and a room key—not a keycard but an actual key. Val hadn't seen one of those in years.

"Checkout is at eleven," Viv said.

"Okay."

"We're not at full occupancy, so I gave you a room that faces the fields instead of the highway. It's on the ground floor."

Val wondered if the "no vacancy" sign had ever been lit. Her knees appreciated being given a room on the ground floor. "Thank you. Can you recommend a good place to eat?"

"In town there's Cabana Sally's if you prefer bar food and sitting outside, or there's the Chat and Nibble if you prefer home cooking."

"Okay, thanks." Val's stomach had started to complain in the last few minutes despite the recent serving of cheesecake at the Monroe sisters' home.

She pulled her car around the back and found her room, number twelve, and parked in the spot directly in front of the tangerine-colored door. With her small suitcase in one hand, she slung her purse over her shoulder and waited until she heard the familiar beeps of the key fob that indicated the car was locked.

She let herself into the room, reached for the switch on the wall, and flipped on the lights. The space was spare. There were two double beds with a nightstand between them. Orange, brown, and gold striped bedspreads covered the bed. There was a desk that looked as if it had seen better days, and a boxy television sat on it, along with an electric kettle and a display of no-name tea bags and sachets of instant coffee. After she locked the door and put on the security chain lock, she dropped her suitcase on the far bed, deciding to take the bed closest to the bathroom for those inconvenient midnight visits.

When she pulled open the lone drawer in the nightstand, she spotted the requisite Bible. It looked as if it hadn't been used much.

She flopped on the bed and stretched out. It was more comfortable than she'd imagined. The paneled walls made the room appear darker, and the overall dark colors made Val feel slightly sad.

Fatigue tempted her, and she thought she'd close her eyes for a moment, then freshen up and head out to grab something to eat. At some point, she had to call Jeff. Based on his tone during their phone conversation the previous night, she was not looking forward to it, but she had to let him know she'd made it safe to Hideaway Bay and had gotten a room. As she wondered whether she should call him before she went for dinner or after, she could feel herself drifting off and she gave in to it, letting herself float away.

Sometime later, her phone rang on the brown laminated nightstand, startling her awake. For a moment she was confused, looking around and not sure where she was. She rolled over, grabbed her phone and glanced at the screen.

Jeff.

She swiped the green "accept call" icon and put the phone up to her ear. "Hey."

"I thought you were going to call tonight." His tone sounded defensive.

"I fell asleep."

"You fell asleep where?" he asked.

"In the hotel room." Where did he think she'd fallen asleep?

"I've been waiting for your call," he said.

"Again, I fell asleep," she said. She massaged her one shoulder; the long drive hadn't done her muscles and joints any favors.

When he didn't say anything, she asked, "How's everything?"

"Fine."

"Good."

"Did you find your grandmother's house?" he asked.

Val hesitated. "I did. I had a nice conversation with the current owners. They're three sisters who inherited the home from their grandmother. Their grandparents bought the house years after Nana had left."

"Uh-huh."

His response was underwhelming.

"Did they have any information for you?" he asked.

"Unfortunately, no. It was before their time, and they don't remember their grandparents mentioning a chocolatier." She hadn't told Jeff about the journal, deciding to keep that to herself for the time being. If she didn't find it, she was afraid he'd say "I told you so."

"Does that mean you're coming home?"

Val blinked, surprised. "What? I just got here."

"But you talked to the current owners, and they couldn't help you."

"I know that. But there might be some people in town who were here when Nana and Poppy were here." It annoyed her that she sometimes had to spell things out.

"Well, how long do you think that will take you?" he pressed.

Annoyance grated her. Not once had he asked how she was. "I don't know, Jeff. I don't know what my plans are. But I promise, you'll be the first to know."

"Val, are you sure you're coming back?"

I don't know.

She was purposefully evasive. "Eventually, yes."

He snorted. "That's encouraging. What am I supposed to do? Sit around and wait until you're finished with your mid-life crisis?"

"No." She breathed deeply through her nose and said tightly, "Move on without me if you feel the need."

Chapter Six

Isabelle Monroe

"I think we should help Valerie Fisher," Alice said over breakfast the next morning.

The three of them sat around the kitchen table, eating Alice's delectable crème brulée French toast and drinking strong coffee from a French press Isabelle had discovered on a trip to Paris with Joe for a writing assignment.

Not this again. Isabelle sipped tentatively from her coffee, but it tasted bitter.

They'd been having a pleasant conversation about Alice's plans for the following summer, when she and her fiancé Jack Stirling would be getting married. Alice was indecisive. Did she want a big wedding? Did she want it at the beach? But then she was tempted by the thought of a destination wedding, too. Isabelle and Lily let her vent, figuring she'd arrive at the right conclusion in time.

Sunshine slanted through the east-facing back window. It made the yellow walls of the kitchen appear almost buttery. The smell of coffee was strong, and the scent of hyacinths lingered in the air from the fresh-cut flowers Lily had picked up the day before, arranged in a vase on the counter.

Alice would not drop the subject of Valerie Fisher and her grandmother's lost journals. That was her youngest sister's problem: she had a big, soft heart and wanted to help everybody. It was a beautiful personality trait. But the harsh truth was you couldn't help everyone or save them all.

"It's not that we don't want to help her, it's just a little more than we can accommodate," Lily said thoughtfully.

Between the two of us, Lily is always more diplomatic, Isabelle thought.

Alice scowled and waved her sister's comment away with her fork. "We only need to take up a few floorboards. We'll take a quick peek and then put everything back as it was."

Isabelle, who liked to think of herself as the voice of reason, said, "But it's never as simple as that. You pull up a few floorboards and you don't find anything there, and so you rip up a few more, and so on and so on until the entire floor is gone and there's nothing underneath."

Alice winced. "Gee, Izzy, that's kind of cynical thinking."

"It's called life experience."

"Who's going to pay for the cleanup and repair if it's needed?" Lily asked.

"I'll pay for it," Alice said.

"No," Isabelle and Lily said in unison. Their tenderhearted sister was not financing this project. She had a wedding to think about, if she and Jack ever got around to setting a date.

"It isn't even the cost so much," Lily said. "It's the disruption. We're all creatures of habit and we like our routines.

None of us wants to come home from work and have to pull out buckets and start scrubbing the front room."

Alice bent her head and sighed. Quietly, she speared a piece of French toast, popped it into her mouth, and chewed thoughtfully. When she looked up, she stared at them. "What if I promise to do the cleanup myself? I'll take time off from work."

"Sparrow, why is it so important for you to help this woman?" Isabelle asked, deciding the coffee wasn't too bitter after all and pouring herself some more.

Alice picked up her teacup, cradling it in both hands and stared out the window. "I don't know. She seemed kind of sad. Did you not pick up on it?"

"Not really, but then I was too focused on the fact that she wants to tear up our house," Isabelle cracked.

Lily laughed but Alice did not.

"She has sadness around her. I can't explain it. I'd like to help if I could."

"Maybe you can help her in other ways," Lily suggested.

Alice tilted her head and smirked. "How? Drop off a pan of salted caramel brownies?"

"Your brownies would make anyone feel better," Lily said with a raised eyebrow.

Isabelle stood and picked up her empty plate and cup. "I've got to get to work. Deadlines and all."

She'd converted a spare room on the second floor into an office for when she wasn't traveling. After she loaded her dishes into the dishwasher, she rinsed out the dishcloth and gave the counters a quick wipe.

Lily and Alice also made moves to get their workdays going. Lily worked part-time with her boyfriend, the writer Simon

Bishop, and Alice shared a law office with Ben Enright over in the plaza off the highway.

The three of them worked around each other: Isabelle wiped the table. Lily loaded the remaining dishes, and Alice put things away in the refrigerator and pantry. When everything was neat and clean, they headed single file down the narrow hallway to the front of the house. Isabelle went up the stairs to her office and Alice, Lily, and Charlie headed out the door, going in different directions.

It was a rare morning that they didn't have breakfast together, and Isabelle enjoyed it thoroughly. But soon Alice would get married and they'd be down to two sisters. Alice had reassured them that she'd still have breakfast with them, but Isabelle was doubtful. She'd be newly married and besides, nothing lasted forever.

Her thoughts drifted to Val and as she reached the second-floor landing, she shook her head, thinking it was an incredible story. Regardless, they weren't tearing up the house to look for a journal that was most likely long gone.

Isabelle hoped that was the end of the conversation, but somehow she doubted it.

CHAPTER SEVEN

Valerie

DESPITE AN AWFUL NIGHT'S sleep, Valerie was anxious to talk to the few townspeople left who might remember her grandparents. It was a long shot, she conceded, that anyone would remember them from so long ago. After all, it was more than sixty years. But she chose to remain hopeful because the alternative was too depressing a thought to even entertain.

After a quick shower, she dressed in a clean pair of jeans and a ruby-red three-quarter-sleeved cotton T-shirt. Carefully, she fixed her hair with a curling iron, concentrating on the left side, where she'd noticed it had been thinning in the last year. Bloodwork taken by her doctor had been normal and she chalked it up, like so many other things, to menopause.

Her phone rang. Renee's name flashed across the screen, and Valerie set the curling iron down and shut it off. She answered the call as she sat on the foot of the bed.

"Hi, Renee," she said.

"Hi, Mom."

"How are you?"

"Don't worry about me, what about you? How are you?" Renee trilled. "Dad called me last night and told me you left."

Valerie rolled her eyes. Why did Jeff have to call her and worry her and make it sound like their marriage was in trouble? Granted, it was in trouble, but her kids didn't have to know that. Yet.

"Mom, what's going on?" Renee asked. "Are you okay? Should I come home?" For being a second child, her daughter could certainly be bossy.

"No, no, that isn't necessary," Valerie said firmly. That was the last thing she wanted. She didn't want anyone disrupting their lives. She could wring Jeff's neck for worrying Renee. And Jeremy? Had he called him too?

"What is going on?" Renee asked again.

Valerie's shoulders sagged. She fingered the pattern on the bedspread. "Nothing. I came to Hideaway Bay to find out about my grandparents. Especially my grandmother. She spoke about Hideaway Bay so much and how much she loved it, but she never told me why they left. And Uncle Chuck doesn't know either."

"And this is important to you," Renee said. That was one thing about her daughter, she cut through all the bull and got right to the point.

"Yes," Val said, closing her eyes. "It's something I've always been curious about. But more so recently."

"I know, you've spoken a lot about Nana when we were growing up, and I wish I could have met her."

"She would have adored you," Val said with a smile. Her grandmother had loved children, and it was a shame she hadn't lived long enough to enjoy Jeremy and Renee.

"And you think you might find some answers in Hideaway Bay? Where is this place, exactly?"

"To your first question, I'm hopeful, and to your second one, it's on Lake Erie, in Western New York, south of Buffalo."

"How did they end up there?"

"That's a good question," Val said. "Poppy's family was from New York City and Nana was from France. There are a lot of gaps in what I know about their lives before they ended up in Colorado."

"They lived all over the place, you said."

"They did. They moved from one town to the next until my father met my mother, and then Nana put her foot down and said she wasn't moving anymore, and they settled down and stayed in Colorado."

"It is curious though, isn't it," Renee said thoughtfully.

Val agreed. She suspected it had something to do with her grandfather. He'd never had a stable job, instead doing the odd thing here and there. Nana had continued to make chocolates and sell them from her kitchen wherever she lived.

"Now, Mom, again, are you all right? Dad says you've been in a bit of a funk these last few months."

Val sighed. "I don't want you to worry."

"Too late. I've inherited that gene from you," Renee said with a laugh.

She didn't know how much to tell her daughter. Didn't want to cause alarm. How did one express general dissatisfaction with one's life?

"First, there's nothing to worry about. I've been rethinking my life, that's all," Val said.

"In what way?"

"You should have been a detective," Valerie said with a laugh.

"Nice deflection, but answer the question," Renee said.

Dare she say it out loud? Dare she share it with someone else?

Val took a deep breath and chose her words carefully. "I want to become a chocolatier like my grandmother." Holding her breath, she waited for her daughter's response.

"Mom, I think that's a great idea!" Renee said excitedly. "Are you talking commercially or more as a hobby?"

"Commercially." Her voice squeaked out.

"Wow, Mom, I am impressed."

"You are?"

"Yes, you have a dream. You have a goal, and you want to pursue it."

"I've been thinking about it for a while. I'm not that old and I still have some life left in me," Val said with a nervous laugh.

Renee laughed. "Mom, who said you didn't? My mind is blown. I, mean, I didn't see that coming. But it's so *perfect*!"

Val felt buoyed by Renee's reaction and was glad she shared it with her.

"I wish I had my grandmother's recipes," she verbalized a thought she had a million times.

"Mom, I remember you making us chocolate candy when we were kids. Whenever I had to bring something into class, the other kids would nag me about bringing in your chocolate for everyone."

"Really?"

"Yes, really, Jeremy and I were the most popular kids in school any time we brought your candy to class."

Valerie smiled. She hadn't known that.

"It's disappointing that you don't have her recipes, but your own chocolate is amazing so start from there," Renee advised.

"Nana made the most delectable chocolate, and they were recipes from her own mother and grandmother." The thought that the family recipes were lost made her sick to her stomach.

Renee was quiet for a moment, and she finally said, "Can you remember anything about how your grandmother made chocolate? Anything at all?"

"Bits and pieces, but there are a lot of missing parts."

"Get a notebook and start writing down what you do remember," Renee instructed. Sometimes Valerie wondered who the parent was.

"I suppose . . ."

"No supposing about it. Just do it."

"All right, boss."

There was encouragement in knowing that her daughter was so supportive in this new endeavor of hers. And it was true: she always loved making chocolate candy and truffles and soft-center candies. She used to spend hours in the kitchen making candy for the kids, losing all track of time.

Renee changed the subject. "Mom, ever since I was little, I have been so interested in everything about France. I knew I wanted to come over and live here someday."

"You've always been a Francophile," Val said with a proud smile. If only Nana could have known that things would come full circle and her great-granddaughter would decide to live in France. But maybe on some plane of existence, she did.

"The point is, I'm living my dream life, and it was you who encouraged me to pursue it. And you know what? I'm really happy."

Warmth and lightness filled Valerie's heart. "That makes me very happy, Renee."

There was a long pause and finally Renee asked, "Do you think you might be suffering from depression?"

"I don't know," Val said honestly. Although as of late, she often felt as if her get up and go, got up and went.

"Promise me that when you get home, you'll go to the doctor. Mental health is very important. And there's no shame in being depressed," Renee said.

"I promise, I will."

"Now, what about you and Dad? Are you having problems?" Renee questioned. "Do you need to see a marriage counselor?"

Her daughter must have been a drill sergeant in a previous life. But she was not about to dump all her marital woes on her. She decided to keep it vague. "We're trying to find our way with our new empty nest."

"Jeez, Mom, Jeremy and I have been gone for a couple of years. Has it been going on that long?"

"No." It had been more of a slow unraveling. "But look, it's nothing for you to worry about. It's probably only a phase. It happens when you've been married as long as we have."

"Are you sure?" Renee pushed.

"Yes!" Valerie did not want to discuss her stagnant marriage with her daughter. No way. Jeff was a good father, and she wouldn't say anything against him to their children.

"All right," Renee said, sounding unconvinced.

"Where are you now?" Valerie asked, shifting toward a more neutral subject.

"I'm sitting outside at a little café, drinking café au lait and eating a croissant. The Eiffel Tower is in view."

"I'm envious. It sounds heavenly," Val said. She could see it so clearly. She and Jeff had gone over the previous spring to visit Renee, and it had been a wonderful time.

"Why don't you come over? We can hang out," Renee said excitedly.

"As appealing as that sounds, I'm going to stay put in Hideaway Bay for right now."

"Maybe when you're finished there," Renee said.

"I'll keep it in mind. Look, we should hang up, you're going to run up your phone bill," Val said.

"All right, Mom. Talk to you later. I love you!"

"I love you too, honey," Val said.

There was no breakfast included at the motel unless you counted the coffeemaker on a small, laminated table in the reception area, so Valerie decided to head into town in search of breakfast. Enthusiasm filled her after the call with her daughter and not only did she feel the uptick in her mood but her motivation to get things done had increased. Before she left her room, she called the number for Lottie Prescott, which Lily Monroe had provided. Lottie, although initially hesitant, perked up when Val identified herself as Delphine's granddaughter. During the course of the brief phone conversation, Valerie asked Lottie if she could recommend a place for breakfast and was told to try the Chat and Nibble on Main Street, and then the elderly woman told her she'd meet her there for coffee afterward. Perfect.

The Chat and Nibble was a diner located directly across the street from the Hideaway Bay Olive Oil Company and Lime's Five-and-Dime. Valerie assumed this was the five-and-dime Isabelle Monroe had mentioned. This was handy. She could talk to Lottie then walk across the street to the five-and-dime, and then circle back to Star Shine Drive and see if Martha

Cotter would be willing to talk to her. Hopefully, among the three of them, someone would remember something about her grandmother.

As she stepped into the Chat and Nibble, a little bell tinkled and she was greeted with the aroma of freshly brewed coffee and baked goods. Her stomach growled and her hands shook. The cheesecake at the Monroes' house had been the last thing she'd eaten. She'd feel better as soon as she had some food in her stomach. The shakiness would cease, and the brain fog would clear. Hopefully.

The hostess asked if she wanted a booth or a table, and Valerie chose the former. She was seated in a booth at the end of the row but with a view of the shops across the street.

She asked for coffee as the server handed her a menu, a thick, laminated affair with several pages. There were options for breakfast, lunch, and dinner, and she was pleased to see that breakfast was served all day. When the kids still lived at home, she sometimes served them pancakes or French toast or eggs and bacon for dinner. Jeff would grouse, but it was what her own parents had done.

Something caught her eye, and she looked up to see an elderly man exiting the five-and-dime. For a moment, she watched him. The apron he wore matched the blue-and-white-striped awning of his shop and covered the front of his crooked frame. On his head were a few wisps of white hair. He walked to the curb, put his hands on his hips, straightened up as much as he could, although he was still somewhat hunched over, and looked up and down the street before disappearing back into the shop.

She returned her attention to the menu and scanned the offerings on the page devoted to breakfast items. Satisfied, she closed it and set it at the edge of the table to indicate to the server that she was ready to order.

In the end, it was the Belgian waffle with chocolate, strawberries, and whipped cream that caught her attention. She opted for it knowing that it would be heavy enough that she wouldn't have to worry about lunch.

When it arrived, she dug into it, her eyes closing in pleasure with the first bite.

When the server appeared and refilled her coffee mug, she asked, "Is everything all right?"

"It's delicious," Valerie replied.

When she finished the last bite, she pushed her plate aside, leaned back in the booth, placed her hand across her stomach, and sighed.

An elderly woman with caramel-colored hair and bright pink lipstick pushed through the door of the restaurant and looked around tentatively. She wore a striking emerald pendant that caught Val's eye. As she was alone, Valerie wondered if this was Lottie Prescott. Just as hesitant, Val threw up her hand in a wave. The elderly woman spotted it, smiled, and headed toward her.

"Valerie?" she inquired.

Valerie nodded. "Yes."

"I'm Lottie Prescott," the woman said, and reached out her hand and shook Val's. On her wrist was a delicate gold bracelet with stars and a moon charm.

As Lottie slid into the booth opposite Val, the server approached again to clear away Val's empty plate and greeted Lottie by her first name, asking if she'd like anything.

Lottie laughed. "Only coffee today, Noreen." She looked at Valerie and said, "My husband and I are regulars. After almost sixty years of marriage, I'm sick of cooking." She made a moue of disgust.

Valerie liked this woman immediately. "I agree."

She pegged Lottie to be around eighty-ish, an attractive woman with bright, clear blue eyes, finely lined skin, and minimal makeup.

Lottie fixed her coffee with two creams and some sugar. She smiled and said, "So you're Delphine's granddaughter."

"I am. Jean-Paul was my dad," Val informed her, pronouncing her father's name the French way.

Lottie sat back against the booth and folded her hands in front of her on the table. "I remember your father. He was just a little boy then. I remember him sitting in his high chair and then as he got older, with skinned knees or bruises. He was always riding his bike or swinging off the tire out back." An expression of merriment flitted across her face.

Val smiled, trying to think of her father in those terms.

"How is he?" Lottie asked. "Of course, he wouldn't remember me, I was a bit older than him."

"He passed away a few years ago. Alzheimer's," Valerie said softly. It was a harsh fact of life, that you never stopped missing people once they were gone.

The smile on Lottie's face disappeared. "I'm so sorry."

"Don't be, you didn't know."

"Where did Delphine go?" Lottie asked, leaning forward, her folded hands sliding across the table.

"They traveled around a bit. From here they went to Indiana and then Kentucky, and then after a few years, they ended up in Arkansas and finally Colorado."

"My goodness, they were the traveling sort."

"I think my grandmother got tired of it, because when they landed in Colorado, she wouldn't budge after that."

"Is that where you live now?"

"Yes, with my husband. My kids are grown and gone," Valerie said.

"I remember that phase of my life. I don't envy you," Lottie said. "All I can say is grandchildren are the balm for the empty nest."

Valerie smiled politely. That was a long way off yet for Jeremy and Renee.

"What would you like to know about your grandmother?" Lottie asked. "I never really met your grandfather, but I do remember your grandmother."

Before Valerie could respond, the server appeared, coffeepot in hand, and refilled their mugs when both women nodded. When she stepped away and after they fixed their fresh cups of coffee, Val said, "Anything at all would help."

Lottie squinted, her eyes narrowing. "I was about ten when I first met Delphine. Of course back then, in 1950, a Frenchwoman was a very exotic thing for Hideaway Bay. So if people didn't know her, they knew of her."

Valerie didn't interrupt; she was content to simply listen.

"My mother used to visit her for chocolate. I had a whole bunch of brothers and sisters, and my mother would buy little boxes of candy for herself and keep them hidden from the rest of us hooligans. And I can't say I blame her," Lottie said with a laugh. She took a sip from her coffee.

Valerie waited anxiously for Lottie to continue with her story.

"Sometimes I'd go with my mother to see Delphine. In Hideaway Bay, if your house faces the lake, the gathering place is usually the front porch." She shook her head and chuckled. "But not with Delphine. We always went to the kitchen. And of course she made the most gorgeous chocolate candy. Again,

I can see why my mother kept it for herself. It was simply divine. I haven't tasted any chocolate that came close."

Lottie paused, collecting her thoughts. "Funny, but I remember she always had this book open on the table, like a recipe book. I tried to read it one time I was there, but it was all written in French."

This was news to Valerie.

"A recipe book," she said. "That's the first I've heard of that. When I was growing up, Nana worked from memory." Another lost item. Her posture sagged against the booth.

"Do you know why my grandparents left Hideaway Bay?" Val asked after a moment. Surely at the time there must have been some talk.

"No, I do not. But whatever the reason, they left in a hurry."

Valerie frowned in confusion. "What do you mean?"

"I was around twenty at the time, so old enough to remember. They were literally there one day and gone the next. Poof! Just like that. I checked with my older sister, Peggy, and she remembers it the same way. She says my mother had visited Delphine just the day before to put in an order for chocolate, and Delphine asked her to come back the following day as she was a little low on stock and planned to make more in the evening."

Valerie digested this.

"Would I be able to talk to your sister?"

"I'm sorry," Lottie said, "but that wouldn't be a good idea. Peggy doesn't like visitors. Actually, she doesn't like people. Been that way her whole life."

Before she could go off on a tangent about her sister's quirks, Valerie asked, "So you never heard anything about why they left in such a hurry?"

"No, not really," Lottie said, but appeared to hesitate.

Valerie jumped on that. "What? What is it?"

Lottie grimaced. "My mother tried to find out what happened to them, but no one knew a thing. Or if they did, they weren't saying. Not even the Marthas on the corner, who were friendly with Delphine. I don't want to speak ill of anyone, but I wonder if your grandfather might have been in some sort of trouble."

Valerie frowned, wondering what kind of trouble he could have been in.

Seeing her expression, Lottie backpedaled. "Like I said, that's purely my own speculation. I don't want to upset you."

Valerie smiled to reassure the older woman. "No, not at all. I appreciate your candor."

Lottie appeared to have shriveled as if she were afraid she might have said too much.

"Can you think of anything else?" Val asked.

"No, but talking about it brings back memories," Lottie said wistfully. And then she added with a twinkle in her eye, "All I can say is that chocolate was never the same in Hideaway Bay after the chocolatier left."

"Thank you for sharing all this with me."

"Who else are you planning on talking to?"

"Mr. Lime," Val said with a nod across the street to the five-and-dime. "And Martha Cotter."

Lottie nodded. "Very good. I'd say Mr. Lime would be your best bet. He would certainly remember your grandmother."

Valerie thanked her, paid the bill, and accompanied Lottie outside. As she waved goodbye to the elderly woman, she looked both ways and stepped off the curb, heading to the five-and-dime.

CHAPTER EIGHT

STEPPING INTO LIME'S FIVE-AND-DIME was like stepping back in time. The place had a fusty smell of sawdust that reminded Valerie of things gone by. It was oddly comforting. Overhead fluorescent lighting brought the store out of the shadows caused by the awning covering the front window, which prevented any daylight from filtering in.

Before she could think of looking for Mr. Lime, she was distracted by the cornucopia of things. Items. Every square inch of space was occupied by various odds and ends for sale. She walked down one row, looking in bins, her footfall light on the old wooden floorboards. Lacy white paper doilies were available in three different sizes to suit the size of your plate. Next to that was a selection of lace doilies in silver foil too. She was amused by the bandages that looked like strips of bacon and the fake mustaches. And she was tempted to purchase a rain bonnet but refrained. It was the Kit-Cat Klock that made her gasp. Nana had had the same one in her kitchen when Valerie was growing up. She wondered what had happened to it. It was black and white, with rolling eyes and a wagging tail.

This she couldn't resist. She picked it up and studied the box, still smiling.

"Can I help you?" asked a papery voice behind her.

Startled, Valerie jumped and slapped her hand to her chest. "You scared me."

"I'm sorry about that, miss," said the man, whom she presumed to be Mr. Lime. There was a twinkle in his eye as he apologized.

Up close, he was wizened, his tall frame stooped to such a degree that he was almost eye level with her.

She looked around the cavernous space. "I'm looking at everything you have here and enjoying your selection."

"Thank you," he said. He nodded to the box beneath her arm. "I see you've found something."

She looked at it and smiled. "I have. I haven't seen one of these in years, and it brings back memories."

"Good for you. Have a look around," he said, and he shuffled back up to the counter, where an old antique brass cash register stood. Next to it was a leather cup holding an assortment of pens and pencils and a metal spike that had receipts skewered on it.

She didn't want to appear impolite and bombard him with questions, especially given his age. On the other hand, if he was still running his shop, he might not be as fragile as he appeared.

She spent ten more minutes browsing and, in the end, she decided on the clock only.

On the counter, a rack displayed all sorts of retro candy and packs of gum: Clove, Beeman's, and Black Jack. Candy she hadn't seen in ages like Mallo Cups, Mary Janes, Payday, Pixy Stix, and orange slices. But the pièce de résistance was the multi-bin selection of Brach's candy. She was tempted but then reminded herself that she'd had cheesecake yesterday and a waffle just that morning. Her ever-increasing waistline could take no more.

"Can I interest you in some saltwater taffy?" he asked, indicating the variety of flavors on display.

"Mmm," Valerie said, studying the assortment and forgetting about her waistline. "Sure."

"Have you ever had saltwater taffy?" he asked.

"No, can't say that I have."

"I'll give you half a pound. What flavor would you like?"

Narrowing her eyes, she scanned the choices, each bin full of individual pieces of brightly colored taffy wrapped in white wax paper. "Um . . . let's try the chocolate."

"Good choice," he said. "Chocolate lover, are you?"

This was as good a segue as she was going to get. "I am. In fact, I come from a family of chocolatiers."

If her eyes weren't glued to him, she would have missed the fraction of a second where he hesitated.

"Is that so?" he asked, busying himself with the task of filling a white paper bag with her selection and weighing it up on the old-fashioned scale. He averted his gaze as he handed her the bag and rang up her order, which included the clock. As she swiped her card along the card reader, he placed her items in a brown paper bag with a handle.

"Yes, in fact I'm here to see if anyone remembers my grandmother, who was a chocolate maker here in Hideaway Bay."

Finally, he made eye contact with her, but something about his expression had changed. The shift was sudden, like looking at the horizon at sunset, seeing a smudge of an orange sun, and then looking up again to find it gone.

"What was her name?" Mr. Lime handed her the bag and his hands trembled slightly.

"Delphine Brandt."

Mr. Lime looked up to the side, appeared thoughtful, and said, "And you say she lived in Hideaway Bay at one time?"

Valerie took the bag off the counter and held it at her side. "That's right. During the fifties." When he didn't say anything, she added, "She was French."

She couldn't imagine anyone in this small town not remembering if a chocolatier had lived there, especially a French one. There certainly weren't too many of those around at any given time.

Either he was dragging his feet and holding something back, or he really didn't remember and didn't want to admit to it. After all, the man was practically a centenarian according to the Monroes. And after eyeballing him, she'd have to agree with that.

"I knew of her, but I didn't really know her that well," he finally said. His voice was soft.

"You don't know why she left or anything like that?" she asked.

"If I didn't know her, I'd hardly know why she left," he said. There was an edge to his voice.

"Someone told me that she and my grandfather left rather abruptly."

He shrugged and looked away. "I wouldn't know."

When she made no moves to leave, he said, "I'm sorry I can't help you."

"Me too." She held up the bag as she walked out. "Thanks for the taffy and the clock."

"Mmm." He said no more, busying himself behind the counter.

It was hard not to be discouraged, and she felt as if she was no nearer to the truth than when she arrived. When she left the five-and-dime, her intention was to go see Martha Cotter. But she got distracted by the sandwich board outside the neighboring shop: an olive oil store with a burgundy awning.

Figuring there was no immediate rush to visit Mrs. Cotter, she pushed through the door, immediately liking the smell of different spices. The interior was done up in dark colors: deep brown hardwood floors and shelving with all the wares on display. A variety of olive oils from around the world dominated one section. Another space was devoted to plain and flavored balsamic vinegars. In the center of the small space was what looked like a distressed barrel with a tabletop. On it were small plastic cups, some containing samples of dipping oil and others holding pieces of fresh-baked French bread. At the back of the table was a variety of dipping oils and to the right, another barrel full of French baguettes in white paper sleeves.

"Don't mind if I do," she mumbled to herself, trying a sample.

Behind the counter, two women, one auburn-haired, the other with brown hair and caramel-colored highlights, conversed easily as they worked. There was a laugh here and there, and Valerie envied them their easy camaraderie.

As she stood there debating whether to buy a bottle and a loaf of bread, thinking about crumbs all over the motel room and the draw of ants, she was approached by both women, who were near her age.

"Can I help you?" asked the auburn-haired one.

"No, I was just browsing," Valerie said, and gave them a quick smile.

"I'm Della Rossi." The woman's smile and the light in her eyes were warm. "I own the shop and this—" She indicated the woman standing beside her. "This is my best friend and able-bodied assistant, Sue Ann Marchek."

"I'm Valerie Fisher, I'm new in town."

Both women spoke at once.

"How long are you in town for?"

"What brought you to Hideaway Bay?"

Valerie laughed.

"Sorry to come on so strong," Della said.

"We don't get out much," Sue Ann cracked, and this resulted in a unified twitter from both women.

"This happens when there's a lull in the shop," Della said, her expression full of mirth.

"My grandmother used to live here in Hideaway Bay," Val said, "and I thought I'd check it out for myself."

"Who was your grandmother?" Sue Ann asked.

"Delphine Brandt. She was a Frenchwoman." That last piece of information might be enough to jog their memories, although it was obvious they were born after her grandmother's time in Hideaway Bay.

Both women appeared deep in thought, and each slowly shook her head.

Della turned to Sue Ann. "Do you know that name, Sue Ann? Your family has been coming here for decades."

"I'm sorry, but it doesn't ring any bells. And my mother and grandmother have passed on. What about your mother, Della?"

Della considered. "She never mentioned anything. But I'll ask her if she remember anyone mentioning a chocolatier."

"Thank you," Valerie said. Not only was the lakeside town beautiful, but the people were friendly and helpful.

"Let me take your number, and I'll call you if I find anything," Della said, turning on her heel and returning to the counter, where she grabbed a Post-it note and a pen.

Valerie followed her over to the counter, rattled off her phone number, and thanked her.

"You should ask Mr. Lime, he's the town's oldest resident." Della nodded her head in the direction of the five-and-dime next door.

"I've already asked him. He said he didn't know her."

Surprise clouded Sue Ann's expression. "Really? That's surprising. He seems to know everyone and everything that goes on in this town."

Della laughed. "That's true."

"In the meantime, if you're going to be here in Hideaway Bay for any length of time, Della has a social club if you'd like to check it out," Sue Ann said. She picked up a flyer from a pile on the counter and handed it to Valerie.

She read it quickly, noting the variety of events on the schedule: a bus going to Niagara Falls, Canada on Sunday, and a genealogy workshop the following month. Curious, she folded the flyer neatly in half and tucked it into the side pocket of her purse. If she did decide to stay in the area for any length of time, she might look into it.

After thanking them both, she headed out, empty-handed except for the bag from the five-and-dime, deciding a crusty loaf of French bread might not be the best thing for a hotel room.

CHAPTER NINE

AFTER SHE PUT HER shopping bag in the trunk of her car, Val slammed the lid closed and decided to walk to Martha Cotter's house. It wasn't that far, and the sunshine was nice. Hopefully, the elderly woman would have some information.

As she passed the Pink Parlor ice cream shop, she glanced in the window, liking the theme colors of pink and gray.

The large house on the corner of Star Shine Drive was Victorian in architecture, and it was pretty with its gingerbread trim and three different colors of exterior paint: cream, pale green, and forest green.

As luck would have it, the elderly woman Valerie guessed to be Martha sat on the front porch, her elbow resting on the arm of her chair, her fisted hand alongside her face. But she was not alone. Another woman sat in the chair beside hers, and they were talking amongst themselves.

With tentative steps, Valerie walked up the driveway to the front porch and waved a greeting to the old woman. Both women turned their attention to her.

"Can I help you?" the older of the women called out.

Valerie sighed, realizing this was the last person she had left to talk to. Standing at the bottom of the porch stairs, she gathered her thoughts. "My grandparents used to live here in town back in the fifties, and I'm hoping to talk to people who knew them when they lived here."

The old woman waved her up to the porch, her arm slender and her wrist bony. "Come on, take a seat."

Valerie stepped up onto the porch and smiled at the younger woman seated next to the elder. They shared the same wide-set eyes. She sat in the wicker chair across from them with her back to the beach.

Up close, the older woman didn't appear as frail, but there was a walker parked next to her chair.

"I'm Martha Cotter by the way," the older woman said. She was dressed casually in a pair of lavender slacks, a matching floral cotton blouse, and a light ivory-colored cardigan. With a smile she indicated the woman seated beside her, who bore a strong resemblance to her and appeared to be in her forties. "And this is my daughter, Martine."

"My name is Valerie Fisher. It's nice to meet you both."

Martha smiled. "My daughter has flown in from Washington State for a visit. It was quite a surprise."

Martine shrugged and grinned. "Mother's reaction when I showed up at her door was so joyful that there might be future surprise visits." Martine winked at her mother.

"I hope so," Martha said. She turned to Val. "Her visit came out of the blue. She and her husband, Edgar, and my grandson, Micah, were here for two weeks at Easter."

"That sounds lovely," Valerie said.

"I'm sorry to bore you with all of this," Martha said.

Valerie couldn't help but smile.

"Now, who were your grandparents?"

"Wayne and Delphine Brandt."

Martha's eyes widened in surprise. "Of course I remember them. The chocolatier!"

Valerie smiled, encouraged by her response.

"I will admit that I didn't know your grandfather at all. But back then, everyone knew the chocolatier in Hideaway Bay. We loved her chocolates!" Martha crowed. "My mother and grandmother were big fans."

To hear her grandmother's work so appreciated warmed Valerie's heart.

"I was told she worked out of her kitchen?" Val prompted. "She didn't have a shop?"

Martha shook her head. "That's right, all her candy was made in her kitchen." She leaned forward in her chair and pointed past Martine to the house that was now owned by the Monroe sisters. "Right there, in that house. Have you spoken to the Monroe girls?"

"I have, but they're too young to remember anything." Val's tone was full of disappointment.

"It was a long time ago," the old woman conceded. She smiled. "My mother and I used to walk down and get a box of chocolate. Your grandmother was a really pretty woman with a French accent, which we all thought was wonderful. She'd sit you at her kitchen table and give you chocolate to try." Martha laughed. "She knew what she was doing, because you'd end up buying things you didn't even know you wanted."

"I'm trying to find out why my grandparents left Hideaway Bay. By all accounts my grandmother loved it here, so I can't understand why they left."

Martha's gaze became unfocused as if she were looking back in time. "It is true they left abruptly. One day they were there and the next day they weren't. My own mother had been down to see Delphine the day before and had ordered several boxes of chocolate because she was throwing a dinner party and wanted to give them as gifts to the guests, but the next day, Delphine and Wayne and their son were gone. They just vanished."

"But you don't know why?" Valerie pressed, feeling her optimism wither like a deflated balloon.

Martha shook her head. "When they left, I was only fourteen, so I didn't know much. If my mother knew, she never said."

"Did anyone live in the house after my grandparents left?" Valerie began to cling to a thought that maybe there was another owner in the interim, between Nana and Poppy and the Monroes' grandparents.

"No. That house was abandoned until Junie and Paul Reynolds bought it." A mischievous smile lit the woman's face. "I used to meet my boyfriend there at night."

Val arched an eyebrow at this and smiled.

"Mother!" Martine said in mock shock. From somewhere deep in the house, a phone rang. Martine stood. "I'll get that. And I'll get us something to drink."

"Nothing for me," Valerie said. "I've had too much coffee this morning."

"Are you sure?" Martine asked. When Valerie nodded, she disappeared into the house.

Martine had just stepped inside when the front door opened again and a teenaged girl appeared, with the same wide-set eyes and heart-shaped face as Martine. "Oh, hi, Gram, I didn't know you had company."

Martha smiled at the sight of the girl, reminding Val of how she'd felt with her own grandmother.

"That's all right, Mimi, come on out. Valerie, this is my granddaughter, Mimi." To Mimi she said, "This is Valerie. Her grandparents used to live in Hideaway Bay a long time ago."

Mimi put up her hand in a wave and smiled. "Hi."

"Hi, Mimi, it's nice to meet you."

It didn't seem as if there was anything more to be gleaned. "I better get going, Martha. Thank you so much for your time." Valerie stood up to leave, but Martha put up her hand. "Hold on one moment, Valerie. I want you to see something." Valerie sat down.

Martha then spoke to her granddaughter. "Would you mind going upstairs, and you know that box in the bottom drawer of the armoire? The one with all the buttons in it?" When Mimi nodded, she continued, "Dump those buttons on the bedside table and bring the box down for me."

"Okay." Mimi went back inside, and the sound of running footsteps on the staircase could be heard from the porch.

"To have her energy," Martha mused, looking at the lake in front of her house.

Valerie smiled and nodded in agreement.

The girl wasn't gone long, and when she returned, she handed the empty rectangular box to her grandmother.

Martha held it in her lap.

"Gram, I'm going over to Kyle's for a little while," Mimi said.

"All right. Dinner's at five."

"I'll be here."

"I'll order Chinese for the three of us. Can you pick it up on your way home?" Martha said.

"Sure, no problem." Mimi turned to Valerie and said, "Nice meeting you."

"You too."

The teenaged girl bounded down the steps and walked along the sidewalk, turning left onto Erie Street and disappearing from sight.

Martha never took her eyes off the girl, smiling. "She lives with me. Before she moved here, I'd never had takeout in my whole life. Now, I'm addicted."

Valerie couldn't help but smile. It was apparent that the two had a great relationship.

"It must be nice to have some company."

"It is. It's a chance for me to fix some things that went wrong in the past." When she didn't elaborate, Valerie remained silent. "And these young people these days. I love them and their ideas. They're so transparent and accepting."

Valerie nodded, glancing at the box in Martha's lap.

"Forgive me, I'm so easily sidetracked." Martha laughed and handed the box to Valerie. "You might like to have that."

Valerie took the box and studied it, her breath catching. It was a white box whose glossy finish had dulled. Scuff marks marred it. But on the front, stamped into the cover in the upper left-hand corner, was a caricature of a woman in the 1950s style with an apron over a dress and high-heeled shoes, holding a tray. Right next to it was stamped the words *Delphine's Chocolates*. She fingered the name and the logo, her throat thickening and her eyes scratchy.

"I've never seen this before."

"Then you must have it," Martha declared. "Our relationships with our grandmothers are very important."

Val stood again to leave. The urge to start bawling was strong, and she didn't want to embarrass herself or this woman who had shown her such a kindness.

She clasped the box against her chest. "I can't thank you enough for this."

"It would be easy for me to say it's nothing at all, but to you, Delphine's granddaughter, it is something. Even if it is just an old box. It's something that links you to Delphine and her past."

Pressing her lips firmly together to staunch the imminent flow of tears, Val nodded.

"I hope you find what you're looking for, Valerie," Martha said.

Val nodded again, the skin on her chin scrunching up.

When she stepped off the porch, she felt buoyed and lighter than she'd felt in a long time. It was amazing what a simple thing like an old candy box could do for you.

The conversation with Jeff later that evening deteriorated quickly. Val relayed to him what Martha had given her. For a moment he was silent and then said, "You're excited over an old box?"

"It's a piece of history from my grandmother's business." It was futile to try and explain to him how important this was to her. It was the only physical thing she had that linked her to Nana's life as a chocolatier and businesswoman in Hideaway Bay. To her, it was concrete evidence that Nana had lived and breathed in this charming town. She decided it wasn't worth trying to explain it to him.

"Did you learn anything more?" he asked.

"Only that she and Poppy left in a hurry," she said.

"Now what?" he pressed.

"I don't know."

"If it's just a bunch of dead ends," he said casually, "you could leave tomorrow and be home by Friday."

Anger flared in her. "Maybe it seems like a bunch of dead ends to you. Maybe you think this is a waste of time. But maybe I'm not ready to come home."

"Haven't you done what you set out to do? What, are you going to stay there forever? Come home, Val."

His insistence irritated her. "Actually, I like the town of Hideaway Bay and I think I might stay." She took in a deep breath. "Indefinitely."

"Indefinitely. What does that mean?" he barked.

"It means that I don't want to come home."

"And what about our marriage?" he demanded.

"That's a good question. What about it? We're like roommates, and that's not what I want."

"It can't always be passionate."

It was frustrating how he sometimes didn't get what she was saying.

"I know that, and I wasn't talking about that. When was the last time you and I did anything together? Went on a trip—"

"We just went to Paris last spring!" he said.

"I mean by ourselves, without visiting family or friends. We never spend any time together."

"I'm tired, Val. I'm coasting to retirement. I'm happy with our routine."

"And I'm fed up. I've asked you many times to go to marriage counseling, and nothing ever comes of it."

"And I've told you many times that I'm not comfortable sharing every detail about our marriage with a stranger."

"And we never did. And here we are," Valerie said. "You've got a wife who doesn't want to come home."

It went silent on the other end of the line and finally, Jeff spoke. "Do you want a divorce?"

Valerie took her time answering. "I honestly don't know. All I know is things can't continue as they are and that I've got to make some changes. If you want to join me, fine, but if you don't . . ." She let her voice trail off.

"That's just great," he said, and he hung up on her.

In all their years together, he'd never hung up the phone on her. But of course, the topic of divorce had never been mentioned before either.

Sighing, she set the phone down, her eyes were wet with tears. It felt as if they'd reached an impasse in their relationship. Uncertainty filled her about the future of her marriage. Like most couples, she'd been so full of hope and excitement on the day she got married, thinking Jeff was the only one for her. No one gets married to get divorced.

It appeared she had indeed arrived at a dead end, in more ways than one.

CHAPTER TEN

V ALERIE SPOKE TO VIV about extending her stay at the motel, and Viv informed her that she could stay as long as she liked. Val made a reservation for another two nights. What was happening after that, she didn't know. Unsure of what to do next, she decided she'd wander around the town and discover what it had to offer, starting with breakfast at the Chat and Nibble.

After a delicious breakfast of eggs sunny-side up and wheat toast, she walked down to the boardwalk she'd seen at the end of Erie Street and walked across its treads, the wood echoing beneath her feet. At the end of it, she removed her sneakers and stepped into the warm, loose sand, which immediately covered her feet. It was cooler below the surface and it felt nice. A good number of people were on the beach, mostly walkers, taking advantage of the sunny May morning. Carrying her sneakers in one hand, she walked along parallel to the shoreline, inhaling the brackish air redolent of lake water and fish but not unpleasant by any means. The lake was calm and grayish-blue in color. Dipping her toes into the shallow water, she was shocked at how cold it was and quickly retreated. Thin, wispy clouds were scattered across the sky but there was no breeze. She looked south and spotted cliffs lining the lakeshore with thick, dense foliage at the top offering glimpses of multi-million-dollar mansions.

Val turned to see how far she'd walked—a considerable distance given how small the houses on Star Shine Drive appeared. She headed back the way she came, but soon she grew a little breathless. *I really have to get this extra weight off.*

Needing a rest, she plopped down in the sand to catch her breath. She stared out at the horizon. Jeff was right about the trip having led to a whole bunch of dead ends. But as disappointed as she was that the whole thing had been an exercise in futility, she didn't want to go home. The thought of returning to Colorado and a tepid marriage depressed her. There had to be more to life. If she died tomorrow, she'd be leaving too many things unfinished.

The temptation to remain in Hideaway Bay was strong. She couldn't shake the sense since she arrived that she felt closer to her grandmother. It was easy to see why Nana had loved the place. Val looked over her shoulder at the back of the buildings that lined Main Street, getting glimpses through the narrow alleyways of the colorful awnings across the street. It was so charming. It was as if she'd stepped into another plane of existence.

In the distance, someone waved to her, and she frowned in confusion. But when she spotted the gentle lope of the Great Dane, Charlie, she recognized the walker as Lily Monroe, the sister with the blond hair. She held up her hand in greeting.

Lily approached her carrying a small pail in her hand. The dog made a dash for Val when he spotted her, and Lily reined him in with the leash. Slowly, Valerie got to her feet to avoid possibly being tackled by the dog.

"Collecting seashells?" she asked with a nod toward Lily's blue plastic pail.

Lily tipped the pail just enough so Valerie could see the contents without them spilling out. The pail was half full of colorful bits of smooth glass.

"Broken glass?" Valerie asked.

"Beach glass," Lily corrected. "You might have seen pieces of it in the sand."

"I have."

Charlie remained at Lily's side, seated, but wagging his tail.

"May I pet him?" Val asked.

"Of course," Lily said with a sideward glance toward her dog.

Tentatively, Valerie reached out and patted the top of the dog's head, and was immediately rewarded with a sloppy wet tongue on the inside of her arm. Caught by surprise, she burst out laughing.

"I wasn't expecting that!"

"Charlie means well, but he has no manners." Lily shook her head in exaggerated resignation.

Val's gaze slid back to the glass in the pail. There were multiple colors: brown, green, and white, and one cobalt blue shard peeked out from the top.

"What do you do with the glass?" she asked.

"I create crafts with it. Christmas ornaments, planters, frames."

"And do you sell them?"

"I do. I have consignments in most of the shops in town," Lily said. Val did not miss the pride in her tone.

"I'll have to check it out," Val said. "Don't you risk the chance of being cut with broken glass?"

"No. Over time, the glass has been tempered by the lake," Lily explained. "My grandfather used to tell us it came from all the boats, freighters, and trawlers that crowded the lake in the '50s and '60s."

Valerie imagined her grandmother standing in this spot, staring out at the horizon, the lake full of boats. It occurred to her that Nana had once stared at this view, had walked in this sand, had breathed this air. A chill tickled her spine.

"It's hard to imagine that there used to be a lot of traffic on the lake. It's so beautiful and peaceful," Valerie mused.

"I know. But I think it's better this way, less industry on the lake."

Valerie had to agree with her there.

"How are you doing with your search?" Lily asked.

Valerie sighed. "Not good at all. I suppose it was too much to ask to try and find out what happened here. Too much time has passed."

"I'm sorry to hear that."

"I spoke to Mr. Lime, Lottie Prescott, and Martha Cotter. Mr. Lime said he didn't know much about Nana at all, and both Lottie and Martha only remember my grandparents leaving abruptly."

"That would explain why the house had been abandoned for years when my grandparents bought it," Lily said.

Valerie nodded. It hadn't been a total loss. She had that candy box from Martha. A physical remnant of the time Nana had lived and worked here was more than she could have hoped for. She'd treasure it. Plus, after all those years of hearing about Hideaway Bay and how much it meant to her grandmother, it was nice to finally visit the place and imagine her grandmother living in the house on Star Shine Drive and walking Main Street and sitting on the beach.

"What was your grandmother like?" Lily asked.

No one had ever asked her this. Not even Jeff, but then she'd told him and the kids so much about Nana there had never been any need to ask.

How did you sum up the importance of one person in your life in only a few sentences?

"When I was with my grandmother, she made me feel loved just as I was. No matter what I did or how I looked or even if I misbehaved, she loved me."

Even that explanation seemed terribly lacking. Woefully inadequate. Childhood, though generally happy, hadn't been easy. She'd been born with a lazy eye that required glasses and two corrective surgeries by the time she was eleven. Kids at school had been merciless in those early years, and there was always refuge with her grandmother, making chocolate. Whenever she'd stepped into that kitchen after school with Nana bustling about, it felt as if all her cares and worries had slipped away. Nana always told her she was the best assistant *ever* but at that young age, Valerie suspected she was more a hindrance than a help.

"Grandmothers are amazing," Lily said softly.

"When I was a teenager and old enough to understand, Nana used to tell me stories about what it was like growing up in France and what the war did to them. She loved the United States though." Valerie, in turn, had told her children those stories. As long as they were alive and continued to pass down the stories, the memory of her grandmother remained alive as well.

"It sounds like she had an interesting life."

"That's for sure." *Much more interesting than mine.*

"What will you do now?" Lily asked. At her side, Charlie spotted another dog, a terrier, and he cowered behind Lily. "It's all right, buddy." Luckily the walker with the dog headed in the opposite direction, and the Great Dane was able to relax.

"I don't know. I suppose there's nothing more I can do here in Hideaway Bay." She swallowed hard and was surprised at the tremor in her voice. "But the thing is, even though I've only been here a couple of days, I don't want to leave."

Lily laughed. "That's what happens to people when they visit Hideaway Bay. They want to stay."

"I might stick around for a little while longer."

"If you like it here, why not?" Lily asked.

And that was a good question.

Chapter Eleven

Lily

THE CONVERSATION EARLIER ON the beach with Valerie played across Lily's mind for the rest of the day. Alice was right; there was an air of sadness and resignation that lingered around the woman. And there was something else about Val that Lily recognized. She seemed lost. Lily was only too aware of how that felt. A while back, she'd been very lost after her husband's death, and coming back to Hideaway Bay had helped her immensely. And although she was sure remaining in town might be a good move for Valerie, it wasn't the whole piece.

It was a rare night that she and Isabelle and Alice were all home together, but tonight their significant others all had other plans. Lily appreciated nights like these; it was nice to hang out with her sisters. Currently, they sat on the porch, watching the sun set over Lake Erie. Charlie slept in front of the door, snoring loudly.

"Does he need some Breathe Right strips or something?" Isabelle asked, casting a glance in his direction. "I can barely hear myself think with that noise."

Lily giggled. "It is loud."

"What did you do to him today, Lily? He's out cold," said Alice.

"We went for three walks on the beach in search of glass for the upcoming Christmas bazaar."

"But Christmas is seven months away," Alice said.

"I know, but remember last year? When I didn't have enough glass for all the ornaments I wanted to make?" Lily winced at the memory of it. There'd been a freak early winter storm in November, and she'd been unable to get out to the beach to collect it.

A comfortable lull settled among them.

"I ran into Valerie Fisher on one of my trips to the beach," Lily said casually.

"Has she had any luck with finding information on her grandmother?" Alice asked.

"No. She's spoken to a few people but hasn't really learned any more," Lily told them.

Alice grimaced in sympathy. "That poor thing."

"She looked a little lost," Lily said.

"I can imagine," Alice said.

Isabelle remained silent, staring at the sunset, not contributing to the conversation.

"Maybe we should pull up a few floorboards to see if her grandmother's journals are there," Lily said, waiting for her sisters' reaction.

That little bomb detonated as expected. Alice jumped up and clapped her hands, startling Charlie, who woke and lifted his head. Deciding it required no further attention from him, he laid his head back down and closed his eyes.

"Oh no, not this again," Isabelle moaned.

Lily cast a side glance at Alice. Her younger sister's expression was bright and open with enthusiasm. Lily winked at her.

"I know it's an inconvenience."

"That's an understatement," Isabelle huffed.

You had to be careful with Isabelle as she could be spiky. You had to know how to approach her.

"Please think about it," Lily said. "If there's nothing under the floor, then we've done everything we can to help her. If there is, then think what a difference that would make in her life."

Isabelle pressed her lips together until all the color had leeched from them.

Alice spoke up. "Maybe there's a story in there for you to write. Journals lost for decades."

Isabelle shook her head. "Nope. I don't write human interest stories." The way she said it, her voice steely, indicated she had her mind made up about it and could not be budged.

"If it becomes a mess, we'll get Dylan Satler out here to replace the whole floor. Alice and I will pay for it." Lily said. "If that's all right with you, Alice."

"Of course it is."

Lily glanced downward. "If it were Gram, wouldn't you want to read her journals or diary from seventy years ago? If Gram's journals were beneath the floorboards of someone else's house, wouldn't you hope the owners would be moved to sympathy to help you out, especially if your grandmother meant so much to you?"

Isabelle turned her head slightly toward Lily and narrowed her eyes. "Oh, that's low, even for you, Lily."

"Just saying."

Their oldest sister didn't immediately answer. Lily and Alice remained silent, waiting for Isabelle to work it out on her own and arrive at the right conclusion.

Isabelle swung her legs off the table, sat up and sighed. "All right. I can see it's two against one. Go get the crowbar from the shed. But if we have to rip up the whole floor, then let's call Dylan and get him to do it so it can be replaced properly and we don't do any further damage."

As Lily and Alice hopped off the porch in a dash for the shed, Isabelle remained seated with Charlie, grumbling about being ganged up on.

CHAPTER TWELVE

Valerie

VALERIE UNPLUGGED HER CURLING iron and left it on the desk of her motel room. It was late morning, and she was hungry. Her plan was to head up to the Chat and Nibble for breakfast and then spend the day at the beach. She'd purchased a bathing suit in town, but the lake was still a little too cold to go swimming. Viv had told her it would be another month before the water was warm enough.

She double-checked her large canvas bag, making sure she had sunscreen, her hat, a beach towel to sit on, her sunglasses, and a couple of magazines to read. She hoped the activity would distract her and ease her mind. The previous night, she'd called Jeff but there'd been no answer. And he hadn't responded to the message she'd left. But then what did she expect? In time, he'd calm down. She hoped.

Later, she would get some dinner at Cabana Sally's and watch the sun set.

A knock at her motel door interrupted her thoughts. She set the bag on the bed and went to the door, thinking it was most likely Viv. Who else would it be? But when she peered through the peephole, she was surprised to see Lily and Alice Monroe standing outside.

Unsure as to why they were there, she opened the door and smiled. "Hi."

The two sisters wore capri pants, T-shirts, and broad smiles.

"Is this a bad time?" Lily asked, her sunglasses perched on top of her head.

Alice stood next to her, holding a blue-and-white-striped canvas bag over her arm.

"Nope." Valerie opened the door wider to allow them in. She caught their gazes bouncing around the room. She was glad she'd made the bed.

"You were right when you said Hideaway Bay needed a B & B," she said.

Both the sisters laughed.

"We won't keep you long," Lily started. They were still smiling, and Valerie thought they were acting strange.

"We have some good news," Alice said.

"Oh?" Val couldn't imagine how their good news could possibly affect her.

Alice set the bag on the edge of the bed. "These things are heavy." She pulled out three well-aged leather-bound books. The edges of their pages were stained and curled.

Valerie's breath hitched, and there was a slight ache in her chest. *It couldn't be.*

"We dug up the floor!" Lily said excitedly.

"And look what we found!" Alice gushed.

Valerie slapped her hands to her face, stunned. Tears filled her eyes as she was overcome with emotion. She couldn't believe it.

Alice laid the journals carefully on the small round laminated brown table beneath the double window. Her approach was careful, slow, and thoughtful. Almost reverent.

For a minute, Valerie could only stare at them. A thought occurred to her. "Are you sure they're hers?"

Lily nodded. "Yes, on the inside covers it says they belong to Delphine Giroud Brandt."

Alice reached out and said quickly, "But we didn't read them."

"We couldn't have, even if we'd been tempted to. They're written in French," Lily added.

Valerie looked at the two women, her heart overflowing with gratitude. The tears spilled. "I can't thank you enough. You have no idea what this means to me." Impulsively, she pulled both of them into a hug and squeezed them hard.

Both women hugged her back.

When they pulled away, Lily took a step back and placed her hand on the doorknob. "We'll let you get on with it. You're probably anxious to dive in."

"Wait." Val said, putting up her hand. "What made you change your mind?"

Lily and Alice exchanged a glance. "We had a good think about it and decided we wanted to help you."

Again, tears welled up in Valerie's eyes. "And what about Isabelle?"

Alice laughed. "She was the one wielding the crowbar!"

Valerie winced. "I hope you didn't have to rip up too much of your floor."

Lily had the grace to laugh. "You'd think your grandmother would have hidden them near a corner or the wall."

"But no, she hid them beneath the center of the floor, right where our coffee table sits. She really didn't want anyone to find them," Alice said.

"I am so sorry. I will pay to repair the floor or replace it," Val said.

But Lily shook her head. "Nope. I think we were just as excited as you to find them."

"Did you find anything else?"

"A couple of buttons and an old black-and-white photo of our grandparents standing on the porch when they first bought the house," Lily said.

"Isabelle said it was worth ripping up the floor just for that!" Alice added.

"We really must be going," Lily said. "I hope those journals give you some of the answers you're looking for. The condition isn't the greatest, but that's due to where they were hidden and for how long."

Valerie nodded, not taking her eye off the stack of journals. "That's to be understood."

Lily opened the door to the motel room, and bright daylight flooded the room.

"Look, before I leave town, I'd like to take all three of you to dinner," Val offered, seeing them out.

"We never refuse a free meal," Alice said.

"Good. I'll talk to you before I go," Valerie said.

They waved goodbye and she called after them, "Again, thank you so much."

She waited until they drove off, and she closed the motel room door and locked it.

Immediately, she pulled one of the two upholstered chairs out from the table and sat down. The fabric on the chair was dated and threadbare but she didn't care. With shaking hands, she pulled the journals closer to her. The leather bindings were dusty, and she wiped a cobweb away from the edging of the pages. She opened the first book and her heart skipped a beat when she came face to face with her grandmother's familiar scrawl. Overwhelmed, she laid her hand on her chest, fingers splayed. In the center of the page, her grandmother had written her name and below it, the years the journal covered. Valerie noted the dates of the books and put them in order. Leafing through the pages, she confirmed they were all written in French. Of course they would be; it was Nana's native tongue. Some of the pages were torn or water-stained and although the ink had faded in some places, it was still legible.

What needed to be done immediately was to get them translated. Val's understanding of French was rudimentary at best.

She picked up her phone and googled "translation services," and soon found one that looked suitable in Buffalo. Excited, she called them and arranged for an appointment the following day.

Even though she was unable to read them, she lay on the bed and leafed through them page by page, her excitement growing. When she got to the last book, she noticed a black-and-white photo with a scalloped white border around it, stuck to one of the pages halfway through. She pried it free and pulled it closer to examine it. It was taken on the porch of the house on Hideaway Bay. Blue ink had been scrawled on the lower border of the photo: *Delphine and Gus 1959.*

A tall, slender man stood on the middle step, relaxed and smiling. Behind him, on the porch, was her grandmother, grinning broadly. She had her arms crossed over her chest, her hands tucked into the crooks of her elbows. She leaned against the porch post and had one leg bent against the other, the tip of her toe touching the porch floor.

Valerie frowned.

Who was Gus?

—ele—

Valerie returned from a few hours at the beach. Despite her curiosity about the journals, she needed to get out of the room for a little bit; it was beginning to feel claustrophobic. The fresh air, the warm sunshine, and the sound of the surf had had a restorative effect on her. On the way back to her room, she stopped at a local deli and purchased a coffee and sandwich to go as she wasn't that hungry for dinner.

Once back in her room, she ate quickly so she could make her phone calls and then spend the rest of the evening going through the journals.

Her first call was to Jeff. She wanted to share her news with him. It surprised her that she was excited to call him and tell him about her news despite their troubles.

But his phone went to voicemail, and she ended up leaving a long, excitable rambling message about the discovery of the journals beneath the floorboards of the house, how she was getting them translated and would be there for a few more weeks and finally, she asked that he'd give her a call just to let her know he was all right.

—ele—

Still wanting to share her great news with someone, she decided to give her daughter a ring. It wasn't too late there yet.

"Hey, Mom, what's up?" Renee picked up on the first ring.

Val relayed her news.

"That's amazing! I can't believe it!"

Tears sprang to Val's eyes for someone else to validate how great a thing this was.

"Have you read any of it?"

"No, it's all written in French, which I should have anticipated," Val said. "I'm going up to Buffalo tomorrow to get them translated."

"Why don't you send them to me? I can translate them for you," Renee offered.

Val appreciated her daughter's offer. But that would mean shipping them off to France, and that was too far away. Plus, her daughter's work as an artist kept her busy full time. It would take weeks if not months to get them back.

Before Val could reply, Renee laughed. "It's okay, Mom, I get it. You couldn't possibly wait *that* long."

"I appreciate your offer, but I want them translated yesterday," Val said.

Renee laughed. "That's okay. Did you tell Dad?"

"I called him, but he didn't answer. So I left a message."

"I'm sure he'll be so excited for you."

"I hope so." Doubt tinged Val's voice.

"Don't be too hard on him. He misses you, that's all, and he's operating from that vantage point."

It had never occurred to Val that her husband might actually miss her. "When did you get so wise?"

Renee laughed. They spoke for a few more minutes before hanging up. Val called Chuck, whose response mirrored Renee's. By the time she went to bed, she had a smile on her face, happy with the day, the most productive one in a long time.

Chapter Thirteen

"Three weeks?" Valerie asked, her heart sinking.

The drive to Buffalo had taken a little more than an hour, and the building that housed the translation service was located right in the heart of downtown. The surrounding buildings had some fine architecture.

The woman behind the desk, whose name was Paula, was a bit older than Val. She looked through the journals and typed on her keyboard.

"Yes, I'm sorry about that."

The office was small, with bookshelves and a sash window that let in minimal light due to the neighboring building being so close. Despite this, there was a large plant in the corner of the room that almost seemed to overtake its space.

"I'd be willing to pay extra to have it expedited," Valerie said. Actually, she'd be willing to give up a kidney to get the translation back as soon as possible.

"I understand your desire to get this back as soon as possible. But the best we can do is three weeks."

Resigned, Val said, "No problem."

Paula pulled sheets of paper off the printer on her desk and went over the terms with Val. When all was finished, Val pulled out her credit card and paid a 20% deposit.

On the drive back to Hideaway Bay, she debated back and forth about how she would pass her time in the beachside town while she waited for her grandmother's journals to be translated. Certainly, she'd be able to find more elderly people to interview in hopes of finding out more information about Nana and Poppy. But probably not three weeks' worth.

The only thing she was certain of was that she was not ready to leave Hideaway Bay.

It was late afternoon by the time Val reached Hideaway Bay, and the sky was a deep, cloudless blue. The sun was so bright it was like a white orb in the sky. The lake shimmered below, bright and sparkling.

What she needed at that moment was some fresh air and scenery so she could think. A phone call was planned with Jeff later that evening, and she'd be lying if she said she didn't dread it. Sighing and pushing thoughts of her husband and her marriage out of her mind, she parked in the lot behind the five-and-dime and walked around front to the main thorough-fare.

Thirsty, she purchased a large coffee and strolled through town, looking at all the shops and loving their colorful striped awnings and signs. The place looked healthy, economically. There were no derelict buildings, and most of the storefronts appeared to be occupied with business tenants. The buildings were a pretty mix of Italianate brick buildings and clapboard-sided buildings with brick fronts.

In the few short days she'd been here, she'd fallen in love with this town. Now she understood her grandmother's fondness for it.

As she considered what she might do for the next three weeks, she thought about the trajectory of her own life, especially the rest of it, and the idea of pursuing a new career in chocolate-making was front and center. Every time she thought about it and the possibilities, the more excited she became. She'd had a vague plan that when she returned to Colorado, she'd seriously start looking into commercial candy making, focusing on chocolates only. But now, here in Hideaway Bay, the pull was strong to start her business right here in the beachside town.

In the past, whenever the fleeting idea of becoming a chocolatier entered her imagination, she'd quickly dismissed it. Her reasons were abundant. She wouldn't be as good as her grandmother. A career employee, she'd never be able to own her own business. She didn't know enough about the business or making chocolate to succeed. She didn't have what it took to become a successful chocolatier. It was too late at this point in her life to start a new career. And her biggest excuse: without her grandmother's guidance, it would never work.

But here she was, with a dual issue that now propelled her in this direction. She still had a good bit of life ahead of her and in the short few months since beginning her retirement, she was bored out of her mind. Her brother was right. She needed a purpose.

As she walked along at a leisurely pace, enjoying the sights and the sounds of the little town, she decided she was going to need a place to stay. If she could find a house to rent in town, she could devote her time to mastering chocolate making with the intent of eventually opening up a shop in commercial premises.

This idea—this dream—filled her with so much excitement that she couldn't wait to get started.

First, accommodation. She couldn't stay long term in the motel. It was fine for a few days but not for anything permanent. Plus, there was no kitchen. A short-term rental would be suitable for now, and she'd ask the Monroe girls if they could recommend a realtor. She'd give herself six months to throw herself into this new venture. There were no kids to look after and no job that demanded forty hours a week of her time. And no marriage to speak of. She could pour all her energy and focus into her new enterprise. And what better place to start than in Hideaway Bay?

It felt right.

But despite her bubbling enthusiasm, she dreaded telling Jeff and her kids. It wasn't that she wanted a divorce, but she couldn't carry on with her marriage and her life as it currently was. It was too depressing. Their routine almost felt robotic. You could tell what day of the week it was simply by what they were having for dinner. They'd turned into creatures of habit.

That ended now.

It was time to start living life again.

With a sigh, she crossed the street, thinking it might be time to get something to eat. She opted for Cabana Sally's, thinking she wanted to celebrate.

Afterward, she headed back to her motel. She could not put off the phone call to Jeff any longer.

Chapter Fourteen

"YOU WANT TO DO what?" Jeff asked.

"I want to become a chocolatier like my grandmother," Valerie repeated.

"Okay. But can't you do that here? In Denver?"

This need to pursue her dream in Hideaway Bay was inexplicable. She couldn't even explain it to herself. "No, I want to do it here."

"For how long?"

"For at least six months. I'm going to see how it goes. And who knows, I may stay here forever." Her mouth was dry, and her hands shook.

"And what about me? What about our marriage?"

She blew out a long breath. "I don't know."

"Do I have any say in this?"

She didn't know how to answer that.

"So are we getting a divorce then? Because it's a little tough to be married to someone who isn't here."

"Do you want a divorce?" she asked.

"I didn't. But now I don't know. I thought when you came home, we could go to counseling."

This came out of left field. How many times over the years had she suggested that very thing.

"Where is this coming from?" she asked, wondering if it was a ploy on his part to get her to return home. That thought held nothing but dread for her.

His tone softened. "I've been thinking about what you said."

She waited, half expectant and half dreading. What if he had changed his mind? Did that give her reason enough to go back? Or was it too late for them?

"Look, you think all you want about it, but I'll be here in Hideaway Bay." She steeled herself, trying not to let him tell her what she wanted to hear. Not wanting him to wear her down to the point where she packed up her car and drove home and back to the way things were. No, this was her chance. The time was now. There might not be an opportunity to do this again.

He sighed. "If you come home, we can think about it together."

The time for that had passed. If only he'd expressed an interest last year, six months, or even three months ago. But it was too late. Things were in forward motion now, momentum picking up.

"I can think about things perfectly right here in Hideaway Bay."

Jeff opted for a different tack. "You're throwing away a perfectly good marriage."

She tilted her head to one side. "Really, you're going to say we have a perfectly good marriage?" When he didn't say anything, she added, "Being in a comfortable rut doesn't make it perfect or good."

"We've got all this time invested in the marriage, and we've got two great kids," he said.

"I know that. But the fact that we've been married almost thirty years and that Jeremy and Renee have turned out to be good people isn't enough." His standards must be very low. A sigh heaved forth. "I need more than co-existing as roommates, Jeff. What we have is not enough anymore. I'm not happy."

There was silence at the other end, and then finally Jeff spoke. "Fine, then."

"Look, I'll call the kids and talk to them," she said.

"Yeah, you do that."

The call ended abruptly, and Val was left staring at the phone for a minute.

Deciding she didn't want to end the day on a downer, she rang her brother and told him her plans. Although he voiced his concerns about her marriage, reminding her that Jeff was a great guy, he also swung his support behind her business idea, telling her it was something that was long overdue.

She had to agree with him.

Chapter Fifteen

"Y ou'll want to talk to Thelma Schumacher," Is-abelle Monroe told Valerie the following morning when she stopped by their house.

On the front lawn was a pile of old floorboards. There was a panel van parked in the driveway. On the side it read "Dylan Satler, Hideaway Bay Home Improvement." Valerie winced when she saw it. Their act of generosity had cost them a new floor.

"And she is . . . ?"

Isabelle's smile was full of mirth. "She was a lifelong friend of my grandmother's. She owns lots of rental property in Hideaway Bay. Some are short term, some seasonal, some long term."

"Would you have a number for her?"

"Sure, but I'll give you her address as well. She lives with-in walking distance of here. And she wouldn't mind if you stopped in."

"Thanks."

"Come on in, but don't mind the mess," Isabelle said, holding the screen door open.

Most of the floorboards had been removed, and a man wearing jeans and a short-sleeved T-shirt was kneeling on the subfloor, laying the new hardwood. The sisters had picked out a wide-plank oak the color of honey. The man turned and gave her a wave of acknowledgement and got back to work.

Not wanting to get in the way, Valerie remained standing by the front door. Isabelle disappeared from the room and returned shortly with a pink Post-it note in her hand.

Val scanned the note. Seashell Lane. This street ran off of Erie, and she had passed it every day as she drove back and forth between her motel room and the town. From the Monroes' house, it wasn't that far of a walk.

With pink note in hand, she pushed through the screen door to get out of the carpenter's way. Isabelle followed her.

"Look, Isabelle, I can't thank you and your sisters enough for all this," she said with a generous sweep of her arm. "I wish you would let me reimburse you for the cost of replacing your floor."

Isabelle laughed and shook her head. "Not a chance. It really was no problem."

"I think having your whole living room torn up might be a little bit of a problem," Val countered.

"It was in desperate need of being replaced," Isabelle told her. "When we pulled some of the floor up, we discovered the subfloor was rotted out in places. So actually, you did us a favor."

Valerie thought she was only being nice but didn't push it.

"Have you gone through your grandmother's journals?" Isabelle asked.

Valerie smiled. "Not yet. They're currently being translated. Unfortunately, I don't speak French." Memories of her grandmother flooded her mind, and her smile deepened.

"How long are you staying?"

"At least six months."

Isabelle laughed. "It sounds like you've been bitten by the Hideaway Bay bug." She stood there with her arms folded against her chest. Valerie envied the younger woman's vitality and realized sadly that she wasn't that much older than Isabelle. She self-consciously touched her hand to her thinning hair as she admired Isabelle's thick, dark mane.

Knowing that Isabelle worked from home, Valerie did not want to keep her. She moved to step off the porch and held up the Post-it note. "Thanks again, I appreciate it."

Isabelle waved her off and disappeared into the house.

Valerie left her car parked on Star Shine Drive and walked to the end of the street, waving to Martha Cotter on her porch as she passed, and turned left onto Erie.

Seashell Lane was a modest area of tidy lawns and well-maintained homes.

Thelma Schumacher's house was a two-story mint green clapboard-sided home. Like all the other homes in town, it had a porch that was deep and wide. Various wind chimes hung from the porch overhang but were currently still as there was no breeze. There were four lawn chairs on the front porch, and ceramic and red clay pots of newly planted annual flowers flanked the ends of each of the steps. A bright orange, red, and yellow flag with the word "Summer" on it hung from a pole whose bracket had been affixed to the porch post. At the far end of the front lawn, a woman stood next to a bird feeder, scooping birdseed out of an open bag that had been placed in a green wheelbarrow. She scooped the seed out cup by cup, pouring it into the feeder. Valerie assumed this must be Thelma. The woman appeared eighty-ish and had a head full of tight iron-gray curls. Her pants were lightweight and ended at her calf. She wore white ankle socks with a pair of sandals. Her red T-shirt was long-sleeved, with little white flowers embroidered along the neckline.

Valerie approached her, and the woman turned around, her expression guarded.

"Can I help you?"

"I hope so." Valerie smiled. "Are you Thelma Schumacher?"

The older woman narrowed her eyes. "And if I am?"

This one was feisty.

"Isabelle Monroe gave me your name and address. I'm Valerie Fisher," Val said by way of introduction.

As soon as she mentioned Isabelle's name, the woman visibly relaxed, and she smiled.

"Are you the one that had them dig up the floor?" She dropped the measuring cup into the bag of birdseed. It was a twenty-five-pound bag, and Val wondered how she managed to get it out to her front yard even with the wheelbarrow.

Val grimaced. "Guilty as charged."

Thelma stood with her hands on her hips. "Interesting story how your grandmother used to live in Junie's house." She shook her head and mused, "It's a small world."

"It is."

"What can I do for you?"

"I'm interested in accommodation, and Isabelle thought you might have a house I could rent."

"For how long?"

"Short term. Six months or so."

"Are you married?"

"Um, separated."

"Sorry, didn't mean to pry. It's just that I run a club for widows and widowers, and I'm always looking to recruit new members," she explained. She took hold of the handles of the wheelbarrow. "Go on and take a seat on the porch, I'll put this away and join you shortly. I may have something for you."

Thelma wheeled the wheelbarrow around the side of the house and disappeared to the back. Hopeful, Valerie stepped up onto the porch and made herself comfortable in one of the plastic chairs. It was made to look like wicker. There were faded floral cushions on each of the seats.

Within a few minutes, Thelma appeared on the front porch from inside the house, pushing her screen door open with her elbow, carrying two tall glasses of iced tea.

"I don't know about you, but I sure could use a refreshment," Thelma said.

Valerie jumped up to relieve her of one of the glasses. With beverage in hand, she returned to her chair and took a sip.

Thelma set her glass down on a little table that sat between two chairs. The top of the table was a kaleidoscope of stained glass. "Hold on a minute."

She went back into the house and returned carrying a purple folder and a pair of glasses.

Once she settled in her chair, she took a sip of her iced tea and set the glass back down. Donning her glasses, she flipped open the folder and spread it out in her lap.

"Actually, I have two properties available for June first. One is furnished and one is not." She looked up at Valerie. "Of course, the furnished one would be a bit more. Both include utilities."

A furnished place would save her the hassle and expense of buying furniture. It would be perfect until she knew for certain what her plans were for Hideaway Bay.

"Could I view the furnished place?"

"I'd require first month's rent and a security deposit," Thelma said firmly, eyeing Val over the top of her glasses. "There's no sense in going over there until you know the cost and whether it fits your budget."

Val thought the rent was reasonable. "Of course."

Thelma nodded. "If you're not doing anything right now, we can drive over and see it. There's no one living in it at the moment. It's up on Starview Drive near the parish hall."

"I left my car over on Starshine Drive."

"That's no problem," Thelma said. "I can drive."

The little cottage, though small, was perfect. It had just enough furniture to get by, and the kitchen was big enough for what she intended to do with it.

Thelma had shooed her away when she suggested going to the ATM to get cash for the security deposit and first month's rent, saying it could wait until the morning. Too tired to fuss about dinner, Val stopped at the Chat and Nibble and had a meatloaf and mashed potato dinner. It was pure comfort food.

Back at the motel, she decided to call Jeremy and Renee. It was time to stop putting that off. It was best they know.

Jeremy was stiff on the phone, asking if his father had betrayed her in any way to make her leave so abruptly and move clear across the country.

Val leaned against the rickety headboard of the motel bed and laid her hand across her belly, wishing the meatloaf dinner would move along her digestive tract.

"Of course your father hasn't betrayed me," she said with a sigh. "We just need a little break."

Jeremy scoffed. "It sounds like you're rebuilding your life in another town without Dad."

When she said nothing, Jeremy asked, "What exactly is the problem between you and Dad?"

"I'm sorry, honey, but that isn't any of your business. That's between me and your father," she said.

He snorted. "It affects me, so it is my business."

"We need some space from each other to evaluate our options," she explained.

"That's code for divorce. Mom, really. You've almost been married thirty years. What's the point?"

It was turning into a circular argument. She wrapped up the phone call, telling him she'd be in touch.

Her next call, to Renee, went a little better. Her daughter was more philosophical about it.

"It's only natural that you and Dad should grow apart. To be honest, I don't see how most marriages stay together."

"Gee, honey, that's kind of cynical."

"Are you the same person today as when you walked down the aisle?"

"Gosh, no." Valerie hardly recognized that fresh college graduate from back then.

"How's Dad?"

"As you might expect," she said wearily.

"Honestly, Mom, although it saddens me that your marriage is floundering, I do think it's great about you pursuing a passion. You're still young, you need to have a purpose in your life. Something that makes you want to get out of bed in the morning."

Tears filled her eyes at her daughter's support. "I think so too," Val whispered.

"Well, you've got my support one hundred percent. I can't wait to see this Hideaway Bay when I come home next time."

"I'd really love that, Renee. I'd love to see you. I can see why my grandmother fell in love with this place."

"On another note, do you have your grandmother's address from when she lived in France?"

"No. Why?"

"I wanted to go visit the place where she lived."

Valerie felt a thrill of excitement. "That would be wonderful. I don't know it. Although I remember her talking about it, I don't recall any names. But you know what, Uncle Chuck might know. Give him a call."

"Thanks, Mom."

CHAPTER SIXTEEN

June 1ˢᵗ

VALERIE PACKED UP HER few belongings from her motel room and settled the bill with Viv at the front desk before making her way over to her new home on Starview Drive.

As soon as she stepped inside, she was hit by the smell of lemon-scented cleaning solution. There was relief in knowing that Thelma had had it professionally cleaned before she moved in, so for now she didn't have to do a thing. After almost thirty years of cooking and cleaning, she was over all that. Maybe someday, she'd be able to hire a cleaner. That would be a luxury.

It didn't take long for her to unpack her few belongings. She took the largest back bedroom with a double bed and one dresser, carefully folding her clothes and laying them in the drawers. There was a washing machine and dryer in a utility room at the back of the house. They looked older, but Thelma had assured her they were in fine working condition.

She added laundry detergent, bleach, and fabric softener to her ever-growing grocery list in preparation for her next task: heading to the big brand-name supermarket out on the highway to stock her kitchen.

It hadn't occurred to her how much of an adjustment it was going to be living alone. She'd never given it a thought as she'd been so consumed with the thought of becoming a chocolatier. After almost three decades of living with Jeff, this living alone was going to take some time to get used to. At times, the silence was deafening. The sound of the television and conversation had always filled the silences back home. To remedy that, she played music or let the windows open to hear the sounds of summer.

It hadn't been easy going forward without her husband. Automatically, she'd slept on the same side of the bed that she always had slept on. She even caught herself at the grocery store, going down the frozen aisle to get his favorite brand of ice cream. Once she realized that that wasn't necessary, she'd hurried out of the aisle.

Despite her desire to pursue her dream, something about it felt a bit 'off' without Jeff at her side. She hoped as time passed it would get easier.

The first week she spent getting ready to dive into the business of chocolate making. She sourced the high-quality couverture chocolate Nana had always insisted on using because of its high cocoa butter content, and she ordered the tools and ingredients she'd need online. The spare bedroom was the coolest of the house. It faced north and there was a big pine tree that had that side of the house covered in shade. She thought this room might be a great cooling room to store the finished chocolate until she sourced a commercial premise. In the kitchen, she cleared a generous space in her cabinets for all her supplies, to keep everything organized and in one area. She kept the old candy box that Martha Cotter had given her propped up against the tile backsplash of the counter to inspire her. She'd taken a photo of it and sent it to Renee who was currently making a modern logo based on that design. Excited, she plunged ahead.

Currently, she stared at the assembled supplies and the stacked bars of chocolate laid out on her kitchen table. The sight of it all improved her mood. She'd had a phone call earlier that morning from Paula at the translation service, telling her one of their employees went out on an unexpected medical leave and therefore they'd need another week to complete the translation. At the time, she'd been disappointed but now, she figured she had enough to keep her busy getting back into the swing of things making chocolate confections.

Butterflies flew around in her stomach. It had been a while since she'd worked with chocolate. But despite the mild anxiety, there was a much stronger feeling of excitement at being back in the kitchen with ingredients and tools she was familiar with and that evoked a sense of nostalgia.

On her brand-new work surface, she used a serrated knife to chop up the chocolate into smaller pieces. Setting it aside, she half-filled the bottom pan of a double boiler with water. She smiled, remembering Nana used to call it a bain-marie.

Val reminded herself that this was all practice to get her back into the habit. It didn't have to be perfect.

When the water boiled, she removed the pan from the stove and set it on a trivet. She took two-thirds of the chopped chocolate and added it to the bowl and set it over the pan of hot water to melt. Once melted, she added the remaining third of the chopped chocolate, divided into three loose piles, called seed chocolate. As she added each pile, stirring it into the melted chocolate with a spatula, she kept an eye on the temperature, making sure it didn't fall below ninety degrees.

As it cooled to the appropriate temperature and she kept a constant watch on her thermometer, it came back to her how her grandmother used to test the temperature by putting a bit of the melted chocolate on her lower lip. Val smiled at that long-forgotten memory.

Using a trick Nana had taught her, she tested the batch by pouring a thin strip over a flat metal spatula. It took longer than she expected for it to harden, and it was dull instead of shiny. She sighed, pushed this sample aside, and started again. Troubleshooting, she speculated that either there were still bits of unmelted chocolate in it, or somehow water from the steam had gotten into the batch. Undeterred, she put the pan of water back on the stove and began to chop more chocolate.

Valerie blew a stray hair out of her eyes. Every window in the kitchen was open, but the heat in the kitchen was relentless. She was on her fourth batch of chocolate that day. Nothing was going right. Over the past week, she'd spent every day in her kitchen, barely stepping outside some days, and had managed for the most part to conquer tempering the chocolate correctly. She had now moved on to fillings.

Despite her tank top, sweat dribbled down the middle of her back. If she was serious about making chocolate confections on a large scale, she'd need commercial premises. But for now, this kitchen would have to do.

Her phone rang, distracting her.

"Ooh," she said, waving her hands around. She only needed the chocolate to drop another degree before she seeded it. She glanced at her screen, hoping she could call whoever it was back later. When she saw the name of the translation service flash across her screen, she momentarily forgot about tempering chocolate and quickly answered it, grimacing when she left a smudge of chocolate on her phone.

When she hung up, she smiled. The journals were translated and ready to be picked up. As soon as this batch was finished, she'd clean up, hop in the car, and head to Buffalo to pick them up. She couldn't wait another day. And as soon as the journals were in her possession, she'd head back to Hideaway Bay, get comfortable, and start reading.

PART TWO

Delphine

CHAPTER SEVENTEEN

1940

Delphine

THE CHURCH BELLS IN the little village outside of Paris tolled furiously.

Fourteen-year-old Delphine Giroud looked over to her mother, who was working with some chocolate in the back room of their little shop in the center of the village. Mme Giroud was hand coating her truffles with a thin layer of chocolate. This was the first step. She had a little bit of chocolate in the palm of her hand in which she rolled the truffle, making sure it was evenly covered before letting it slide off the palm of her hand to cool. But at the sound of the church bells, she straightened and stared at the window. Finally, she dipped her chocolate covered hands into a bowl of water at her side before wiping them on the large white apron that covered her dress. Her beautiful auburn hair was pulled tightly off her face, a large plait wound around the top of her head like a crown. Her eyes were green, and they appeared wary. Their shop, a golden-colored stone building with shutters on the windows and flowers growing in abundance around it, opened out onto the cobblestone street, and she stepped outside to see what was going on.

There was a preponderance of women among the villagers. Many of the men had been killed in previous war and many others had gone off to fight in the current war. But there were still those young men under the age of sixteen, boys really. The only middle-aged men left behind were either badly wounded from the first war or not fit for the second. There was Maurice from the butcher shop and the haberdasher, Jacques. The seamstress, Amelie, stepped out as well, her tape measure draped loosely around her neck.

Suddenly, one of the boys from the village, Claude, came tearing through town from the north side as if he were on fire. The butcher stepped out into the street, grabbing hold of the boy as he sailed past and halting his forward motion. Mme Giroud stepped off the curb and held her arm back, indicating that Delphine was to remain in front of the shop. Her light perfume floated past Delphine, a comforting scent. Mme Giroud's heels clicked along the cobblestones as she joined the butcher, the haberdasher, the seamstress, and other villagers as they circled around Claude.

Claude was Delphine's age, and she'd never been keen on him. He was prone to exaggeration and self-importance. But still, she'd like to be part of that little circle to hear what he had to say. Slowly, she inched her way closer to the crowd, standing behind her mother and out of sight. She strained to listen.

"What are you saying?" Maurice asked.

"There's no way the German army could have broken through the Maginot Line," declared the haberdasher.

"It's true, it's true," Claude said vehemently. "They're here. The Germans are here."

Amelie put her hand to her throat and whispered to Mme Giroud, "What about what happened in Poland, Marguerite?"

Mme Giroud was quick to reassure her. "Amelie, what we heard was awful. But we don't know how true it is."

Amelie looked unconvinced, and a ripple of fear spread through Delphine. She'd listened to the grown-ups since the war started. The horrendous stories about how the Nazis had invaded Poland and had resorted to rape and murder. That couldn't happen here, surely. Could it?

As quickly as Claude had come into town, the group of villagers broke up and dispersed. Their strides were clipped as they returned to their stores and slammed their doors, bolts sliding into place.

Mme Giroud took Delphine by the elbow and forced her into the shop, and like the other shopkeepers, she shut the door and bolted it. The sign in the front window indicating the shop was open was removed and fluttered to the windowsill. The shutters were closed.

"What is it? What's happening?" Delphine asked several times, but her questions fell on deaf ears. Her mother scurried around the shop, her brow furrowed, a deep scowl lining her forehead, the chocolate in the back room forgotten. She muttered under her breath as she ran about the shop. Before heading to the upstairs flat where they lived, she paused, put a hand on Delphine's slim shoulder and said, "Stay right here. Don't move." It was that tone she used when she didn't want to be disobeyed.

Delphine nodded quickly but wordlessly. Her mother disappeared up the stairs. Alerted by an unfamiliar noise, Delphine turned her head toward the front of the store as a threatening rumbling increased in the distance.

Her mother flew down the stairs. In one hand, she held the small leather-bound book of her chocolate recipes. As Delphine was growing up, her mother had painstakingly written down all the recipes that had been handed down to her by her own mother and grandmother. The two of them would sit at their small kitchen table in the flat above the chocolate shop, listening to the latest broadcast while Delphine did her homework and her mother carefully transcribed family recipes. As time went on, the broadcasts turned ominous, the threat of war looming, and her mother would snap off the radio and sigh.

Mme Giroud set the book down behind the counter and took some chocolate and wrapped it hurriedly with brown paper, looking repeatedly toward the front window. She emptied the black metal box of the day's takings, some of the coins rolling along the counter and others dropping to the floor with a clatter and a ping. Hurriedly, she picked them up and added them to the pile. Carefully, she tucked the recipe book inside of it. She picked up a handful of coins from the ones scattered across the counter.

It was surreal to Delphine. She had no idea what war would be like. Surely this would all come to an end quickly, and everyone would stop being so tense. Wouldn't they?

Mme Giroud heard the rumbling as well. It sounded like thunder.

"Mon dieu."

Delphine's eyes widened; her mother never swore. Mme Giroud looked toward the front window and swallowed hard.

Suddenly, she herded Delphine to the back of the shop and thrust the chocolate and the box containing the recipe book into her daughter's hands. In the past, Delphine had never been allowed to touch the book, the reason being that it was a "keepsake" and "very important."

Her mother threw open the back door, which opened out onto a vista of French countryside, gently rolling hills and mature trees now full with leaves. But the scenery was marred by heavy funnels of black smoke in the distance. Mme Giroud momentarily forgot about Delphine as she took in the scene, gasping. But the increasing rumbling and the sound of squealing brakes as cars pulled into their village forced her to focus.

Mme Giroud's eyes were full of tears.

She bent down in front of Delphine and folded her hands over her daughter's as they held the metal box. "You must listen very carefully. This is life or death." There was fear in her eyes and Delphine took a step back, alarmed, but her mother didn't let go of her hands.

Outside, the rumbling increased in volume, and added to that was the steady beat of marching footsteps.

"Listen to me!"

Delphine turned her attention back to her mother.

Mme Giroud knelt in front of her, her chin quivering and voice shaking. "You must run and hide." She shook Delphine's hands as if to add emphasis. "I want you to hide this book for me," she said.

"Will they steal it?" Delphine asked. What would the German army want with a recipe book about chocolate truffles?

Marguerite shook her head. "No, but it might get . . . damaged." Panic laced her mother's voice. "Put this in your pocket." She dropped the coins into the pocket of Delphine's apron.

Delphine stood there, frozen, unable to move. Fear and dread made it feel as if her legs weighed hundreds of pounds. All she could do was stare at her mother.

"Delphine!"

She nodded quickly but still made no effort to move.

Sudden banging on the front door of the shop startled them both. Mme Giroud looked over her shoulder toward the front door, where the banging continued but then suddenly stopped. The sound of wood splintering made Delphine peer around her mother's form, and she spotted the butt end of a rifle pushing through the door.

She was still watching the action at the front of the shop when her mother jumped up, shoved her out the back door, and hissed, "Run!"

The door was slammed closed in Delphine's face, and she stood there for a second. The air smelled acrid, and there was a blood-curdling scream from somewhere in their tiny village. That noise spurred her to pivot and run as fast as she could.

Delphine got farther and farther away from the village, but the fear didn't abate inside her. She kept running, ignoring the stitch in her side, ignoring her parched mouth and most of all, ignoring the urge to go back and check on her mother.

Even in the distance, the rumbling and the booms continued, and something else was there now: *pop-pop* noises studded the other unfamiliar ones, which she recognized as gunshots.

As she ran through the open field, she spotted the line of vehicles, heavily armored trucks and tanks, rolling toward her village in single file. She collapsed to the ground to stay out of sight. Unsure whether they'd spotted her or not, she crept through the field on her belly, keeping her head down.

The disparity of the day was not lost on her. The sky was an endless blue and a soft, warm breeze floated along her back as she crawled through the sweet-smelling grass. After twenty minutes of this, with the front of her apron grass-stained and dirty, she lifted her head slowly and looked over her shoulder.

The column of vehicles was no longer visible, but she did spot large plumes of black smoke rising from the village. And even at that distance, there was the muffled sounds of shouts and screams.

She kept going, spurred on by fear and the importance of her task. As she made her way, she clutched the metal box so tightly her fingers began to throb.

Her grandparents' abandoned former home—or what was left of it from the previous war—was located about two kilometers outside of the village. If she could make it there without being seen, there would be tons of hiding places.

Once she cleared the crest of the hill, she lifted her head and shoulders to look around. Seeing no one, she got on her knees and rolled over on her back, trying to catch her breath. She lingered for a few minutes; the warmth of the sun felt good on her face. Sighing, she sat up and scanned the area, still not seeing another soul. She put her hand along her eyebrows to shield her vision from the sun, and spotted the ruins of her grandparents' former home. From her vantage point, it looked quite tiny, the huge stones scattered around the property looking more like little ones.

Still unsure as to where the soldiers might be, Delphine kept low to the ground. She continued to crawl, or sometimes she stood to stretch and work out the kinks that were forming in her muscles, but then she'd lower herself to a crouch and run a little faster.

The former home of her grandparents had been a two-story stone cottage with window boxes and shutters and lots of flowers. Or that's what her mother had told her. It had been destroyed in the last war, and her mother and grandparents had been displaced from a home that had been in her grandmother's family for generations. They had lived in town ever since. Often, Delphine's mother would bring her out there for a picnic and tell her stories of what it was like growing up there.

But now the house had been reduced to rubble and destroyed furniture, which lay in a pile to one side. There was one chair her mother had been able to salvage, and she used to sit in it, stare at her house, and lift her face toward the sun, always with a smile. The chair wasn't much—exposed to the elements, it was starting to deteriorate as had everything else.

Behind the house was an orchard of apple and pear trees. But the trees, as if sensing the impending doom, had not produced any fruit last year. When they were last out here weeks ago, her mother had inspected the blossoms on the trees, fingering them, and had been hopeful for a crop this year.

Delphine took the weathered chair, dragged it out of sight behind the big pile of rubbish, and sat for a moment. She set the metal box down on a somewhat flat stone beside her and unwrapped the chocolate. Her mother's beautiful creations had formed into a pile of goo with the heat. Delphine didn't care, for she was hungry, and she scooped it up with her fingers and ate it all, licking her fingers and even the brown paper. Finished, she crumpled up the paper and threw it into the rubbish pile.

Her search for the perfect hiding spot began in earnest. She'd been entrusted with one task, and she wasn't about to let her mother down. At first, she'd contemplated the large rubbish pile, thinking she could bury the box deep at the bottom, but she quickly dismissed that thought when the black smoke on the horizon reminded her that everything was going to be burned. Also, there might be rodents about, and she couldn't take the chance that they might find their way into the box and chew through the leather cover and the notepaper. She lifted the box and, clutching it to her chest, she looked around, searching for something. The problem was there really was nothing. How could you hide something when everything was out in the open? She remembered the old disused root cellar out back and ran toward it. It had been built into the natural curve of a low hill generations ago. It was largely overgrown, the wooden door no longer visible, as grass and hanging branches covered it. Her mother had tried to access it before, but it had proved too difficult. But now, Delphine had to try.

First, she had to locate the thing. She tried to think back to where her mother had stood, but her guess was off. She set the box down in the grass behind her and plunged both hands into the overgrowth, wincing when a sharp edge pinched her hand. Moving her hands along, she patted the surface, hoping to find anything that resembled a wooden door. Having never seen it herself and only going on what her mother had told her, she continued to seek it out. A dual sense of urgency and fear propelled her, and she scrabbled along until at last, her right hand landed on what she thought was a piece of trim wood. Her hand moved along, feeling the peeling paint on the otherwise smooth surface. But the scrub that covered it was three to four inches in depth. She tried not to despair, but how was she going to access it with her bare hands?

Instead, she gave up on it for a moment and dashed back to the ruins of the house. It was imperative that she hide this recipe book. Never had a task felt so important or daunting. She stared at all the loose stones, some the size of boulders, and had an idea.

Starting with the largest stone, she tried to move it, but it wouldn't budge. She worked her way down until she found one she could move. Beneath it was a hollow pocket created by the bottom of the large stone. That would work, she thought, if only temporarily. If only it were a bit deeper. The rubbish pile stood before her, practically beckoning. She sifted through it, hunting for something she might be able to use as an implement. A broken chair leg caught her eye, and she reached her arm in, wincing when her flesh came into contact with something wet and squishy. She pulled the chair leg from the pile and used it to dig the hole a little deeper. It was not as easy as she thought it would be. When she was satisfied with the depth, she placed the box into it, hoping it would protect the book. She covered the hollowed-out space with the dirt she'd disrupted. Grunting as she heaved the boulder back into place, she stepped back, admiring her handiwork with a nod. It was as good as any hiding place.

Besides, it wouldn't be for long.

Now, she needed to hide herself.

In the weeks that followed, confusion reigned supreme. The German army took control of Paris and the rest of France, except for the southwest where the Vichy government had been set up. Information was scant, and rumors took on a life of their own and swirled around the town. The most pervasive was the belief that this would all be over soon. That a peace agreement would be signed and France would regain her autonomy. As they waited for this to happen, a slow trickle of Northerners began to appear, almost as if on a pilgrimage. Delphine stood outside the shop and watched them. In the beginning, there was the odd pushcart carrying a family's belongings as they headed for what they thought was safety in the Southwest of the country. But soon that trickle turned into a full-blown gush as the number of French people fleeing the north and the east of the country sought safe haven in the south.

If there had been a shortage of men before, they'd totally disappeared with the arrival of the German army. Those fighting in the French army were quickly shipped off to German prisoner-of-war camps. And those men not fighting, especially young men, were drafted and sent off to work in German factories. That left a surplus of Frenchwomen alone with the German army.

From the beginning, Mme Giroud had given Delphine advice.

"Do not engage with them at all. Stay out of their way," she warned. "Remain silent and do not look them in the eye."

Delphine had nodded and tucked this piece of advice away and like everyone else, she waited for it all to be over with so things could go back to the way they were.

CHAPTER EIGHTEEN

Winter 1941–42

DELPHINE WOKE IN THE kitchen at the back of their shop. It was cold, but not as cold as the upstairs or the rest of the building. She and her mother had taken to sleeping in the kitchen, laying blankets out on the floor by the stove every night, as coal and gas were hard to come by and the stove was their only source of heat. She rolled over and looked out the back window, watching the snow fall. In the past, she would have loved the novelty of it but not this year. It had made a bad situation worse.

She got up, in no hurry to leave the relative warmth of the blankets. But the cold, empty space next to her told her her mother was already up. Quickly, she folded the blankets and piled them on a chair in the corner, out of the way. Her mother sat at the table, mending an old coat. It was practically threadbare, but she had turned it inside out and was currently repurposing it.

The doors to the chocolate shop were closed to keep the heat in the kitchen. Mme Giroud had not made any chocolate in a long time. There was a shortage of ingredients. There'd been a shortage of just about everything.

When the commanding German officer of the area had arrived and announced his love of fine chocolate, they'd been buoyed, but that enthusiasm was tempered by the thought that their neighbors might think they were collaborating with the enemy, not that they had any choice. The high-ranking officer had arranged to get the supplies Mme Giroud needed to make chocolate but before they arrived, he'd been transferred to a command at the Eastern Front and the supplies, when they did arrive, were shipped off to Germany. His replacement had pronounced chocolate frivolous. And since then, the shop had been shuttered.

"Eat," Marguerite said with a nod toward Delphine's breakfast.

It was the same as yesterday and the day before that: two small pieces of stale bread and a cup of "coffee," which was actually chicory that was desperately trying to pass for coffee and failing miserably. Delphine narrowed her eyes at the bread and asked, "What about your breakfast, Maman?"

"I already had mine earlier," her mother said, tugging the needle through the stiff fabric.

This was the lie that had passed between them every day since the rationing began. Marguerite pretended she'd already eaten, and Delphine went along with it because she'd protested once, knowing her mother was giving her part of her share, and her mother had flown into a rare pique of temper. Delphine never questioned her again.

"I'll finish here and go get bread and sausage," Mme Giroud said.

"No, I'll go, Maman, it's too cold out," Delphine said. Her mother was a shadow of her former self. Last week, Delphine had waited four hours in line for sausages.

Her mother didn't argue, and Delphine was glad of that; she didn't have the energy. She dipped the stale bread into the lukewarm chicory coffee to soften it and ate it quickly.

"Delphine, don't rush your meal," her mother chided.

Delphine snorted. When she was finished, she carried her cup and plate over to the sink and set them on the drainboard.

She pulled on a pair of wool stockings that were at least three years old and that had been darned in many places. Her mother had pulled an old overcoat of her father's out of mothballs and refashioned it for Delphine's size. Before she slipped on her shoes and the coat, her mother lined her shoes with newspapers to keep her feet warm. When Delphine pulled the coat on, her mother stuffed more newspapers down into the sleeves. She pulled on her gloves and then pulled her mother's gloves over her own.

"I'm ready," she said, heading toward the front of the shop.

Marguerite unbolted the door carefully. They'd done the best they could to repair it after the Nazis had smashed through it on their arrival. "Do you have the coupons?" she asked.

Delphine patted her front pocket in response.

"Don't lose them," her mother advised.

To lose them would mean they wouldn't eat for that week.

The shop had the smell of must and disuse. The familiar scent of chocolate had been relegated to memory. Dust and shadows covered every surface. An image of a hot cup of chocolate floated before her, but she quickly banished it from her mind; there was no sense in torturing herself.

Her mother opened the front door and they were hit immediately with a blast of cold air. Delphine shivered despite being bundled up, and Marguerite peered out slowly. "Go on. And remember, don't talk to anyone."

This was her admonishment every time Delphine stepped out of the house. You didn't know who you could trust. You kept your opinions to yourself, especially those opinions about the Nazi occupier. There were rumors through the village that someone was running an underground Resistance ring. That thought both excited Delphine and scared the life out of her. No one knew who it was or if it was even true. And they were better off not knowing. The flip side of that was that no one knew which villager was supplying the German army with information about their neighbors.

No one could be trusted.

"Go back inside, Maman," Delphine said. She almost added, "I'll be right back," but they both knew she wouldn't be back for hours.

The snow crunched beneath Delphine's feet as she made her way to the butcher. She hoped she wouldn't have to wait in line as long as last week. It had taken her two days to warm up after she'd returned home.

If the cold hadn't penetrated right down to her bones, she might have thought the village looked quite pretty all covered in snow. But currently, her attention landed on the line outside the butcher's shop, and she groaned. There was nothing else to do but get in line. She couldn't risk coming back later as the sausages might be gone and they'd have no meat for the week.

Maurice, the butcher, opened the shop, let one customer in, and closed the door quickly behind him. Inside, Delphine knew a German sentry was posted, who would review every order. When the rationing first started, Maurice was known to give extra. Maybe a few extra links if they had young children at home, or a fine soup bone with the meat still on it, but the occupiers soon got wind of it and made an example of Maurice. And he now had a permanent limp, courtesy of the occupying army, to show for it.

Delphine took her place at the end of the line, watching other villagers slowly make their way to the butcher's as well. She shoved her hands in her pockets, trying to keep them warm. After a few minutes, she stamped her feet in place where she stood to ward off the chill. The longer she stood there, the more she lost feeling in the tips of her fingers and her toes. She despaired of their current situation ever ending.

CHAPTER NINETEEN

1944

THE VILLAGE HAD GROWN quiet after the fleeing of the Germans. People began to move freely around the town square and congregate in small groups. Delphine remained behind the closed doors of the shop, peering out the window. Despite the rumors that the Americans were in France, she wouldn't believe it until she saw it.

Hunger gnawed at her, but she was so used to it she paid no attention to it. If the Allies were coming, she hoped they were bringing food. The last few years had been lean ones.

In the distance was the rumbling again, caused by tanks and jeeps and other armored military vehicles. Delphine opened the door of the shop and stood on the stone step, watching the reaction of the others. But no one ran, no one screamed. An excited buzz whistled through the town. It reminded her of fetes and carnivals from years ago, before the war. That had been so long ago it was nothing more than a faint memory, but still it was a familiar type of excitement. One that had been absent for the last four years.

She folded her arms across her chest, rubbing her upper arms. One of the town's barn cats, a beautiful striped black-and-gray tom, wound itself around her legs, purring.

"Go on now, Simon, I have nothing for you," she scolded. She could barely feed herself. But they both knew she'd eventually cave in and give him a morsel or two. It was a game the two of them played. He continued to purr and leaned all his weight against her leg.

"All right, then." She slipped her hand into the pocket of her apron and pulled a piece off the heel of stale bread and tossed it to him. He batted it aside and tackled it, hunched over, eating it. She'd learned the hard way years ago that it was best to keep some food on her person; you never knew when you were going to have to run. Or hide.

In the beginning, when the German army first arrived, people walked on eggshells, trying not to run afoul of the occupying force. But things worsened after 1942, when the Gestapo took over the policing of the country. The butcher, Maurice, had been executed for ties to the Resistance movement. And the rumors were that it was Jacques, the haberdasher, who'd turned him in to curry favor with the Gestapo.

The thunderous rumble grew louder and the drone of the villagers' voices, tinged with excitement, rose to match it. Impatient, she stepped off the stoop and onto the cobbled street, standing on her tiptoes to see past the heads of the villagers gathered in the square by the waterless fountain in front of the church.

Suddenly, the group threw their hands up in cheers, and a current of energy zipped through the air. Still slightly mistrustful, Delphine was not convinced yet. The crowd parted, allowing for vehicles to pass through, the noise of the convoy and cheers of the people now deafening. It wasn't until she spotted the American flag hanging off one of the vehicles that her legs buckled in relief.

It was true. The Americans were here, and the occupation was over.

She stepped back, stumbling, her legs unable to support her weight, and managed to trip up onto the step outside the shop, where she leaned against the rotting doorframe, bracing herself.

Tears filled her eyes and quickly spilled over. Her smile was so big and broad she felt like she was using muscles in her face she hadn't used in many years.

People standing on the cobblestone street backed up to give the vehicles room, some having to lean against old buildings. In front of Delphine the cat looked up, his ears flattening, and he disappeared behind the building.

American GIs were sitting on the outside of tanks as they rolled through, or were packed in the back of jeeps. She couldn't move her eyes fast enough to take it all in. It was not lost on her how very different the day was from the one when the Nazis arrived. She swallowed hard, emotions threatening to engulf her.

They all looked so healthy. Although the soldiers looked haggard and dusty, not one of them was skin and bones.

If they'd only arrived a year earlier, they might have been able to save her mother.

As they passed her, she waved heartily, smiling.

"Hey, beautiful!" called out a soldier perched on top of one of the tanks.

Delphine looked up and saw the well-built soldier grinning at her, flashing white teeth in a stubbled, dusty face. His eyes blazed blue, and the hair peeking out from beneath his helmet was as black as midnight.

He winked and tossed something to her. "That's for you."

She caught the item with both hands and looked at it.

It was a Hershey Bar. American chocolate.

Oh.

She hadn't had any chocolate since that day long ago when she buried the recipe book at her grandparents' abandoned farm.

She looked up, wanting to thank him, but his tank was out of hearing range. His gaze was still locked on her. She held up the chocolate bar and shouted, "Merci!"

He nodded and disappeared down the road.

CHAPTER TWENTY

LIKE EVERYWHERE ELSE IN France, they began the process of rebuilding not only their town and village, but their lives as well. Like most of her neighbors, Delphine had assumed the food would start increasing in volume with the liberation. It did and it didn't, more of a trickle than a flow. There were still some things you couldn't get. Margarine was still being substituted for butter, and chicory for coffee. What she wouldn't give for a decent cup of coffee and a baguette slathered in real butter.

During the occupation, most goods like potatoes, sugar, eggs, meat, and milk were redirected for the German army. As long as she lived, Delphine swore she'd never eat a cabbage again. The thought of it made her gag.

She waited outside, seated on the step, smoking a cigarette. The American soldier who'd thrown her the candy bar was around frequently to see her. And he always brought something with him. Last week it had been a pack of cigarettes, a guilty pleasure of hers. The week before that, it had been a little bit of sugar. When she questioned him about how he obtained these items, he'd shrug, grin that grin of his that absolutely made her melt, and say "I have my contacts."

His name was Wayne Brandt.

She heard him before she saw him. It was the whistling. Some American tune that he'd told her the name of but that she could not remember. She stubbed out the cigarette on the ground beside her and sat up straighter in anticipation of his arrival. She always looked forward to seeing him, and tonight was no different.

And there he was. In the bright sunshine and the façade of the church as his backdrop, he strolled down the street, nodding to other villagers who greeted him as they passed. From where she sat, she could see his grin and the cigarette between his fingers.

As he approached, she jumped up, eager to see him. His unit wasn't stationed far from her, and he walked down to see her a few nights a week. Currently, he was teaching her English. It was painstakingly slow, but she was determined to learn it.

He took one last drag on his cigarette before flicking it away. His grin broadened as he sat next to her on the step.

"Bonjour," he said.

She leaned into him, liking the solidness of his form next to her: it was sturdy, dependable.

He smelled of tobacco and male sweat, and considering there'd been a lack of both in the village for the last four years, she found it intoxicating. So this was what an American male smelled like.

She brought out the English starter book he'd somehow managed to procure and opened it up. For the next hour, he instructed her. This was how they spent their late afternoons together. Then afterward, they would go for a stroll around the village or sit on the step, smoke cigarettes, and stare at the starry sky.

But tonight, he was quiet. More so than usual. Though their ability to understand each other fluctuated, Wayne was usually quite chatty, and she liked the sound of his voice: deep with a strong American accent. But the words were few and he smoked cigarette after cigarette, often lighting the next one off the first.

Halfway through the lesson, she took the book from her lap and closed it, setting it aside. He looked at her, confusion shadowing his features.

"Delphine?"

She stood from the step, stepped back, and held out her hand. "Come on."

He jumped up, flung his cigarette away, and took her hand in his. She led him around the back of the shop and landed on the well-worn path through the fields. They walked hand in hand in companionable silence through the field of sweet grass she had once crawled through. But things were different now.

"Where are we going?" he asked.

"You'll see," she said, looking up at him with a smile.

"All right, then," he said agreeably.

The pile of rubble that had once been the home of her grandparents remained, surprisingly undisturbed by the Nazis during their occupation of the town. And her mother's recipe book remained untouched beneath the boulder that stood at what used to be the front wall of the house.

"Was this your home?" he asked.

She explained in broken English that it had been the home of her grandparents but had been destroyed during the First World War. He nodded, looked around, kicked at a pebble on the ground. Seemingly satisfied, he sat on the boulder above the recipe book and pulled out two cigarettes. He lit them with his Zippo lighter, clipped it shut, and handed one to her. Amused at his choice of seat, she took the cigarette from him, his fingers brushing along her fingertips.

"You're quiet," she said, studying him through the plume of bluish smoke she'd exhaled.

He shrugged and looked away.

Now she was concerned. "What's wrong?"

He looked up at her, taking a long drag off his cigarette. "We're heading out."

She frowned, not understanding.

"My unit is leaving, shipping out. Moving on," he explained.

"Are you going home?" she asked, fearful.

He shook his head and laughed. "Not quite yet." He paused and added, "Hopefully soon."

She looked at him, gape-jawed.

Just when you thought the war was over and you couldn't endure any more loss, it came out of nowhere. Granted, she knew the troops were never committed long term to France, and he'd told her previously that some were already heading back to the United States. She wondered if it had been his way to let her know that this—this thing between them—wouldn't last forever. But Delphine knew that all too well. Nothing lasted forever, not the Germans, not the chocolate shop, not her grandparents' house, not the liberating forces, and not the young American soldier with the wicked grin who went out of his way to bring her things and help her with her English.

She knew of impending loss, the heavy sense of doom that enveloped you at what was coming down the road. She'd known it before. When her mother was dying, she'd felt helpless. And now, she felt that way again. Things out of her control. Besides, who was she? Just a girl from a French village. In the whole scheme of things, she was simply going along for the ride.

"I should get home," she said hurriedly, choosing not to wait for him and marching off in the direction of the shop and the flat above it where she lived.

Wayne pushed off the stone and caught up to her, tugging at her hand and pulling her into his embrace. She liked it there, liked the way his arms slid around her and held her close against the solidness of him. He kissed the top of her head, and she closed her eyes. She looked up at him when he cupped the sides of her face, his hands smelling of tobacco. She held onto his wrists with her hands. Slanting his head to one side, he pressed his lips against hers. His kiss was warm and demanding, and she liked how her body responded to his, how it yielded to him. His hand traveled along the length of her arm, then landed at her waist, working its way up to her breast. Delphine broke away, breathless.

She started walking again toward the shop, with Wayne at her side.

"Do you know when you're leaving?" she asked.

"Couple of weeks," he said quietly.

She'd probably never see him again. He'd get home, and with all the pretty girls in America, he'd forget all about her. It had been a wonderful couple of months, something she'd remember for the rest of her life.

Behind the shop, in the lavender twilight, Wayne stopped, put his hands on his hips, and looked around. She stared at him, waiting.

"How would you like to live in America?" he asked. The grin was gone.

She wished he wouldn't tease her, it was hurtful. She laughed it off. "I'd love it. I'd love to live in Hollywood." It was the only real thing she knew about America, aside from the Statue of Liberty.

"I can't offer you Hollywood, but I can offer Queens, New York."

She shook her head, not comprehending.

He crossed the distance that spread out between them and stood in front of her, so close she could see all the hairs of his eyebrows: dark, thick, and framing those sapphire blue eyes of his.

"What are you saying, Wayne?"

"I think we should get married before I ship out," he said, watching her reaction.

Her mouth fell open. Of all the things for him to say, she hadn't expected that. Of course, she might have wished for it, but she never expected it. If anything, the war had taught her not to expect anything good to come in her direction. But now . . .

Before she could answer and gush a "yes," she flung herself at him and jumped into his arms, wrapping her arms around his neck tightly and smothering his face with kisses.

Wayne laughed and wrapped his arms around her waist in response. Through her avalanche of kisses, he whispered against her ear, "That's my girl."

CHAPTER TWENTY-ONE

1946

New York

DELPHINE CLUTCHED TIGHTLY TO Wayne's arm, still in a state of disbelief that she was walking down a sidewalk in New York City in a borough called Queens.

A mixture of nervousness and adrenaline fueled her, lifting her out of the fog that had encompassed her since she boarded the ship to sail to America. The journey had been long and arduous, for she had suffered seasickness. The irony was not lost on her. To have survived the degradation and deprivation of a world war only to be crippled by nausea and vomiting. By the time the ship had pulled into the New York Harbor, doubt had filled her. What if he didn't show up? What if she didn't like it there? But as soon as she spotted Wayne as she disembarked, all fears, worries, and doubts dissolved.

She hadn't seen him for more than a year. He'd been trying to get her over to the United States, but the red tape had seemed almost insurmountable, and Delphine had nearly given up hope. But the War Brides Act had passed in December of 1945 and suddenly, things were moving.

For March, the weather was chilly in New York. Despite the dampness, it was sunny. As they walked arm in arm toward Wayne's mother's house, she tilted her head several times to the sun to feel its warmth.

"Mother is so looking forward to meeting you," Wayne said reassuringly. "I'm so glad you're here. I can't believe it, Delphine!"

When he departed from France, he'd paid the parish priest, who'd been educated in London, to continue with Delphine's English lessons. Her speech was still broken at times, but she had a clearer command of the language. When she'd asked how he'd been able to afford to pay for those lessons as she knew Fr. Lavigne to be quite cheap, he'd laughed and said, "I had something he wanted to trade for." She questioned him no further, deciding it was none of her business. It was no secret that if you wanted something you couldn't get, Wayne Brandt was your man, for he had connections. And during times of war, people had to do what they had to do to survive.

As soon as the Germans had left France, Delphine had gone to her grandparents' former home and had heaved the boulder from its resting place, revealing the black metal box still inside the hiding space. Currently, the recipe book was in her satchel, which Wayne carried.

New York was unlike anything she'd imagined. The sky-scrapers gleamed in the sunshine, their height astonishing. The sidewalk had a slight downward incline, and on the horizon, the city was as clear as a bell. Gray and black buildings against a gray-blue sky. She'd never seen so many buildings and people in one place. The street where Wayne lived was lined with tidy two-story redbrick homes. Their features were interesting. The first floors of the houses were bricked but the second floor was wooden cladding, most painted white. But there were a few homes that deviated, and the paint was a pale yellow or a pale green.

"Here we are," Wayne said proudly, standing at the foot of his driveway. At the end of the narrow driveway stood a bricked garage. The neighboring houses were so close you could throw your arm out the window and touch the house next door. It was obvious they'd sacrificed outdoor space for larger living quarters.

The house where Wayne lived with his mother resembled the other houses. White lace curtains hung at the windows, and a small front porch was sheltered beneath arched brickwork. The front lawn was the size of a postage stamp, and its emergence from winter was evident: soggy yellow grass and a muddy flower bed with bare rosebushes lined the front of the house.

As Wayne stepped forward, Delphine pulled him back. He regarded her with a curious look, a frown marring his beautiful face, the dark eyebrows slanting downward.

"Delphine?"

"I'm nervous," she admitted.

He pulled her to him and kissed her forehead tenderly. "Nothing to be nervous about, darling. We're together, that's the main thing."

She nodded and gave him a quick smile to reassure him that she was all right, even if she wasn't totally convinced of that herself.

He pulled her arm tighter to him as they walked up the driveway and then up the front steps. Butterflies flew around in her stomach, and the nausea she felt on the ship returned as a fine sheen of perspiration broke out on her brow. She wished she and Wayne could afford a place of their own, but Wayne had said he was saving money for that. This—living with his mother—was only temporary.

They stood in front of the door and Wayne looked at her. "Ready?"

She nodded, plastering a bright smile on her face. Tenderly, he squeezed her hand in reassurance.

Wayne opened the door for her and as she stepped forward into her new home, she reminded herself that if Mrs. Brandt was anything like Wayne, everything would be okay.

CHAPTER TWENTY-TWO

WILMA BRANDT WAS NOTHING like Wayne. Her gray hair held none of the magnificent black like Wayne's, and her eyes were hazel rather than the stunning blue of her son's. Wayne must strongly resemble his father, Delphine concluded.

Mrs. Brandt had an imperious air about her, which immediately made Delphine shake in her shoes. It was nothing she said or did outright, but it was the way she held herself: head high, chin up, shoulders back, her hands clasped in front of her. She seemed to regard Delphine with curious dismissiveness.

Wayne introduced them, all smiles, his arm around Delphine's waist. "Mother, this is Delphine, my wife." She thought she would never tire of Wayne introducing her as such. She stepped forward to embrace Mrs. Brandt, but the older woman preempted that move by sticking her hand out for Delphine to shake.

Delphine blinked, stepped back next to Wayne, and shook Mrs. Brandt's hand.

"It's nice to meet you," Delphine managed to croak out, her voice quivering.

"And you." Mrs. Brandt was a short, stout woman with a mighty bosom. Her dress was long-sleeved, navy blue with a white lace collar, and she wore sensible black shoes. Over her shirtdress, she wore a clean, pressed apron of pale yellow.

Delphine stared at the carpet beneath her feet. It was a floral design with colors of gray, burgundy, and black. She glanced up and took note of the living room, whose design was stark. Framed black-and-white photos were placed evenly along the white walls that showed no blemish. A red corduroy sofa and two easy chairs were grouped around a redbrick fireplace. Centered on the mantel was a walnut-cased clock. Two eight-by-ten framed photos flanked the clock, one on each side. On the left was a photo of what Delphine presumed to be Mr. and Mrs. Brandt on their wedding day. Mr. Brandt was the image of Wayne and a curvy, younger Mrs. Brandt was adorned with a voluminous wedding dress and headpiece and veil. The photo on the right was one of Wayne, his service photo, taken in uniform. Delphine couldn't help but smile at that.

"I suppose you might want to have a rest after your long journey," Mrs. Brandt was saying, diverting Delphine's glance from surveying the rest of the room. "Wayne can show you where you'll be sleeping."

It was at that inopportune moment that Delphine's stomach gurgled and growled.

Mrs. Brandt raised an eyebrow and Delphine flicked a glance at Wayne, who grinned. He rubbed her back and said, "Maybe you'd like something to eat first."

She nodded quickly. She hadn't eaten much on the journey as she always seemed to be throwing it up.

"Very well, then," Wilma said with pursed lips. "You better come on back to the kitchen." Without waiting for a response, she marched toward the back of the house.

When Delphine looked questioningly at Wayne, he smiled and said, "She'll defrost once she gets to know you. She's not used to having another woman in the house."

And he led her back to the kitchen for something to eat.

But the older woman did not warm up, or she was taking her sweet time to do so. She was polite and civil to Delphine but there was no warmth or welcome, not really. Delphine felt conspicuous in the house and took to going for long walks as spring progressed into summer, generally trying to stay out of Mrs. Brandt's way. No matter how hard she tried to be a help around the house, it was never good enough. She didn't use enough starch in the clothes when she ironed, she peeled the carrots the wrong way, and she left her stockings hanging all over the bathroom. Delphine solved the latter problem by having Wayne loop a wire from one corner to the other in their bedroom, and she hung her stockings and delicates there.

But that was the other problem. Wayne was gone a lot. He didn't have a regular job, but he worked "odd jobs" as he put it. This fact seemed to bother Mrs. Brandt a great deal, but Delphine could not understand why. He brought home money, they were building up a savings account, and there always seemed to be enough to go out dancing on Friday and Saturday nights. Sunday mornings were treacherous for her with the knowledge that she had to suffer through the whole long week until Friday night for some fun.

The worst was when Wayne didn't make it home in time for supper. It forced Delphine to sit in stony silence with her mother-in-law as they made their way through some kind of roast. And it was always potatoes, carrots, and peas. When Delphine offered to cook to help out, Mrs. Brandt scowled and said that she wouldn't care for Delphine's French cooking.

When Delphine was in the house, which was most of the time, she kept to herself in her room, looking through magazines and newspapers Mrs. Brandt had discarded. Wayne had brought her a journal with blank, lined paper, and every day, she wrote in it, feeling that she could express herself openly in French because neither Wayne nor Mrs. Brandt spoke it. There was freedom in that, pouring her heart and soul out on paper.

At least in the summer, she could go outside and sit on the porch. The next-door neighbor was friendlier to her than her own mother-in-law. And on those blessed days when Mrs. Brandt went out to see her sisters or play bridge on Monday nights, Delphine snuck downstairs and sat in the living room.

By October, she'd begun to dread the coming of winter, when the weather would deteriorate and she'd be stuck in the house. Plus, the baby she so desperately wanted wasn't happening. At least with a baby she'd have something to keep her occupied. As much as she begged Wayne to find a place of their own—so she could breathe—he'd always say "not yet."

After a particularly trying day when the rain was incessant, forcing her inside and stuck up in her room, she appeared listlessly at the dinner table, trying to summon the courage for another meal. Wayne had not come home. He'd said earlier that morning that he might be late tonight.

The meal was the usual: roasted meat—chicken tonight—with mashed potatoes, sliced carrots with butter, and peas. They ate in stony silence as Delphine pushed her food around on her plate, not interested.

"You'd think with the way you people had no food during the war, you'd be grateful for a good meal," Mrs. Brandt declared, having no difficulty eating the food on her plate.

Delphine felt as if she'd been slapped. Her cheeks burned and she summoned all her strength to keep from bursting into tears and giving the other woman the satisfaction.

"Unfortunately, Wayne is like his father," Mrs. Brandt said with a sigh.

Delphine stared at her, waiting for an explanation, but none was forthcoming. Mrs. Brandt resumed eating her meal in silence. Delphine hurried through the rest of her meal, refusing an offer of apple pie, and cleared her plate, setting her dirty dish on the drainboard as previously instructed. She'd once washed the dishes, but then that task was taken away from her when Mrs. Brandt declared she didn't use enough soap.

She retreated to the haven of their bedroom, closed the door behind her, and leaned against it, bursting into tears. She didn't think she could go on like this. Although it was early, she dressed for bed. There was never any need to go downstairs in the evening, and she wanted to complete her nightly ablutions before Mrs. Brandt retired to bed later that evening.

Back in the bedroom, she hung her stockings out to dry and lay on the bed. It wasn't even seven in the evening and here she was, ready for bed when she was young and should be staying up till all hours.

Her thoughts drifted to France and the flat above the shop and of course, her mother. Images of her father were vague as he'd died when she was young. Leaning back on the pillow, she closed her eyes as she tried to recall everything about her late mother. The way she wore her hair. The way she smiled and the way she smelled: a combination of a light perfume and chocolate. Tears rolled out of the corners of her eyes and soaked the pillow. If only she were back in France in their shop, making chocolate like her mother and grandmother used to make. But she was as far away from her homeland as possible.

It wasn't lost on her that she didn't have a lot of options. She had no money of her own and she was married. And although she loved Wayne more than anything, she couldn't live like this. She had left war-torn France and the German occupation behind to live like this. She shuddered at those past remembrances.

As the night darkened, she rolled over onto her side and turned on the switch for the small porcelain bedside lamp with the fussy shade. With her elbow tucked under her head, she pulled open the drawer of the bedside table and pulled out the leather book she'd brought with her all the way from France.

Under the inadequate light of the small lamp, Delphine paged through the book, smiling at her mother's delicate penmanship, the entire book written in her native language. It was heartwarming to see both. It reminded her of home and the love that had once been there.

As she fingered the pages and read through all the recipes and notes her mother had made in the margins, the tears began to fall again, but this time with force until she was downright sobbing.

The door opened and Wayne appeared, startling Delphine. Hurriedly, she closed the book and set it on the bedside table, swinging her legs off the bed as he closed the door and rushed around to sit next to her. She reached in the pocket of her robe for her lace-edged handkerchief and hastily swiped at her eyes and sniffed.

"Delphine, what is it?" He draped his arm around her shoulder. "Are you hurt? What's happened?" There was a faint trace of whiskey on his breath, but his tenderness caused a torrent of tears to reappear.

He remained silent, inching closer to her on the bed so he could hold her close. As she cried, he rubbed her back. Finally, when it seemed as if no more tears would come, she wiped her eyes and blew her nose heartily, which made him laugh. Embarrassed, she looked away, but he cupped her chin with his finger and tilted it until she faced him.

With a smile, he said, "You're still beautiful to me."

She gave a smile but felt as if more tears might be on the way.

Suspecting as much, Wayne said, "Now, why don't you tell me what's going on so we can figure out what to do about it?"

As she poured out her story about her troubles with his mother, how she spent all day up in the bedroom trying to stay out of her way, Wayne listened intently, nodding here and there. As her story progressed, his frown deepened to a scowl, and a muscle ticked along his jawline. When she finished, she wailed, "Can we please get a place of our own?"

He bit his lip and took her hand in his. "No, we can't right now."

Her shoulders sagged. What did it take for him to see that she couldn't continue like this. "Please, Wayne, send me back to France, then."

An alarmed expression appeared on his face, and he hugged her hard. "You can't go back to France. I'd miss you too much." When he pulled away, he took her hands in his and clasped them. He looked deeply into her eyes. "I promise you, you will not be mistreated in this house any longer. And if anyone ever mistreats you again, you're to let me know."

She nodded but she was doubtful. She didn't believe any-thing would change in his mother's treatment of her, but he was so sincere she smiled, thinking he meant well.

"What's that?" he asked with a nod toward the leather book on the nightstand.

"It's my mother's recipe book for the chocolate she used to make," she said.

"May I see it?"

"Of course," she said, picking it up off the bedside table and handing it to him.

As he flipped through the pages, she said with a sigh, "I miss the shop and the chocolate making."

"It's all in French," he noted.

She laughed. "That's all right, I can read it."

He grinned at her and despite everything, she wanted to melt.

"Why don't you start making chocolate here?" he suggested, still looking through the book.

She snorted. "And where would we find a kitchen for me to use?"

Not comprehending, Wayne said, "The kitchen downstairs of course, silly."

Her laugh was brittle. "As if that would ever happen." She couldn't picture his mother allowing it.

But he ignored her response, still leafing through the book. "And what would you need to start making chocolate candy?"

Not taking him seriously, she rattled off her list. "Cocoa beans, vanilla, sugar, butter, milk . . ." Her voice trailed off.

"Noted," he said, and he snapped the book shut and handed it to her.

CHAPTER TWENTY-THREE

After falling asleep in Wayne's warm embrace, all cried out, she woke in the morning to an empty bed and raised voices downstairs. Frowning, she flipped the bedcovers back, grateful for the heat emanating from the vents in the floor, and felt around for her slippers along the rug. She stood, pulled her robe off the edge of the bed, and tugged it on, belting it around her waist. Quietly, she pulled open the door and tiptoed to the landing.

Wilma was saying something, her tone hard but the words indistinguishable. However, Wayne's words were not.

"Why is my wife locking herself up in the bedroom all day long?"

They must be in the kitchen. Delphine got comfortable on the top step and listened. With his mother's reply, Wayne said, "It wasn't what you told her to do, but it is how you've made her feel."

His mother said something, and Wayne exploded, which made Delphine rear back and put her hand to her throat.

"I don't care that you don't trust foreigners," he yelled. "Do you have any idea the horrors of war? I've seen things I wish I'd never seen, stuff to give me nightmares for the rest of my life. But here's the thing: so has Delphine. Things you can't even imagine. The Nazis occupied her village for four years. Four years! What do you think that was like?"

Delphine strained her ear to hear Mrs. Brandt's response but was unsuccessful.

"You're damn right it wasn't nice," Wayne raged. In all the time she'd known him, she'd never seen him angry.

"When I first met her," he continued, "she was skin and bones. I was afraid to hold her hand for fear I might break it," he said loudly.

His mother said something that caused the volume on his voice to lower a bit, but Delphine could still hear him:

"She suffered enough during the war. I won't have her hurt again."

There was no response from Mrs. Brandt.

"I want to put that war behind her and me," Wayne said. "I wanted her out of there and far away. And I won't let her be mistreated by anyone, including you." Disappointment and sadness tinged his voice. "Of all people, I never expected you to treat her so badly. If you can't find any room in your heart for her, then we're out of here."

From her position on the top of the stairs, she clearly heard Mrs. Brandt gasp.

When the conversation downstairs ceased, Delphine pulled herself up and headed back to the bedroom to get dressed.

This would now go one of two ways: Mrs. Brandt would despise the fact that she'd tattled on her, and the situation would grow worse, or things would improve. Delphine actually hoped for the former; it might motivate Wayne to look for a place of their own. Her movements to get dressed and make the bed were painstakingly slow, for she dreaded going downstairs and facing her mother-in-law.

After Wayne left for the day, Mrs. Brandt attempted to make conversation with Delphine. It wasn't as if she prattled on and on but when Delphine came down for breakfast, she was greeted with a plate of bacon and eggs and two pieces of lightly buttered toast. Her mother-in-law turned from the counter, where she was wiping out the cast iron frying pan.

"Good morning, Delphine."

"Good morning, Mrs. Brandt."

"I trust you slept well?"

"I did, thank you."

That was the most conversation she'd ever had with the woman at breakfast. Granted, there was no smile to accompany her words, but Delphine supposed it was a start. Hopefully, she'd taken Wayne's words to heart. Delphine's posture relaxed and she tucked into the meal in front of her, hungry.

Finished, she leaned back and said, "Thank you, that was delicious." She stood and carried the plate over to the sink, where Mrs. Brandt had her hands deep in dishwater, washing the breakfast ware.

"I can dry." In the past, Delphine had offered to help all the time but was always point-blank refused.

Mrs. Brandt went to protest but apparently thought better of it and relented, pulling her hands from the dishwater and giving them a quick dry with the towel lying on the counter next to her. From a drawer, she pulled out a clean towel and handed it to Delphine.

Delphine stood next to Mrs. Brandt at the sink, drying each dish thoroughly and stacking them on the kitchen table. At first, she was anxious in case there'd be some criticism, but none came and gradually she relaxed.

When Wayne returned at dinnertime, his mother was mashing potatoes with a hand masher and Delphine was setting the table. They'd made a little progress. Mrs. Brandt had actually asked Delphine for assistance with the dinner.

In his arms was a large brown cardboard box and he nodded to Delphine and said, "Honey, pull out that chair for me."

Curious as to the box's contents, Delphine set the silverware down and pulled out the chair at the end of the table, the one they didn't use. Wayne set the box down with a grunt and Delphine peeked in. Even Mrs. Brandt stepped away from the counter to inspect.

The box was packed with bags of sugar and chocolate, bricks of butter, small bottles of vanilla, and large glass bottles of milk.

"What's all this?" Mrs. Brandt asked with a sniff and a scowl.

Wayne put his hand around the back of Delphine's neck and gave it a gentle squeeze. "This is for Delphine. She's going to start making chocolates."

Delphine could hardly believe her ears or eyes. Her heart beat faster with excitement.

Mrs. Brandt scoffed. "And where is she going to do this?"

Wayne leveled a gaze at his mother. "Right here in this kitchen."

His mother went to say something, but Wayne thrust up his hand and said firmly, "Delphine can use the kitchen after breakfast until you need it to get things ready for dinner."

"And lunch?" Mrs. Brandt lifted her chin and folded her arms across her chest.

Delphine flicked a nervous glance to her husband, feeling the goodwill that had existed between her and her mother-in-law withering on the vine like a dried-out grape.

"Mother, you can certainly make yourself a sandwich at the kitchen table," Wayne said.

A sigh escaped Mrs. Brandt's lips.

"Come on, Mother. Did you know that Delphine's mother and grandmother were chocolatiers back in France?"

Mrs. Brandt moved her head ever so slightly toward Delphine but said nothing.

Delphine jumped in. "I'll clean everything up when I'm done."

"That's my girl," Wayne said, leaning over and nuzzling her cheek.

"It's time for supper," Mrs. Brandt announced, and turned her back to them and began portioning out the dinner among three plates.

As they sat down, Delphine asked eagerly, "May I start tomorrow?"

Mrs. Brandt lifted her head and made eye contact with her son, who sat across from her. "I suppose."

Delphine was awake before the birds. As soon as she'd heard Wayne snoring the previous night, she'd flipped the bedside lamp on and pulled her mother's recipe book out of the top drawer of her nightstand. It wasn't until she couldn't keep her eyes open anymore that she slipped it back into the drawer and turned off the light, settling back on her pillow with a big yawn.

Ideas filled her head about what kind of chocolate confections she wanted to make. It was important to start simply and not jump too quickly into too many different types. It had been many years since she'd helped her mother in the kitchen of the shop back in France. Her mind drifted back, thinking of those days before the war when the time was simpler and much happier. But there had been happiness again at the end of the war, and that had come in the form of Wayne.

"Someone's up early." Wayne sat on the edge of the mattress, reaching for his trousers on the chair next to his side of the bed and pulling them on. He stood, tucking in his undershirt, and adjusted the belt around his waist.

Delphine sat in the other armchair across the room, sitting on her hands, trying to tamp down her excitement, but failing. She was dressed and ready to go.

Wayne pulled her from the chair, wrapped his arm around her shoulders, and pulled her close, kissing her temple. "Go on, go down. I'm sure Mother's up already." He playfully swatted her bottom as she walked by him. "I'll be down in a minute."

Down in the kitchen, she gulped down her breakfast.

"Don't eat so fast, Delphine, you'll get indigestion," Mrs. Brandt advised her.

Delphine slid a glance at Wayne, who'd taken his seat at the table and was shaking his head, laughing.

"She's anxious to make candy," Wayne teased.

"Mmm," Mrs. Brandt spread butter over her toast.

Delphine hesitated. "Yes, if that's all right."

Mrs. Brandt pressed her lips together. "I guess."

Beneath the table, Delphine nudged Wayne's elbow and when he lifted his head to look at her, she raised her eyebrows and nodded toward his plate, indicating that he should hurry up.

"Okay, okay," he said with a laugh. He stood with half a piece of toast hanging from his mouth and pulled on his coat. He planted a quick kiss on Delphine's cheek. "Good luck. I'm expecting all sorts of wonderful things from you when I get home."

She hadn't been this excited since the Americans rolled into her little village back in '44.

Mrs. Brandt stood and began clearing the table. Delphine helped, putting the jar of milk away in the icebox and setting the crystal dish of butter on the counter. After the table was clear, she pulled off the white-and-gray tablecloth with pink flowers, took it out the back door, and gave it a good shake over the porch railing. Back inside, she folded it up and set it on one of the chairs.

As her mother-in-law washed the dishes, Delphine ran upstairs and retrieved the family recipe book. When she returned, Mrs. Brandt was hanging the towel on the rack to dry.

"Well, I'll leave you to it," she said.

"Thank you," Delphine said, breathless from the run up and down the stairs.

As soon as her mother-in-law was out of sight, Delphine set her recipe book on the table and opened it to the page she needed. She gathered all her supplies and lined them up on the countertop. Finally, she rummaged around the cabinets for pots and utensils. When she dropped a heavy pot on the floor with a resounding clang, she winced and picked it up quickly.

"Everything all right in there?" Mrs. Brandt called from the living room.

"Fine," Delphine called back.

The morning and early afternoon flew as Delphine worked tirelessly around the stove and table, using a combination of the recipe book and her own recall from her memories of helping her mother in the shop. It amazed her how much came back to her as she got into the process. Soon the aroma of chocolate filled the air.

Wayne had only been able to get her a large jar of maraschino cherries and when asked, Mrs. Brandt had supplied her with a small bottle of amaretto. She'd opened it, sniffed it, and although the bottle was dusty, she wiped it down and went ahead anyway. She'd experimented making chocolate truffles, using the cocoa powder to dust them. Her head was so crammed with ideas.

"My goodness, it smells good in here," Mrs. Brandt said from the doorway of the kitchen. Her gaze bounced around the room. Chocolate covered every available space on the table and the counters.

Delphine had only planned to make one batch. But once she got started, she couldn't stop.

Tentatively, she looked at her mother-in-law, hoping she wasn't too upset at the mess that had engulfed her kitchen. She didn't appear to be. Delphine looked up to the clock and gasped.

"Is it that late already?" she asked.

"It is."

"I'll get out of your way as soon as I can," Delphine said, trying not to panic but failing. If she didn't keep to her part of the agreement, would Mrs. Brandt not let her use the kitchen anymore? "I'm so sorry, I didn't realize what time it was."

Mrs. Brandt waved her away. "Don't worry about it. Take your time. We can eat dinner a little bit later."

Delphine was damp from all her exertions, especially tempering chocolate all afternoon over the double boiler, but she was pleased with the dark, luxurious, satiny texture of the finished chocolate.

"Can I do anything to help?"

"I need a place to put all this chocolate, so they're out of the way. Or at least until we can eat dinner," Delphine said, looking around.

"How about the dining room table?"

Delphine nodded. "Yes, that'll do." She hesitated. "Would you like to try one?"

Mrs. Brandt's eyes sparkled. "I was hoping you would ask."

Delphine took down a small saucer from one of the upper cabinets and put one of each kind of candy on the plate: a cherry cordial and a chocolate truffle, and handed it to her mother-in-law, her hand shaking.

Mrs. Brandt studied the offering, picked up a piece, and bit into it. Delphine held her breath, her stomach in knots. Her chocolatier career might end tonight if the feedback wasn't good.

The older woman chewed thoughtfully and raised one eyebrow. When finished, she took the other piece of chocolate and popped that into her mouth, closing her eyes. Delphine took that as a good sign, but she didn't want to count her chickens too soon. The silence was maddening.

When Mrs. Brandt finished, she declared, "I must admit, Delphine, that that is the nicest piece of chocolate I've ever had." And she gave her a slight nod.

Delphine couldn't help but beam. They were probably the kindest words Mrs. Brandt had ever spoken to her. It meant a lot to her.

"I'll finish up quickly," Delphine promised, pivoting on her heel to do the cleanup.

"I'll carry these finished pieces to the dining room table for you," Mrs. Brandt said.

"That would be appreciated." Delphine smiled as she hurriedly rinsed out pots and scoured them with a steel wool pad. Mrs. Brandt walked back and forth between the kitchen and dining room, carrying out trays of chocolate. In no time, Delphine had wiped down the table and counters and picked up the folded tablecloth off the chair and spread it out over the table.

When all the dishes were put away, Mrs. Brandt pulled out the bags of potatoes and carrots.

"Can I help?" Delphine asked.

She shook her head. "I'd think you'd be exhausted by now. Go put your feet up. I'll see to dinner."

"Are you sure?"

"I am," Mrs. Brandt said with a smile.

Wayne's return at dinnertime woke Delphine up. She'd fallen asleep in the living room, her head against the back of the sofa. She sprung forward and wiped the corners of her mouth, aware that it had fallen open in her sleep. The smell of roasting meat emanated from the kitchen. Her stomach growled and saliva filled her mouth. In her busyness to make chocolate, she'd skipped lunch, choosing instead to keep going, spurred on by the pleasant memories of making chocolate with her mother back in the shop in France.

"Something smells good!" Wayne announced as he strode through the door.

She bounced up and ran to his embrace, hugging him tight. If it hadn't been for him, she would not have had her first wonderful day in the United States.

Pleased, he laughed, wrapped his arms around her, and kissed her on the forehead. "Did you have a good day?"

She squeezed him and closed her eyes and smiled. "The best."

"I'm glad."

Mrs. Brandt appeared in the room, an apron covering her dress. "Dinner's almost ready."

Embarrassed at being caught in an intimate show of affection, Delphine quickly pulled away from Wayne, but he kept his hand on the small of her back.

"Delphine, have you shown him the chocolate?" Mrs. Brandt asked.

She shook her head. "Not yet."

"Wayne, you really must try some. It's the best I've ever had," Mrs. Brandt pronounced, and she disappeared into the kitchen.

Wayne laughed and raised an eyebrow at Delphine. "High praise indeed."

Delphine took him by the hand, pulling him into the dining room, where his eyes widened at the sight of all the chocolate candy laid out before him.

"My, you have been busy," he said. He stood near the edge of the table and picked one up, turning it around between his fingers, inspecting it with a frown before tossing it into his mouth. "Wow," he said simply.

Her smile was broad. His opinion mattered to her. He'd given her so much and more than anything, she wanted him to be proud.

He helped himself to a second and then a third and when he reached for a fourth, Delphine reached for his arm, shook her head, and cast a furtive glance toward the kitchen. "No more, you'll spoil your dinner."

He ignored her, laughing, and ate one anyway.

"Aren't they wonderful?" Mrs. Brandt asked from the doorway.

"They are," Wayne agreed.

"Come on then, dinner is on the table."

The meal that evening was pleasant, more than pleasant, Delphine thought. It made the food taste better than it usually did. Mrs. Brandt asked questions about her mother and their lives as chocolatiers. Wayne reached beneath the table and gave Delphine's knee a squeeze. She rewarded him with a smile that was just for him.

Later that night, when she went to bed, she realized it was truly the happiest she'd been in a long time. She couldn't remember the last time she'd experienced such outrageous contentment; it had definitely been a long time ago. Before the war. As soon as her head hit the pillow, she was fast asleep; she didn't even have the energy to write in her journal as was sometimes her habit before bed.

Chapter Twenty-Four

DELPHINE MADE MORE OF her confections over the next two days, and while the family was eating it, there was far too much for three people. It piled up on the dining room table and soon, they had to clear room on half of the kitchen table for the overflow.

As Delphine stood at the stove, stirring a pot of chocolate, Mrs. Brandt looked around with her hands on her hips and declared, "We're running out of space."

Delphine paused, the wooden spoon mid-stir. Her heart sank as she feared her mother-in-law might call a halt to the chocolate making.

Mrs. Brandt appeared lost in thought and then snapped her fingers. "I've got an idea. I'll be right back."

"Do you want me to stop?" Delphine asked, afraid of the answer.

Mrs. Brandt turned and looked at her as if she wasn't making any sense. "Of course not. Why would you think that?" She exited the room and returned wearing her wool coat and tying her scarf under her chin. Without another word, she went out the back door.

Delphine shook her head and continued stirring. *Curious woman.*

Mrs. Brandt wasn't gone long but when she returned, she was not alone. Delphine heard them before she saw them.

"You must try her chocolate," Mrs. Brandt was saying as she led a group of neighbors in.

Shyness gripped Delphine and she wanted to run upstairs, but she was tied to the pot on the stove.

Mrs. Brandt appeared with three women in tow. One of them, Mrs. Nixon, lived next door and always waved to Delphine whenever she sat out on the front porch. The other two, Mrs. Brown and Mrs. Kimmel, Delphine knew by sight.

"It smells wonderful in here." Mrs. Nixon spotted Delphine and smiled. "Are you responsible for all this?" Her smile was warm and generous, and Delphine felt herself relax. She nodded.

"Would you look at all that chocolate." Mrs. Kimmel pointed to the kitchen table, which was half covered in candy.

"Sit down, sit down," Mrs. Brandt said with a broad sweep of her arm, indicating they should take a seat at the kitchen table.

All three removed their coats and hung them on the backs of the ladderback chairs.

"I'll make some tea." Mrs. Brandt turned to Mrs. Brown and said, "Or would you prefer coffee, Peggy?"

"No, if everyone is having tea, I'll have tea as well."

"It's no problem at all," Mrs. Brandt said.

At the stove, with her back to them, Delphine raised an eyebrow. She didn't know what her mother-in-law was up to. But she knew better than to interfere.

Mrs. Brandt set about making tea for four, including Delphine, and one cup of coffee for Mrs. Brown.

As the kettle boiled, she pulled a tray from the top shelf of one of the cabinets and placed a white lace paper doily on it. She assembled some chocolates on it and set it in the middle of the table. With a nod, she said to her neighbors, "Go on, try one." She caught Delphine's eye and gave a conspiratorial wink.

As the neighbors sampled the chocolate, Mrs. Brandt passed around steaming cups of tea and coffee.

The women marveled at Delphine's creations, helping themselves to a second and third. All were in agreement that the chocolate was divine.

"I shouldn't, but I can't resist," Mrs. Nixon said, helping herself to another one.

"The mix of chocolate and coffee is irresistible," Mrs. Brown pronounced.

Delphine cocked her head to one side, contemplating Mrs. Brown's comment, thinking it could be another flavor to experiment with.

"Is the candy for sale?" Mrs. Kimmel asked. "My sister's birthday is this weekend, and she would love a box."

Delphine froze and hurriedly looked to her mother-in-law.

"Yes, of course it is. Delphine sells it by the pound," Mrs. Brandt told them.

"How much?" asked Mrs. Brown.

Delphine's eyes widened and she looked again at Mrs. Brandt, uncertain.

Her mother-in-law came to the rescue and quoted them a price per pound.

"That's a little pricey," Mrs. Brown said with a sniff.

"This isn't factory-produced chocolate, mind you," Mrs. Brandt countered. "Delphine comes from a long line of French chocolatiers."

That was a little bit of a stretch to the truth, but Delphine kept her mouth shut, figuring her mother-in-law knew what she was doing.

Mrs. Brown cast a sideways glance at Delphine, as if she were skeptical.

"Besides, everyone knows that before the war, France was noted for their fine chocolate," Wilma said.

They were?

To assuage the women, she showed them the recipe book. "This book has been handed down generation to generation among the women in Delphine's family, from mother to daughter."

Delphine bit her lip to suppress a chuckle as she removed the chocolate from the stove to let it cool down. That statement wasn't quite truthful. Only her mother and grandmother had been chocolatiers, and it was her mother who'd penned the recipe book.

"Make up your mind, either way," Mrs. Brandt said sternly. "I've got some women from the next street over coming in an hour."

Delphine shot her a look. The woman was absolutely fierce.

"I'll take a pound," Mrs. Kimmel said. "Do you have a box to put it in?"

Delphine panicked. She had nothing to put it in. She couldn't just hand them a pound of fine chocolate and send them on their way. She didn't have so much as a bag to put it in.

"When do you need it by, Lorraine?" Mrs. Brandt asked.

"Saturday."

"I'll tell you what. We'll have boxes by then, and I'll personally drop it off to you if you place and pay for your order today."

"All right." Mrs. Kimmel peered at Mrs. Brandt. "And you'll drop it off?"

"I said I would."

Both Mrs. Brown and Mrs. Nixon followed suit, each ordering a pound themselves.

After lunch, Mrs. Brandt returned with four women from one street over and by the time they left, they'd placed orders for six pounds of chocolate.

At the end of the day, Mrs. Brandt counted up all the money, placed it in an envelope, and handed it to Delphine, who couldn't believe all the cash.

"There you go. You've earned it," Mrs. Brandt said proudly. But Delphine pushed the envelope back to her and shook her head.

The older woman looked aghast and put her hand up. "That's your money, Delphine, I can't take it."

But Delphine knew that if it weren't for the older woman, she wouldn't be holding that envelope of cash in her hand at that moment. And she was grateful. It was certainly more than she started the day with.

"Besides, Wayne's fortunes may come and go, and you're going to need a nest egg," Wilma said thoughtfully.

That was a curious statement, but Delphine thought she'd reflect on it later. There was more than plenty of money in that envelope. She pulled out the bills and counted them, divided them into two equal piles, and handed one of them to Mrs. Brandt. But the older woman still refused.

"Delphine, that isn't right."

The young woman searched her limited English vocabulary for the right word. If Mrs. Brandt brought in the customers, then Delphine would make the chocolate. Questioningly, she said, "Partners?"

Her mother-in-law beamed, and with reluctance took the cash Delphine offered. She stuck her hand out and shook Delphine's. "Partners."

The business grew out of that little kitchen in Queens, the arrangement suiting both Delphine and Mrs. Brandt. Wayne knew someone who could get them one- and two-pound candy boxes, and they invested in a premium kitchen scale. Initially, it was the neighbors and family who were invited to the kitchen for tea, coffee, and chocolate, and most, if not all, were repeat customers. No one left without making a purchase. Soon, Delphine's customer base mushroomed by word of mouth and the pile of cash grew, the envelope in the top drawer of the bureau getting thicker.

Six months in, Delphine and Mrs. Brandt were planning a trip to the wholesaler in New Jersey to look at their supplies and order more. They'd take the train, investigate the warehouse, order what they needed, and have some lunch before returning home. Delphine was excited and looking forward to it. Other than going out dancing and drinking on Friday and Saturday nights, there hadn't been much time for anything else. It might be nice for a change to go out in broad daylight, she mused as she gathered her belongings from her bedroom. She snapped open her purse and pulled out her wallet, a real leather one Wayne had given her for Christmas.

Thinking about all the stuff she had to do in New Jersey, she pulled open the top drawer of the bureau, rooting around for the envelope of cash. A frown of confusion spread over her face as she pulled out the familiar brown envelope but minus the cash. Her eyes widened as she looked inside the empty envelope. Panicked, she pushed her underwear around in the drawer, looking for the wad of cash. Where had all that money gone? There'd been hundreds and hundreds of dollars there.

"No," she whimpered. She groped around the inside of the drawer, feeling for the cash, but came up empty. Frantic, she pulled the drawer out of the bureau, upended it, and dumped the contents on the bed. After a quick glance, she knelt on the bed, going through everything, but still no cash.

"Delphine, are you ready? We're going to miss the train," Wilma called up the staircase.

Hunched over the pile on the bed, Delphine straightened and called back, "Be down in a minute." She slid off the bed and pulled out every drawer of the bureau, rifling through them. Getting down on her hands and knees, she checked beneath the bureau in case she'd dropped the money. By now strands of hair had loosened from her carefully constructed hairdo and framed her face.

Wilma appeared in the doorway, startling her. "Whatever on earth is going on?"

Delphine had been on the other side of the bed, searching underneath it, and she popped her head up. "I can't find it."

"Can't find what?"

"My money," Delphine wailed.

Wilma's lips pursed and her eyes narrowed. "Where did you last have it?"

Delphine pointed to the bureau. "There."

Wilma Brandt did a cursory survey around the room but did not dig further. "Wayne must have taken it." Her voice was quiet, and just beneath the surface the tone was accusatory.

Delphine blanched. "He would never."

"Come on, we'll be late," Wilma said.

"But I have no money," Delphine cried.

"Don't worry about that. I'll pay for the supplies and lunch," Wilma offered. "Come on, now." Gently, she wrapped her hand around Delphine's upper arm and helped her up. She guided her by the elbow out the bedroom door, retrieving Delphine's hat and handbag off the bed.

As Wilma propelled her down the stairs, Delphine muttered, "I don't know why he would do such a thing. Why would he take the money without telling me? He knows I need it for supplies."

Wilma's silence was telling, and that frightened Delphine. How many nights had she lain in bed with Wayne, discussing her plans for her little chocolate shop, with him being so encouraging.

When they landed at the front door, the horn of a taxi blared outside.

"Fix your hair and put your hat on, Delphine," Wilma encouraged, holding her hat in her hand. She stood behind Delphine in the mirror.

"Unfortunately, Wayne is like his father," Wilma said softly. "He is charming and very handsome. Almost roguish. But also like his father, he's a dreamer and a gambler."

Looking at her mother-in-law over her shoulder in the mirror, Delphine stopped brushing back the stray hairs and stared at her, open-mouthed. "But I . . ."

"Yes, I know, you didn't know," Wilma said. "But you were bound to find out sometime."

Granted, Delphine knew he didn't work a "real" job. Whenever she'd questioned him, his answer was vague: "a little bit of this and a little bit of that." But a gambler?

"Why didn't you tell me?" she asked.

Wilma shook her head. "It wasn't my place. This was something you had to find out for yourself."

The cab driver laid on the horn outside and Wilma sighed, tut-tutting. She opened the front door to signal him and held Delphine's coat for her. As she slipped it on, Wilma said, "I loved Wayne's father with every fiber of my being, but he almost destroyed us with his gambling. I couldn't make the money fast enough, and I was horrified. When we purchased this house, I had to put my foot down and have only my name on the deed. At first, he refused, but I had to threaten to leave him to finally get him to agree. We wouldn't have a roof over our heads if I'd left it up to him."

"Did he ever quit?" Delphine asked as they stepped out of the house onto the porch.

"No, he didn't. And I cannot tell you how ashamed I felt to feel nothing but relief when he died." Wilma closed the door behind her, turning the doorknob to make sure it was locked.

"But I don't know what to do," Delphine said as they walked side by side to the waiting taxi idling at the curb. She certainly didn't want Wayne to die; she loved him. But she couldn't have him taking her money without her knowledge. The missing money had caused her to feel fear and panic, and it slammed her back to those years in her village during the war, of being without. And that was something she never wanted to feel again.

"Don't worry about it now, Delphine," Wilma advised with a pat of her hand. "Tonight, when we get home, we'll come up with a good hiding place for you too."

Delphine stopped outside the bright yellow taxi before she climbed into the back seat. "Don't tell me you have to hide your money from Wayne?"

Wilma gave her a tight smile. "I may be his mother but when he's in need of money, that really doesn't matter."

Delphine's stomach twisted and she felt as if she might throw up as she got into the taxi. How could she not know this about her own husband?

Wilma pulled the cab door shut behind her and gave directions to the driver. She turned to Delphine. "To be honest, I'm surprised this didn't happen sooner."

When the taxi pulled away from the curb, she said no more.

"But how could you?" Delphine demanded of Wayne later that evening when they'd retired up to their room.

Wayne sat on his side of the bed and tugged his shoes off, letting them fall with a soft thud to the floor. He looked over at her standing at the end of the bed. "I told you, I needed some money so I took it."

What made her irate was that he couldn't see what was wrong with his actions.

"But you didn't ask me! You knew I needed that money to buy more supplies," she cried.

"You're my wife. I don't need to ask you for your money. What's yours is mine and what's mine is yours," he snarled.

Delphine took a step back. This was a side of him she'd never seen before. Sure, they had their little spats, but he'd never responded with a sneer. The irony was not lost on her: he'd committed the crime but was angry because she'd called him out on it.

"You should ask me before taking things," she said, this time her voice barely above a whisper, not wanting to provoke him.

He remained silent.

"Can I ask what my money was used for?"

"Your money," he said with raised eyebrows and a smirk. "Now it's *your* money?" He pulled off his shirt and tossed it on the chair. "You forget, Delphine, that I put a roof over your head, and I bought all those supplies when you were first starting your business."

To placate him, she rephrased her question. "What did you use it for?"

"I invested it so we can buy our own house someday," he said smoothly.

She ignored the carrot dangled in front of her in the form of the promise of their own house and asked, "Invested it in what?"

"You wouldn't understand," he said evasively.

"Try me." It infuriated her to think that people, especially her husband, thought she was stupid because English wasn't her native tongue.

"I'm tired. Turn off the light." He stood, stepped out of his pants, and threw them on the chair as well, stuffing his socks into his shoes. Slipping into bed, he pulled the covers up to his shoulders and said again, "Turn off the light, Delphine."

She turned the light out, shrouding the room in darkness, but remained standing at the foot of the bed, watching her husband drift off to sleep. She curled her hands into fists at her side. Never again would she let this happen. She was too familiar with the feeling of deprivation and of things being taken away from her. No, never again. No matter how much she loved Wayne, she would never let herself be put in this position. In the future, if he needed money, he'd have to ask her for it.

Maybe Wilma would show her a hiding place to safeguard her money, but Delphine knew a thing or two about hiding things that were of value.

By the following year, the cottage industry from Wilma's kitchen had blossomed, and it wasn't long before Delphine had recouped her earnings. She kept it well hidden from Wayne. There were times when she knew he'd searched their room; her belongings in her drawers had obviously been pushed about. And every time he came up empty-handed, he darted down the stairs and left the house with a slam of the front door.

By 1949, the event she'd been waiting for finally happened: she was pregnant. Fear had had her believing they'd never have a child. And those days waiting for the baby were happy, joyous times for both her and Wayne. Despite their issues in the past, it brought them closer together.

It was late summer, and Delphine was starting to show. She was glad the cooler weather was on its way. Unlike all the horror stories she'd heard from the women who stopped in to purchase pound boxes of chocolate, she'd never had morning sickness or fatigue. If anything, her appetite had increased, and she felt more energetic than ever before. Wayne had started talking about buying a house, but Delphine kept kicking the idea down the road, suggesting they wait until after the baby was born. The truth was, she didn't want to leave Wilma. Sometimes she thought she and Wilma got on better than she and Wayne did. It had got to the point where Delphine and her mother-in-law were able to anticipate the other's needs, practically reading each other's minds. While Delphine made all the chocolate and experimented with different flavors, Wilma ran the business side of things. She alone was responsible for getting Delphine's Chocolates out in front of people, whether it was paying for a stall at a Christmas bazaar or a lawn fete. The woman's mind never stopped, and she was the singular driving force behind their thriving chocolate business.

They'd gotten the idea to open up a shop with a big kitchen in the back, and they were currently on their way back from visiting their third site. This one ticked all the boxes, right on a main thoroughfare with a nice shop window and kitchen already in situ. The bonus was that it was within walking distance of the house. Delphine and Wilma talked excitedly about their plans. There had already been meetings with an accountant and a lawyer to do things "properly," as Wilma insisted. The only dark cloud had been when Wilma advised Delphine not to put anything in Wayne's name. That had hurt a bit, but she understood fully.

A new baby, a new business . . . it was all coming together, Delphine thought excitedly as the house came into view. She had enough cash saved in various spots in the house that she'd be able to put a generous deposit down on the shop and buy some equipment.

As they approached the house, they noticed a man standing on the front porch, pressing the doorbell.

"Can I help you?" Wilma called out.

Upon hearing her voice, he turned to them and smiled.

Delphine followed Wilma up the porch steps.

The man was in his late forties or early fifties. His dark suit was impeccable, his collar stiff and his shirt a pristine white. There wasn't a hair out of place or a wrinkle to be found anywhere. On his pinkie finger he wore a signet ring with a large black onyx.

"I'm looking for Wayne." His voice was deep and gravelly. Up close, his eyes were as dark as the night, with hair to match. His complexion was heavily pockmarked, but it did not detract from his looks. It did make him appear more menacing, however.

"You must be Wayne's wife," he said, his grin wolfish.

Opting not to confirm, for there was something about this man that made her uneasy, Delphine simply said, "Wayne isn't here right now."

"I see. Tell him Tony called."

"Do you have a last name?" It was quite possible Wayne knew more than one.

"Dukaski."

Wilma said nothing, brushed by the man, and inserted the key in the lock. Her hands shook as she opened the door, and Delphine wondered if she should be more afraid than she was.

Wilma pushed through the front door with Delphine hot on her heels.

Tony lifted his hat off his head. "Good day, ladies."

Once inside, Wilma firmly closed the door and locked it, something she'd never done before. During the day, the doors were usually wide open. As for Delphine, she shrugged a few times, trying to shake off the sense that that man knew what she looked like in just her knickers.

"He's kind of scary," Delphine said.

The air was tense.

"He'll be back, I'm afraid."

"What makes you say that?" Delphine said, unable to imagine the reason the man would keep returning.

Wilma removed her coat, pulled out a hanger from the hall closet, and draped her coat around it, tucking her scarf in the sleeve and hanging it in the closet. With both hands, she smoothed down her hair. Delphine was slow to remove her coat, feeling a chill that had nothing to do with the weather.

"Because Wayne probably owes him money." Wilma glanced at her wristwatch and headed into the kitchen. "I better get the dinner on."

Delphine followed her, forgetting to remove her coat. "Why do you say that? How do you know Wayne owes him money?"

"Why else would he be here? It surely isn't a social call." Wilma grabbed her apron off the hook near the back door and tied it behind her. She pulled a pan from a lower cabinet and laid it on the stove.

"Do you think he owes him a lot?" Delphine asked. The idea that Wayne owed someone like Tony Dukaski money was unfathomable to her. How did he get mixed up with the likes of him?

"How much do you think he owes him?" Delphine repeated when Wilma was not forthcoming.

Wilma shrugged as she sliced a cooking onion on a chopping board. "He'd hardly make a house call for a small amount of money owed."

This troubled Delphine. How could Wayne owe anyone money? He always seemed flush with cash, and they still went out dancing almost every Friday and Saturday night.

Wilma shot her a glance and a quick smile. "Wayne's a big boy. He can take care of himself. Besides, you don't need the extra worry. You need to think about the baby."

Delphine nodded. Moving slowly, befuddled with confusion and questions, she removed her coat and walked to the closet as if she were sleepwalking. Even the distraction of sitting and peeling vegetables at the kitchen table did not calm her down.

All talk about their visit to the premises for the new shop had been forgotten. That seemed so long ago now.

Wayne was his usual outgoing self when he appeared at dinnertime. He leaned in to kiss Delphine, but she turned her head so his lips landed on her cheek. Wilma was quiet as she laid the meal out on the table. When they all sat, he asked, "How did it go with the shop?"

"Good," Delphine said evenly, not looking at him.

Wilma remained silent.

"You'd think the two of you would be more excited," he said, forking a lump of mashed potatoes and gravy into his mouth. "It's all you've been talking about."

Wilma stared at her plate and said nothing. But Delphine felt the need to address their afternoon visitor.

"Someone came by the house looking for you," she said.

"Really?" He picked up a slice of bread and slathered it with butter.

"Yes. Tony Dukaski." Delphine did not remove her gaze from her husband's face.

The butter knife in Wayne's hand froze for a fraction of a second before it picked up again, spreading butter to the edges of the bread. He did not look at her. "Did he say what he wanted?"

Wilma, who'd been unusually reticent since they'd returned home earlier, scoffed. "What do you think he wanted? You most likely owe him money."

Wayne waved her comment away, dismissive. "It's only a misunderstanding."

Delphine and Wilma spoke at the same time.

"Is it?" Delphine asked, the food on her plate untouched.

"You either owe him money or you don't," Wilma said sharply.

"He didn't seem like a very nice man," Delphine said.

"Look, don't worry about it. I'll go see him tomorrow." Wayne reached for Delphine's hand, but she drew it away and let it fall into her lap. He sighed and resumed eating his dinner.

Later, before they went to bed, when she brought up the subject again, he reassured her that he would take care of the problem and she'd never have to see Tony Dukaski again.

But Tony Dukaski returned the following day. The day after that, he appeared in the morning, in the afternoon, and in the evening. And every single time, Wayne was out. She couldn't figure out if Tony was unlucky or if there was another reason for the increasing frequency of his visits. Wayne heard about each visit, the muscle ticking along his jaw, and promised repeatedly to take care of it. But he never did.

Finally, on the fourth day, when the doorbell rang, both Delphine and Wilma looked toward the front door.

"I'll get it," Delphine said. "Would you mind taking over here?"

Wilma took the wooden spoon from her and continued to stir the pot of chocolate on the bain marie.

Wiping her hands on her chocolate-stained apron, Delphine marched to the front door, reminding herself that she had lived under Nazi occupation for years, so she should be able to handle this man.

When she opened the door, he stood there on the front porch, dressed impeccably as always. She hadn't seen him in the same suit twice. Out front, against the curb, sat a shiny black Cadillac with a driver in the front.

"I'm sorry, but Wayne isn't here," she told him blandly.

"That's my tough luck. But then I don't mind the scenery." His gaze raked over her from head to toe and then back up again, his grin predatory.

Although fear filled her, she straightened her spine and gritted her teeth.

He took a step closer to her, closing the gap between them. Bending his head, he sniffed. "You smell nice, like chocolate or something."

She refused to budge or be intimidated. Tony moved in closer, until she could feel his breath on her neck.

"You tell your husband to pay up what he owes, or something unpleasant might happen to his pretty wife," he whispered, and stepped back with a laugh. He lifted his hat and turned to step off the porch.

She'd gotten through the war only to be intimidated by this jerk?

She called out after him, "How much does Wayne owe you?"

He stopped, pivoting to face her, his expression grim. When he revealed the amount, Delphine paled and a slight gasp escaped from her lips.

"That's what your husband is getting up to behind your back."

There was only one thing to do. She'd have to use the deposit money to pay him off, or they'd never get rid of him. And Wayne might get hurt. Or herself. She was going to be a mother soon and she had to protect her child.

"Come back tomorrow and I'll have your money for you," she said simply.

This resulted in Tony narrowing his eyes and stepping closer to her. "Are you trying to play me for a fool?"

Indignant, Delphine said, "Of course not. I give you my word. You'll get your money tomorrow."

He regarded her for a moment, deciding whether she was being sincere or not. Delphine waited and held her breath.

"All right, then," he said. "I'll be here at one sharp."

"I'll be here," she said with a nod. And before he could say another word, she slipped inside, closing the door behind her and leaning against it. Shaking, she sucked in a deep breath.

~❧~

"What did you do?" Wayne asked, his eyes sparking with anger. Delphine had never seen him so furious in all the years they'd been together.

Reflexively, she took a step back. She didn't think Wayne would hit her, but one could never be too sure. If she'd learned one thing, it was that people could be unpredictable and cruel.

"I don't know why you're so angry." Truly, she was at a loss. She thought he'd be glad to get the likes of Tony Dukaski off his back. To not have him coming around every day, pestering his wife and mother.

"Do you know how it looks when my wife pays off my debt?" he yelled.

They were up in their bedroom. When he'd arrived home, he'd landed in the kitchen in a state of fury and said tightly, "Delphine, upstairs. Now."

But if he was going to continue yelling, then there'd been no point in hiding up in their bedroom.

"He wouldn't leave us alone," Delphine cried. She didn't want to tell Wayne how someone like Tony made her feel. As if he were eyeing her up like she was his next meal.

"I told you I would take care of it." There was a cutting sharpness to his tone.

"But you didn't!" she cried. "So I did. I had to use my deposit money for the shop to pay off your bad debt!"

"You've humiliated me in front of other people," he said.

His male pride was going to be their undoing. She rolled her eyes and said quietly, "And you put your wife, mother, and unborn child in danger."

He stared at her, seeming to contemplate what she'd said.

"I took care of it because you didn't," she said coldly, and marched out of the bedroom and returned to the kitchen so she could finish her dinner. Lately, her appetite had been formidable.

"There's more there, Delphine," Wilma said with a nod toward Delphine's empty plate.

"No, I shouldn't," she said, despite feeling as if she could easily put away another plateful.

Wilma pressed her lips together, opened her mouth, and then closed it again, clearly struggling with something she wanted to say. "I know you meant to help him," she said. "But don't ever pay off his debts again."

Delphine didn't understand. "But he's my husband."

"Yes, but now there'll be no limit to the money he'll borrow if he knows at the back of his mind that his wife will rescue him."

She was at a loss for words.

"Early in my marriage, I did the same thing. Bailed my husband out. But in the end, it was throwing good money after bad, and I had to leave him to his own devices. If he got a beating, that was his own doing. Yes, it bothered me when he ended up with broken bones, but for my own sanity I had to stop rescuing him."

Delphine flinched at the mention of broken bones.

Abruptly, Wilma pushed her chair back, stood, and began clearing the table. But she'd left a lot for Delphine to think about.

The shifts in her relationship with her husband were sometimes subtle and sometimes explosive. But each time, she was left with the sense that she liked him less, that he wasn't the man she'd met back in her little village when he came rolling in with his unit. But there was nothing she could do about it. She was truly stuck. To return to France was out of the question and besides, there was nothing to return to. Whatever relatives were left were either elderly or scattered all over the country. To go back as a single mother would require money, lots of it, something she didn't have. And she'd grown to love America; she didn't want to leave.

He was her husband. They had a baby coming and hopefully more children after that. So she continued to make chocolate in the kitchen with Wilma's help. Surely Wayne would settle down and become responsible once the baby was born.

CHAPTER TWENTY-FIVE

1949

DELPHINE BOUNCED THE BABY on her hip in an attempt to soothe him. But she supposed five-month-old Jean-Paul had picked up on her anxiety. She hadn't slept for the last two nights and as a result, she felt shaky and irritable.

Wayne hadn't been home in days. There'd been no word from him either. When the crying baby woke her before dawn three mornings ago, she'd been startled to see that the other side of the bed was empty. She reached out, feeling Wayne's side of the mattress, but it was cold, no warmth at all. Unconsciously, she'd worried her bottom lip as she pulled the baby out of the crib that was next to her side and brought him into bed with her. When he was finished nursing, he fell asleep, milk still dribbling down his chin. Usually, she liked to enjoy this time with her baby, running her forefinger down the side of his face, relishing how soft his skin was or fingering his fine dark curls that were beginning to grow. He was truly a gorgeous baby. She could stare at him all day, unable to believe that he was a part of her. But now, worried about Wayne, she gently stood and placed the baby carefully back into his crib. There were still a couple more hours of sleep in him before his day began.

She shrugged her robe on and slowly opened the door and peeked out. The upstairs hallway was darkened, but the small lamp at the bottom of the stairs that was kept on all night gave her enough light to see. Carefully, she tugged the door shut behind her, not wanting to wake either the baby or Wilma.

Tiptoeing to the top of the landing, she peered over the banister but was met with shadows. No lights on. Now outright concerned over her husband's whereabouts, she made her way down the staircase, careful to avoid the creaks.

The kitchen was cold and quiet. No sign of Wayne. She went to the living room, where she peered out from behind the drapes to see if his car was parked on the street. But it wasn't out there.

She heard a door open upstairs.

Wilma stood at the top of the stairs and called down in a loud whisper, "Is that you, Delphine?"

Delphine rushed to the bottom of the stairs. "It's me."

"Is everything all right?"

"Wayne never came home last night."

This was met by a gasp, and Wilma descended the staircase in her quilted baby blue robe, holding on to the banister. A crown of tiny rollers wrapped around her head, held in place with a black hairnet.

Delphine hated worrying her, but it would be a little hard to hide Wayne's absence when he didn't show up for breakfast.

"What do you mean, he didn't come home?"

Delphine sighed. Her worry over Wayne made her irritable and annoyed but she knew Wilma would be just as worried as she, so she bit her tongue and didn't retort with a sarcastic reply.

"He's not upstairs and he's not down here, either."

"Well, where could he be?" Wilma asked.

"That's a good question."

"Is his car outside?"

"No." She went to her mother-in-law's side. "There's no sense in worrying. I'm sure he'll be home soon. We should go back to bed. We've got a long day ahead of us."

"I don't know if I could go back to sleep."

"Try." They did have a long day ahead of them; they had a big chocolate order to fulfil, and the baby kept them busy. It would do neither of them any good if they were dragging all day.

After a few moments, she convinced Wilma to go upstairs, and she followed her up. But when Delphine climbed back into bed, she found it hard to settle. She snuggled into her pillow, but sleep was evasive.

An hour later, now exhausted from trying unsuccessfully to fall back asleep and with her stomach in knots over Wayne, she forced herself to get up and out of the bed.

After a quick wash at the bathroom sink and a haphazard brush of her teeth, she dressed and headed downstairs, leaving the door to her room open to hear if the baby cried.

She put the kettle on, standing next to it, not wanting it to get to the stage where it blew its shrill whistle.

As she sat at the kitchen table, drinking a hot cup of tea, she mused that she really had no idea how her husband spent his days. He sometimes rattled off names like Lester, Brownie, Joey B, and Slim, but who they were and what he was doing with them, she had no idea. It occurred to her that she had no number for any of them and did not have a clue as to where to begin to search for her husband. Was he all right? Was he hurt? Was he unable to get home? Was he lying in a ditch somewhere?

The overhead light went on and Delphine blinked. Wilma entered the kitchen and went straight for the stove. "I couldn't go back to sleep either," she commented, turning the burner on beneath the kettle.

When she sat down at the table with her cup of tea, she said, "I checked on the baby on my way down. He's fast asleep. He's such a love." A genuine smile appeared on Wilma's lips.

"Has Wayne ever done this before?" Delphine asked, fingering her teacup. The tea had now gone cold. Before the war, Wayne had had a life and she was pretty sure it was similar to the one he was living now, except now he had a wife and baby.

"Not in a very long time." Wilma's deep sigh blew the steam over her tea off course.

"What if he's hurt?"

There was a grim set to Wilma's lips. "Sadly, with the characters he consorts with, that is a strong possibility."

Delphine's stomach felt like lead. If anything happened to Wayne, what would become of her and Jean-Paul?

"Look, there's no sense in getting all worked up, he's probably tied up somewhere," Wilma said.

"Tied up?"

Wilma shook her head. "I'm sorry. Poor choice of words. I mean, he's probably busy. Or otherwise engaged." She pursed her lips in disapproval.

"Do you think he's with another woman?" Delphine's worst fear was that he was dead, but this one was a close second.

Wilma looked genuinely surprised. "Of course not. If he's not hurt, he's out gambling somewhere. But with another woman? Never. I see the way he looks at you." She reached over and patted Delphine's hand. "Don't ever worry about that. He'd never cheat on you with another woman. Cards, yes, but not another woman."

There was no consolation in those words.

Wilma finished the remainder of her tea and stood, carrying her cup over to the sink. With a sigh, she said, "I'll call the hospitals and the morgue."

Delphine's heart lurched at the last word, but her mother-in-law's tone seemed matter of fact. Was this how her own married life to Mr. Brandt had been? How had she stood it?

By the third day, when there'd been no sign, Delphine reassured herself with the fact that neither the hospitals, the police, nor the morgue had any record of him. As the baby fussed on her hip, she looked at all the candy they needed to box up. She was so tired she wanted to cry.

When the front door opened and she spotted Wayne, she exchanged a glance with Wilma. Without a word, she handed the baby over to her mother-in-law and marched to the front room.

He still wore the suit he'd left in three days ago, but now it was rumpled and there were dark stains in his armpits. His eyes were bleary, either from lack of sleep or too much booze. He looked like she felt: shaky and exhausted. But it was the smile on his face that sent her over the edge. To come strolling in after being missing for three days, and smiling instead of being sheepish and apologetic?

She flew into a rage. It was so unexpected she heard Wilma gasp behind her, and the baby started crying.

Wayne took a step back and put up his hands. "Whoa, whoa, what's this all about!"

Furious, she slapped his hands away. "I'll tell you what this is all about, you've been gone for three days, and we've been worried sick about you! Your mother has been calling the morgue and the hospital every single morning to see if you were there. We didn't know who to call."

"Slow down, and say it in English," he said. "Actually, don't. I get the gist of it."

She'd been so consumed she'd reverted to her native tongue. "Where have you been? Why didn't you call us?" she demanded in English. "We've been out of our minds with worry."

"I was busy," he said.

"Busy? Too busy to call us? Let us know you were all right?"

"I said I was busy," Wayne said. His defiance and his own anger made her furious.

"You're mad because I'm angry that you disappeared for a few days?"

"I said I was busy, and that should be good enough."

"Is there someone else?" she asked, hands on her hips. She didn't think so, but she had to ask.

The question caught him off guard, and his confidence wavered. He scowled. "No, no, of course not. How could you even think something like that?" He appeared shaken at her question.

Well, good. Now he can know how it feels.

She folded her arms across her chest and waited.

He tipped his hat back on his head. The tail of his shirt hung untucked from his trousers on one side. He was a mess.

He stared at the floor. "Look, Delphine, I'm sorry."

"Where were you?" she asked again. She knew he wanted to go upstairs and crash on the bed, as did she, but he wasn't going anywhere until he answered some questions.

"I was at a high-stakes poker game for the last three days," he said. He scratched the back of his neck.

Delphine blinked. "What? All this time?"

"Yes."

"Where did you get the money for that?" she cried. She wasn't bailing him out again.

"Shh, shh." He held his hands up in front of him as if to placate her. She hated when he did that. Like she was eight years old.

"Did you borrow again?"

"No—well, I did, but I was able to pay the loan back with my winnings." He grinned as if this would make it all right. "And I have some good news."

No good news could improve her mood that morning. He reached into his pocket, pulled out a brown envelope, and handed it to her. His excitement eased the exhaustion on his face.

"We own a house!" he announced.

Delphine scowled and wondered what he was talking about. He must have passed the point of complete exhaustion. She took the envelope from his hand. On the outside in neat penmanship was written *12465 Star Shine Drive, Hideaway Bay, New York*.

Inside the envelope was a set of keys.

Delphine read the address out loud. "Hideaway Bay?" Granted, she wasn't from Queens, but she'd never heard of the place despite living here for a few years.

"More like Getaway Bay," Wilma muttered behind them.

If the last few days hadn't been so exhausting, Delphine would have grinned, but she was too tired to think straight. "Where is this place?"

"It's on Lake Erie." Wayne removed his jacket and took the envelope from her, stuffing it into his jacket pocket and draping the coat over the newel post.

"Where's that?" she asked.

"That's on the other side of the state," Wilma said. "You're not going to move there, surely! Why, it's too far away."

Delphine flicked a glance at Wilma, noting her upset. No, she wouldn't be moving to the other side of the state. In the last few years, she'd created a life, a family, and a business in this house. And she wouldn't leave Wilma; the older woman had been too good to her.

"We don't have to move there, don't you see?" he said. "We can sell it and use the money to buy a house here."

She rubbed her forehead and sighed. That was the problem with Wayne. He had these pie-in-the-sky dreams, and they were at heights that were impossible to reach. It always *sounded* good and promising, but usually everything fell through. Or he ran out of money. Right now, she was tired, and she couldn't hitch her wagon to his star. The baby would be up soon, and she needed to get to work.

"I'm going to bed," he said with a yawn. Stretching, he raised his arms above his head, showing the dark stains beneath his arms. He took off his suitcoat, flung it over his shoulder, and walked up the stairs, scratching his forehead.

Five minutes later, he called out from the bedroom, "Delphine, the baby's awake!"

It was going to be a long day.

***

A month later, Delphine was fast asleep in her bed despite the unrelenting heat. Before settling in, she'd pushed the windows up as far as they would go, but it had been futile. There wasn't so much as a whisper of a breeze. Wayne was gone for the night, and she wasn't sure what time he'd be home. The baby was fast asleep in his crib, wearing only a diaper. His fine hair clung to his face and neck, poor thing.

A car speeding down the street woke her. She tried to read the bedside clock in the weak light that shone in from the streetlamp out front.

She sat up when she heard the car screech to a halt in front of the house. Hurriedly, she went to the window and peered out, standing in the shadows of the room.

A Buick idled in the middle of the street as three men got out and opened the rear passenger-side door. They spoke hurriedly in clipped voices and to her horror, they dragged a man out of the back seat and tossed him onto the front lawn. To her continuing horror, she realized it was Wayne.

"Oh no," she muttered, dashing out the bedroom door and down the stairs. She heard the slam of car doors and the squeal of tires as the Buick sped away.

She threw open the front door and ran outside to the front lawn, where her husband lay curled in the fetal position under the glow of the streetlamp.

"Wayne!" Her voice sounded loud in the middle of the quiet night.

A groan emitted from Wayne's lips.

She rushed to his side and knelt down. Gently, she rolled him over and leaned back and gasped.

His face was unrecognizable. His beautiful blue eyes were swollen shut. Bright red blood stained the 'o' that was his mouth. He clutched his hands over his stomach.

"You need to go to the hospital," Delphine whispered.

He managed to get out a weak "no."

"Wayne!" she hissed. It was obvious that his injuries were serious. Serious enough to require medical attention.

She felt so helpless. She started to get up. "I'm calling an ambulance."

"What's going on?" Wilma demanded from the porch. "Is that Wayne?"

Delphine looked up and peered at her in the darkness. In a loud whisper, she said, "Yes. He's badly hurt."

Wilma ran down the stairs, holding up the hem of her robe so she wouldn't trip. Even in the darkness, Delphine saw her eyes widen in horror, and she threw her hand to her mouth and gasped. "I'll call an ambulance," she said, and ran back into the house.

Wayne groaned, turning once again onto his side.

Delphine continued to kneel beside him, holding his hand. "Don't worry, Wayne, we'll get you fixed up," she said softly.

He said nothing, but his face was contorted in a grimace.

Delphine's heart beat so fast and so hard she could hear it in her eardrums. She looked up and down the street, looking for any evidence of the car and the men that had so unceremoniously dumped her husband on the front lawn.

The low whine of an ambulance could be heard in the distance. *Thank God.*

The ambulance pulled up and parked against the curb, and the attendants got out and ran over to Wayne with a canvas stretcher. He did not resist their attempts to help, not even when they loaded him into the back of the ambulance. When she attempted to get into the ambulance with him, he weakly waved her away, muttering, "Stay with the baby."

As Delphine stood by Wilma near the steps of the front porch, they watched in disbelief as the ambulance carted Wayne away. One by one, lights had begun to flick on in the houses across the street and on either side of them. From the upstairs window came the cry of Jean-Paul.

"I'll get him a bottle." Wilma rushed back into the house before Delphine could respond.

Wayne ended up staying in the hospital for a few days. He had two broken ribs and a fractured eye socket. He needed stitches at the corner of his mouth. When he came home, he was quiet and sullen and did not leave the house.

Initially, Delphine was happy he was around. She thought it would be a good opportunity for them to spend some time together. But Wayne wasn't interested in that. He spent much of his time sitting on the porch, and although he was attentive to Jean-Paul when he was around, he did nothing extra with him.

Delphine suggested taking trips to the zoo or the park, but he said no. He slept poorly at night, tossing and turning and keeping Delphine up in the process. When she expressed concern about his state of mind, he brushed her off, annoyed with the question. She'd never seen him so irritable before. Even as his health improved and the bruises faded, he remained aloof.

She and Wilma packed up candy orders, and Wayne moved listlessly around the kitchen, picking things up, inspecting them as if he'd never noticed them before. Delphine exchanged a glance with her mother-in-law, who wore a heavy frown.

At one point, Wayne picked up a box, lifted the lid, and helped himself to a piece of chocolate.

"Wayne! That's part of an order," Delphine wailed.

"If you want to eat some of the chocolate, it's all laid out on the dining room table and you can help yourself," his mother said.

He didn't respond, didn't even return the lid to the box. He looked at both of them, said nothing, and walked into the dining room.

"But don't handle the chocolate at the far end of the table. It's setting and you'll leave fingerprints," Delphine called out after him.

Chapter Twenty-Six

As the weeks went by, there was no more talk about the house in Hideaway Bay. Somehow, Wayne once again became flush with cash, and Delphine saw even less of him than before. But this was always cyclic, she knew. This was how it was. When the winnings were large, he was hardly around, explaining that he was out there trying to parlay his winnings—or "earnings" as he called them—into more. And when the chips were down, he ran the gamut of morose to hyper, all these ideas abounding. And he'd be hanging more around the kitchen, and getting in the way. Finally, she'd told him to spend more time with Jean-Paul so she could focus on the candy-making. For orders continued to increase, and she'd built a nice nest egg, which she continued to hide in various places around the house.

But a month after he'd won the house in Hideaway Bay, he arrived in the bedroom in the middle of the night and flipped the light on. The brightness immediately woke Delphine, and she squinted against it.

"Turn it off," she hissed. "You'll wake the baby." She rolled over and glanced at the clock. It was a little after one in the morning.

Wayne either didn't hear her or ignored her as he knelt on the floor on his side of the bed and pulled out the small suitcase they kept beneath it. He set it on the bed and opened it, its lid landing on Delphine's hip.

"Get up, Delphine. We have to go." He pulled some but not all of his clothes from his bureau drawers.

She sat up, propping herself on her elbows, groggy. "What?"

"Get your stuff, get stuff for the baby. We have to go."

"What are you talking about?" He wasn't making any sense. Was he drunk?

The last thing he took from the bureau was the brown envelope with the keys to a house in Hideaway Bay, tucking it into the pocket of his coat. He hurried around to her side of the bed and sat on the edge, the mattress dipping beneath his weight.

His eyes were dark and bloodshot. There was no smell of whiskey on him. Only the all-too-familiar scent of fear. It immediately took her back to those years living under German occupation. "We need to leave right now," he said.

"Right now? Why? Can't this wait until morning?"

"No." His tone was frightful. Fearful and nervous. "We have to pack up and leave now."

"For how long?"

"For good."

She shook her head and sank back amongst the pillows. "I'm not leaving. Not like this. No, Wayne, I won't do it."

He grabbed her arms forcefully and dragged her back up to a sitting position.

"You're hurting me," she said.

"Listen to me good, Delphine. I'm in trouble and we have to leave," he said thickly.

"What kind of trouble?"

"I can't explain it now, there's no time. If I don't get out of here, the next time they throw me on the front lawn, you'll be a widow."

That startled her into action, and she jumped out of bed and began to dress. She threw just enough clothes for her and Jean-Paul on top of Wayne's things in the suitcase. Along the sides she tucked in the cloth diapers and the diaper pins. On top of their clothes, she laid her recipe book and her journals. For who knew when they'd be back.

Once the suitcase was packed, she began to make the bed and Wayne waved her off. "Don't worry about that. Get the baby and let's go."

His fear and anxiety were contagious.

"What about your mother?" she asked.

"I'll wake her now and meet you downstairs." He disappeared out of the room and left the door open. She heard him knock on his mother's bedroom door, open it, and then there was the sound of muffled voices.

Gently, she lifted the baby from his crib, his warmth and baby smell pure sweetness, and set him on a blanket she'd laid out on the bed. He didn't so much as stir while she swaddled him. When he was safely in her arms, she picked up two of his favorite toys and made her way downstairs.

"Ready?" Wayne asked.

"Yes, but the suitcase is still upstairs."

She waited for him in the front parlor, her coat on and her handbag over her forearm, holding the baby close to her as he raced up the stairs and returned with the suitcase. Wilma followed him down in her bathrobe and hairnet.

"What have you done now?" she asked her son, her expression angry and disgusted.

"I can't go into it now, Mother, but we have to leave." Wayne headed for the front door with the suitcase in his hand. He looked at his mother. "All of us. Together."

Wilma shook her head, a grim set to her lips. "This is my home. I won't be run out of it."

He stepped closer to her. "It's too dangerous. Come with us."

She shook her head and stood rooted to the spot, resolute. "No, Wayne, I'm not going."

"Wilma, please come with us," Delphine pleaded.

Wilma's expression softened. "No, Delphine. I won't leave my home."

"Please."

"Wait a minute." Wilma stood between Wayne and Delphine, and she put an arm around Delphine. "You go, Wayne, but leave Delphine and Jean-Paul here with me."

Delphine liked that idea. She and Wilma would get along fine without him. They were already doing it. But Wayne shook his head. "The same people who want to kill me would think nothing of hurting Delphine and the baby."

"What kind of people have you gotten yourself involved with?" his mother cried. "How could you put your wife and child in harm's way?"

"Mother, we don't have time for this," Wayne said. He held open the front door. "Come on, Delphine, get in the car."

She looked back and forth between her husband and her mother-in-law. Her hesitancy caught Wayne off guard and part of his expression crumpled as he realized she was torn. Suddenly, he looked very fragile and vulnerable. Her preference was to remain there with Wilma. But Wayne was her husband and she'd vowed never to forget all that he'd done for her and given her: a new life and a baby. She had no choice.

Delphine went to Wilma and still holding the baby, who was beginning to stir, wrapped one arm around her mother-in-law as the both of them looked at each other and sobbed.

"I'm sorry." Tears streamed down Delphine's face. In a pleading voice, she said, "Come with us."

Wilma shook her head. "No. You must hurry and get out of here."

Wayne took the baby from her arms to hurry things along and stepped outside to put the baby into the car.

Mrs. Brandt enveloped her in the warm embrace of her bosom and whispered in her ear: "Now, Delphine, if you find Hideaway Bay isn't to your liking, let me know and I'll wire you the money for a train ticket to come home."

That kindness brought tears to Delphine's eyes, and she nodded rapidly, her chin quivering, trying to blink away the tears.

"Delphine!" Wayne said, popping his head back through the front door.

"All right," she hissed, and reluctantly she pulled away from Wilma.

"Mother, it might be a good idea for you to go visit your sister in Ohio for a few days," Wayne suggested on his way out.

Wayne took hold of his wife's arm firmly and tugged her away, practically pushing her out the door. "As soon as it's safe, we'll be in contact, Mother. And it goes without saying, do not tell anyone where we've gone."

Wilma stood there, her shoulders sagging and her arms hanging by her sides, looking the way Delphine felt: shattered.

They hurried out the door and off the porch, Wayne's eyes constantly scanning up and down the street, traveling right to left.

Once Delphine got settled into the passenger side of the front seat, he took their sleeping baby from the back seat and handed him to Delphine. He ran around to the driver's side, still looking furtively around, and slammed the car door, breaking the silence of the middle of the night.

They drove well into the night, the silence between them tense. Delphine was too tired to care. Her arms grew weary from clutching Jean-Paul so tightly to her chest. He'd woken once, stirred, fussed, and she'd nursed him until he fell back asleep. Initially, Wayne was hunched over the wheel, continuously looking in the rearview mirror, and it wasn't until they cleared one hundred miles that he began to relax.

Delphine sat forward and let out a little cry.

Wayne looked at her sharply. "What is it?"

"I left all my chocolate-making equipment back at your mother's house." She looked over her shoulder as if she might be able to see Wilma's house behind her. "We need to go back."

Wayne shook his head. "I'll get you new stuff when we get there."

"Do you know what condition this house is in?" she asked. Her fear was that the house would be in ruins, uninhabitable. And another, equally unappealing thought occurred to her: the house in Hideaway Bay could already be occupied. She voiced these fears to Wayne.

"Nope. He assured me that the house has been empty for years. It was his parents' summer home, and they left it to him when they died, but he had no interest. He didn't even seem to care that he lost it playing cards." Wayne smiled to himself.

"He must be a lousy poker player," she muttered.

Wayne looked briefly at her. "It wasn't that at all. I'm a better one."

That was nothing to brag about. Trying to work out a kink in her arm, she shifted the baby to her other side, stretching and flexing her free hand, making it into a fist and then releasing it.

"You're not going to be able to hold him for six more hours," Wayne said. "Why don't you make up a bed for him in the back seat?"

"Six more hours?" she asked. "I thought you said this was in New York?"

"It is, but it's on the other side of the state. About five hundred miles west."

Her heart sank. They'd be in the car all night. He was right of course; she couldn't hold the baby all night long. She was sleepy herself. And her arms were already stiff. She indicated to Wayne to pull over and when he parked on the shoulder, he got out, opened her car door, and took the baby from her. She got into the back seat and made up a small bed for Jean-Paul, nestling him between her hip and the suitcase.

Wayne restarted the car, looked over his shoulder, and pulled back out onto the road.

Delphine stayed awake for as long as she could, but her eyelids grew heavy and the monotony of driving, of being the only vehicle on these back roads, made her sleepy. She wished Wayne had a real job like other husbands. She knew of neighbor women whose husbands went off to work shifts at Con Edison or for the police or fire department. They complained about them, how they had to stretch to make ends meet, how their husbands always seemed to be working. It was a problem Delphine wished she had. She was certain not one of them had to leave their home in the middle of the night because their husband had gotten involved with the wrong kinds of people. How lucky they were!

Her thoughts drifted to France—France before the war—and happier times when her mother and grandmother were still alive. In her mind, she tried to recall every detail of that point in her life: of the three of them in the kitchen while the chocolate was being made. The smell of chocolate and vanilla always reminded her being back in that kitchen with them. Her mother's angular face, the color of the lipstick she wore, the light perfume she wore. It was these thoughts that lulled her eventually into sleep.

When she woke hours later, the morning sun was bright, and there was the shrill cry of seagulls overhead. Groaning, she sat up, her hair a tangled mess around her face. Immediately, she noticed Jean-Paul was not next to her. Her heart skipped a beat as she looked around, frozen with fear. Wayne was gone as well. Slowly, she opened the car door and looked around.

They were parked on a street next to a beach of all things. In the distance, she could see Wayne standing in the sand in his good shoes, holding Jean-Paul and pointing to the narrow strip of blue horizon on the lake. The baby was wide awake and had a pacifier in his mouth. But by now, he must surely be hungry. Knowing he was safe, she slowly got out of the car and stood, stretching her back and rubbing the nape of her neck. After smoothing out her skirt, she turned away from the lake and, shielding her eyes from the bright morning sun in the east, she looked around and wondered if they'd arrived at their destination.

The street opposite the beach was lined with grand houses, some set back, all ornate with gingerbread trim, turrets, and wide, sweeping front porches. Her gaze landed on the house directly across the street from her. It was not as grand as the others, but it was still larger than their house in Queens. It was three stories, the uppermost floor smaller because of the slant of the roof, likely an attic, with dormer windows. Although the house looked uninhabited, it appeared to be in decent condition. There was a generous porch. On one pillar of the porch were the numbers 12465 in black wrought iron. This was it. She sighed, hoping the inside was as decent as the outside.

She swept her gaze southward, toward the end of the street, and spotted a small town. She glanced at her wristwatch—a Christmas gift from Wayne—and saw that it was nine thirty. From her viewpoint, she could see a few pedestrians along the town's street.

Wayne strolled back toward her, lifting his hand in a wave. As they walked, he spoke to the baby, smiling. Moments like this warmed Delphine's heart and prevented her from leaving him altogether.

"You're awake," he said. The baby reached out his arms for Delphine, and she took him into her embrace.

"I'll need to feed him," she said, looking around.

Wayne opened the car door. "Go ahead. No one's around."

She sat in the back seat and unbuttoned her blouse, looking around to make sure no one was nearby before lifting her breast out of her bra. She pulled the baby to her until he latched on and, feeling modest in front of her husband, she draped the baby blanket over her shoulder until it covered her bare breast.

"How long have we been here?" she asked Wayne. He stood outside the open door with his back to her to give her some privacy.

"About half an hour. I thought you'd want to sleep. I took Jean-Paul for a walk and showed him the beach. We'll have to get one of those new things they have, a stroller."

That would be nice. They'd left the buggy behind in Wilma's garage and pretty soon, he'd be too big for it.

"So this is Hideaway Bay," she said.

"It is. Nice little town. Later, after we get situated, I'll take you for a drive around. It's a nice place, and town is within walking distance."

"Have you been inside the house?"

He shook his head. "Not yet. I wanted to wait until you woke up."

When Jean-Paul was finished nursing, he dozed back off. Delphine put herself back together and got out of the car, lifting the sleeping baby out with her.

"You can probably leave him in the car," Wayne said.

Delphine clutched the baby closer to her and shook her head. As charming as the town looked, she wasn't taking any chances with him.

They walked side by side across the road with Wayne's hand on the small of her back. They climbed up the steps and stood at the front door. The clapboard siding was covered with dust, and bits of sand covered the bare front porch. Forget about a stroller, she thought, the first thing she'd be purchasing was a broom.

The door creaked when Wayne unlocked it and pushed it open. They stepped into the front parlor and looked around. It was sparsely furnished, but there was a fireplace with book-shelves, a sofa that had seen better days, and two armchairs with sagging seat cushions. It smelled musty, like it was in dire need of open windows and a bucket of soapy water. She followed Wayne through a narrow hallway and spotted a dining room on the right with built-in cabinets. There was a long table but no chairs. He led her through to the back of the house, and they stepped into the kitchen.

It was a bright, sunny room, and Delphine smiled for the first time since he'd woken her up to leave Wilma's house. The walls were painted pale yellow, and there was a white ceramic double-basin sink. Against the one corner was an American Electric stove covered in white enamel. Half curtains, faded and threadbare, hung from the windows with a matching valance above. She could so easily picture herself making chocolate here. So far, she liked the look of the kitchen. There was a lot of promise there.

And they owned the place. Their first home.

There were plenty of bedrooms upstairs, and there was also one dead mouse, which she grimaced at. Wayne spotted her expression and laughed. "I'll take care of him."

In the largest bedroom, she walked over to the window and looked out at the lake. The sky was deep azure, the water beneath it navy. Small foamy waves landed on the shore. The sand was darker where the water had swept over it, but it was loose. There was one person on the beach, a tall, thin man with a head of dark hair, walking along the shore, his gaze every so often drifting out to the lake. He soon disappeared from sight.

"Have you ever been to the beach before, Delphine?" Wayne asked.

She shook her head. It was on her trip over to America that she'd first laid eyes on the Atlantic Ocean. And she'd seen a fair bit of it, looking at it from the side of the ship as she vomited into the vast expanse.

The lake was crowded with freighters, trawlers, and tugboats off near the horizon. Closer to shore were small fishing boats, looking placid on the still water.

"Where is everyone?" she asked.

He shrugged. "They may not be up yet."

She frowned at him, skeptical. In her experience, Americans were up early. Too early sometimes. She never understood getting out of bed when it was still dark out, especially if you didn't have to. It seemed to go against the laws of nature.

"I'm hungry," she announced.

"Okay." He headed out of the room. "I spotted a grocer in town. Do you want to go with me?"

She shook her head.

"We could walk over. I'll carry the baby," he offered.

"No, I'll stay here." Her tone indicated that she didn't want to argue about it.

Now that she was inside the house, she didn't want to leave. Looking around, she saw so much that needed to be done. She didn't know where to start. The chocolate making would have to wait until things were better organized.

Chapter Twenty-Seven

For the first week, Delphine spent most of her time cleaning. She'd quickly realized that Wayne was better at minding the baby than doing housework, so she'd hand off their son, and Wayne would take him for walks around the block, talking to their new neighbors. Delphine remained in the house, unsure of how they would welcome a foreigner in their midst, if they'd welcome her at all. Besides, she was too busy cleaning and sprucing the place up to take a stroll. She'd worry about going to the beach, going to town and whatnot, once she'd gotten the house the way she wanted it.

But every day, Wayne went up to Main Street to use the payphone to call his mother. She hadn't taken Wayne's advice and gone to her sister's house in Ohio, choosing instead to remain at home. Apparently, a trio of men arrived on the doorstep every day, looking for Wayne but Wilma told them she had no idea where her son had gone, telling them he had disappeared into the night. Finally, the neighbor across the street, a NYPD detective, who'd noticed the car and the men in it had walked over when they were on the porch and had asked Wilma if everything was all right. After that, they had not come back.

From dawn until dusk, she tackled one room at a time, starting with the kitchen, washing everything down with bucket after bucket of soapy water. The icebox did not work, and Wayne managed to move it out to the backyard. For now, they would have to do without. But the stove worked, which meant she could cook and make meals. She hung the rugs out on the back line to air them out. Wayne dragged the wringer washing machine outside, and she went through all the bedding, washing it and hanging it out on the clothesline. She mended the curtains as best she could. More than once, she wished Wilma were there. She'd know what to do. She'd take charge. But she wasn't there, and Delphine had no choice but to take charge herself.

Each night when she climbed into bed, she groaned, the muscles in her body stiff and aching. She still had not ventured out to investigate the town, despite Wayne's encouragement. She used the excuse of all the work that still needed to be done. Wayne would just laugh and say "It's clean enough!" But still she remained indoors. She would love to go to the beach, to see what it was like, but there was fear there. She still wasn't sure how she would be accepted. And even more than that, she didn't want to get attached to the town, no matter how charming it looked. She still had her heart set on returning to Queens.

On the tenth day, while Wayne sat on the porch keeping the baby occupied, Delphine sat at the kitchen table, writing in her journal, trying to catch up. So much had happened in such a short time, she was still trying to process it all.

Female voices out on the front porch alerted her that there was someone out there other than Wayne. She froze, fountain pen mid-stroke. Heart beating faster, she closed the journal and pushed it aside. She stood, smoothed the skirt of her dress, and crept to the doorframe of the kitchen when she heard the screen door creak open.

"Come on in, ladies," she heard Wayne say. "Delphine's in the back, in the kitchen. Go right on through."

Delphine quickly returned to her seat, not wanting to be caught spying, and picked up a torn curtain she'd been mending.

Two women arrived in the kitchen, one in her late twenties, the other in her fifties. They so strongly resembled each other with their wide-set eyes and heart-shaped faces that Delphine concluded they must be mother and daughter. The younger woman held a pie in her hands.

Delphine jumped up, wishing she could hide, but there was nowhere to go. The thing she'd been avoiding, meeting the people of Hideaway Bay, was now happening. Although Wayne had told her repeatedly that they wouldn't be returning to New York City any time soon, she'd been holding on to the hope that one day he would announce things had been smoothed over in Queens and they'd be able to return, picking up where they'd left off with her and Wilma running their little business out of their kitchen.

The truth was, she didn't want to like Hideaway Bay. From the front windows of her house, with that magnificent view of the beach, especially in the evenings when the sun set over the lake, it was truly mesmerizing. But what if she got attached and then they had to leave here too? Only weeks ago, she'd been tooling happily along, saving money for a shop, making plans for their future, and all that was gone now.

Delphine stepped back, her hands behind her, until she felt the stiff edge of the counter against her back. Embarrassed at being caught wearing a headscarf and an apron that was in need of a wash, she smiled tentatively at the two women.

The younger woman stepped forward, holding out the pie toward her. It smelled divine, and its crust was golden brown.

"We've met your husband, Mrs. Brandt, and we wanted to come by and welcome you to Hideaway Bay. I've made you a blueberry pie." When Delphine didn't take it from her, she set it on the table, which shook slightly due to its uneven legs. The piece of cardboard Wayne had placed beneath the one leg had improved it somewhat, but it was still imbalanced.

"Thank you." Delphine's voice was barely above a whisper.

"I'm Martha Hahn and this is my mother, Martha Dorschel."

The older woman smiled warmly. "How do you do?"

Delphine nodded. "Fine. I'm Delphine Brandt." Fear kept her stuck against the counter, and she didn't move forward to shake their hands. She stood there, gripping the edge of the counter behind her.

"We live in the house on the corner," the younger Martha said. "Your baby is beautiful. I have a four-year-old daughter myself. Also named Martha." She twittered.

"All the firstborn daughters in our family are named Martha, after Martha Washington," Mrs. Dorschel said proudly.

Delphine wondered how they kept it all straight. She remembered her manners and said, "Would you like to sit down?" She swept her hand toward the three mismatched chairs at the wonky table.

Both women sat and pulled up their chairs to the table. Delphine realized she would have no choice but to join them. Before she sat, she asked them if they would like tea. But they refused, saying they could only stay a few minutes. Relieved, she sat down and joined them. She didn't know what to say, but she needn't have worried. To her great relief, Mrs. Hahn took control of the conversation.

"Your husband said you were from France," she said.

"I am. I met Wayne over there."

"Of course, during the war," Mrs. Dorschel said. She made a *tsk-tsk* noise. Delphine was confused, not knowing if her disapproval was directed at Delphine having lived in France or at the war in general.

"Our ancestors on my mother's side were from France. Long ago though," said Mrs. Hahn. She named some region Delphine had never heard of, but Delphine nodded politely.

"Before the war, we went to Paris a few times," Mrs. Dorschel piped in. She glanced at her daughter and smiled. "Those were fun times, weren't they, Martha?"

"They sure were. It's such a shame to hear that Paris and the rest of the country were occupied by the Nazis during the war. Very distressing."

The women were friendly and put Delphine at ease, but she couldn't help but feel as if she were a bystander to their conversation. True to their word, they didn't stay long, and Delphine jumped up from her chair when they stood to leave.

As she walked them out to the porch, she stepped outside, and the warmth hit her. From where she stood, she could hear the surf hitting the shore.

"We live right over there, Delphine," Martha Hahn said, pointing to the grand house on the corner.

"Stop down sometime and visit," Martha Dorschel said.

"And bring your beautiful baby," her daughter cooed.

The two women stepped off the porch, the younger one first, and walked side by side down the footpath to the sidewalk, talking as they went.

Wayne appeared from around the back of the house with Jean-Paul tucked sound asleep against his shoulder. "What did you think of Martha and Martha?" He was grinning. When she saw Wayne like this, her heart melted.

"They were very nice."

"You should take them up on their offer. Go down and sit with them. They're always sitting out on their porch. And they like to talk."

She'd gathered that much.

"Was that a pie they brought over?" he asked.

Delphine nodded. "Blueberry." She was distracted by the beach and the pull of it.

"I think I'll go for a walk on the beach," she said. Suddenly, she didn't want to be cooped up in the house anymore. She pulled off her headscarf and shook her hair out, then removed her apron and laid them both on a porch chair.

The sound of the surf was a lure. Overhead, seagulls cried as they swooped and dived.

"Go ahead," Wayne said. "I'll put the baby down for his nap."

But she was only half listening as she stepped off the porch and crossed the street. She walked through the short grass until her shoes hit the loose, heavy sand. For a moment she stared at it. She took a few steps forward, surprised by the weight of it. She took off her shoes and held them in her hand. The sand was warm on her feet, and she was surprised at the extra effort it took to move through it. A sharp breeze blew in off the lake and lifted her hair from her shoulders. Curious, she approached the water and waded into the surf, not going any deeper than her ankles so she wouldn't get her skirt wet, surprised at how warm the water was. Further along the shore, a young mother and her two toddlers played in the surf. The three were sitting at the edge of the water, letting it roll over them. All three laughed joyously, and it brought a smile to Delphine's face. The young mother caught sight of Delphine and gave her a hearty wave. Smiling, she waved back.

After a bit she walked on, collecting the tiny seashells that littered the beach and gathered them in her hand. With a fistful of seashells, she walked on past the rear of the shops on Main Street. She'd yet to go into any of them, despite Wayne's encouragement. Not even the grocers. From where she stood, she could barely see her house off in the distance. She walked on further until Main Street ended, and she spotted a white gazebo on a green space and behind that, more houses. Every house she'd seen in Hideaway Bay had a porch. Sitting on one's porch was almost like an art form here.

She plopped down in the sand, her shoes scissoring in her hands, one going one way, one the other. She shifted around until her bum made a depression in the sand, and she stretched her pale legs out in front of her. She realized as she sat there, leaning back on her hands, that she'd hardly had a moment alone since Jean-Paul was born. It wasn't a complaint, for no greater thing had ever happened to her.

A man walking through the sand caught her attention. He was tall with a slim build, and his back was ramrod straight. His hair was dark, and he had strong Roman nose. His linen pants and shirt were cream-colored and crisp, not a wrinkle in sight. The wind had picked up and whipped against him, but his step did not falter. As Delphine pushed a strand of hair off her face and tucked it behind her ear, she wondered about his destination that his stride was so purposeful and efficient. She recognized him as the man she'd spied through the upstairs bedroom window back on that first day they arrived.

As he continued northbound along the shoreline, she turned her head slowly, watching him. As with all men she came across, she wondered about them. She couldn't help it. Did they have wives and children at home? Did they come home late at night, smelling of whiskey? Did they cycle through periods where they were flush with cash one day and then having to rob Peter to pay Paul the next? Did their wives live with the uncertainty of how the bills were going to be paid and how food was going to be put on the table? Somehow, she doubted that. She'd learned early on that her marriage wasn't normal. Waiting for Wayne to come home for dinner was an exercise in futility, because you never knew when he was going to stroll through the door. So, on Wilma's advice, dinner was at a fixed time he was aware of and if he wasn't there, his plate was covered in tin foil and placed in the oven. Wilma said it was his fault if his meat was as tough as shoe leather when he got home.

Delphine pushed her hand through the sand, making big piles. Tired, she laid back, feeling the warmth of the sun and the coolness of the breeze on her. She supposed she should get back, but her body was so relaxed she didn't want to move. Eventually, she closed her eyes, trying to figure out a way to get back to Queens.

Chapter Twenty-Eight

After a few months, Delphine began to settle in. The stroller Wayne had ordered from the Sears catalogue arrived—and just in time, as Jean-Paul was getting heavier by the day—and on sunny days she pushed the baby around town. People called out to her or greeted her over white picket fences as she walked by. Everyone was so friendly, she mused. On the days when it wasn't too hot, she took the baby to the beach, although pushing the stroller through sand was a lot harder than she'd imagined. She'd sit at the shore with her legs stretched out in a V shape, the baby sitting between them.

Some days, she went over to the Marthas' on the corner. They'd sit on the porch and chat while Martha Hahn's young daughter sat with the baby on a blanket laid out on the front lawn. The baby was fascinated by grass, and young Martha liked to mind him. Little Martha's friend, Cal Cotter, sometimes joined them, and his mother, Ernestine, would sit with the three women on the porch as they drank tart lemonade and ate slices of pie with golden crusts and juicy fillings.

They were currently sitting on the shore, the day overcast but warm. The surf rolled in, washing over them, and Jean-Paul squealed with delight, clapping his chubby hands. He turned his head to look up at her with an open-mouthed smile, showing off his brand-new baby teeth. She tousled his blond hair and kissed the top of his head. He brought her so much joy.

Wayne had gone up to Buffalo two days ago. She hadn't heard from him since.

And so it began. Again.

All that fresh air made Jean-Paul tired, and it wasn't long before he grew cranky, no longer impressed with the beach. She snuggled him, put him in the stroller, and returned home to give him lunch and put him down for a nap in the crib Wayne had brought down from the attic. He'd given it a good wash and painted it white. The fresh coat of paint had really spiffed it up.

As the baby slept, she got comfortable on a kitchen chair out on the front porch, her feet up on the church rail, and wrote in her journal, looking up every once in a while to stare at the lake and gather her thoughts.

Wayne was encouraging her to pick up her chocolate making again. Since they'd arrived in Hideaway Bay, she hadn't even looked through her recipe book. In fact, it was still in the suitcase in the upstairs closet. With every day that passed, the hope of returning to Queens and Wilma grew dimmer. She sighed, letting the sound of the surf roll over her. It wasn't long before she nodded off in the chair.

The baby's crying startled her awake, and she sat up, unsure of where she was for a moment. She went upstairs to her crying baby and pulled him out of his crib. His face was beet red, and his skin felt as if it was burning up.

Concerned, she laid him back down and ran to get a couple of washcloths, which she ran beneath the tap, letting them get soaked with cold water. She wiped the crying baby down with the cold cloths, trying to keep a compress on his forehead, but he kept moving his head away. She hurried downstairs to heat a bottle, brought it back up, sat on the bed and held him close, and put the bottle in his mouth. Soon, he fell asleep in her arms, but his body still burned. Carefully, she stood, trying not to wake him, and laid him gently back in the crib. She needed to get some help. A doctor. She waited at the side of the crib, seeing if he would stir. When he did not, she ran down the stairs, out the front door, and off the porch. As she rounded the end of the driveway, she collided with a man walking by on the sidewalk.

"Oomph!" she said.

The man stopped her propulsion and held her by the upper arms. It was the tall man with the distinctive nose she'd spotted twice already on the beach.

"Whoa, slow down. Where's the fire?" he asked with a laugh.

The words exploded from Delphine's mouth. "My baby is sick. And my husband is out of town, and I need a doctor." She brushed her hair back from her forehead.

The man smiled at her reassuringly. "Your French is lovely, but do you speak English?"

For a moment, she stared at him blankly.

"English?" he repeated, his voice as soft as the whisper of a breeze.

Hurriedly, she repeated what she'd said, but this time in English.

"Ah," he said, satisfied. "You need a doctor."

She nodded quickly. "Where can I find him?"

The man opened his mouth but before he could say anything, a sharp wail from the upstairs bedroom pierced the air.

"Jean-Paul," Delphine said.

"Go to your baby, Miss," the man said, "And I'll fetch the doctor."

She watched for a brief moment as he sprinted toward Main Street. Once he disappeared, she turned and ran into the house, dashing up the stairs to get Jean-Paul.

As she continually put cool compresses on him, working against him fighting them off, she hoped the man would return with the doctor.

She was in the kitchen when she heard the knock at the front door. Relief filled her and with the baby in her arms, she raced to the front of the house. At the door stood two men: the one from earlier and another she presumed to be the doctor.

"Come in, come in," she said, remembering to speak in English and pushing the screen door open to allow them entrance.

The doctor was elderly, with eyes that twinkled and a halo of snow-white hair. When he spoke, his voice boomed, startling her.

"My name's Dr. Morley. What's this I hear there's a sick baby in this house?" he asked. His tone was jovial.

"Delphine Brandt," she said.

"All right, Mother, will you lay the baby down on the kitchen table so I can examine him?"

She carried the baby back to the kitchen and laid Jean-Paul on the table. The baby let out a shriek in response. Dr. Morley set his black medical bag on an unoccupied chair and opened it, removing a thermometer and stethoscope.

Delphine stood back, supporting her elbow with her arm as she chewed on her fingernail. The tall man with the dark hair hovered in the doorway, concerned.

The doctor examined the baby, frowning. This made Delphine's heart race. Finally, he looked up and said, "Mother, sit in the chair and hold the baby so I can listen to his lungs."

Delphine did as instructed, cooing and shushing the crying baby. Within moments, Jean-Paul began to settle.

The doctor bent over and listened intently to the baby's lungs, frowning. Finally, he straightened, and his jovial tone was gone when he spoke. "This baby is very sick," he said, folding his stethoscope up and putting it back into his bag.

Delphine could feel tears forming in her eyes but said nothing, trying to stay calm and not wanting to break down in front of these men, who were strangers.

Dr. Morley set his bag on the floor and pulled out a small bottle of medicine and his prescription pad from his bag. He scribbled instructions on it and held out the bottle in front of Delphine. "Four times a day for the next ten days. Keep trying to get the cool compresses on him and make sure, above all else, he drinks. If the milk is too heavy for him, give him some sugar water."

Delphine nodded.

"I'll give him his first dose of medicine before I leave." He looked around the kitchen and said, "Do you have a bottle handy? It's bitter tasting."

There was a bottle she'd warmed up, cooling on the counter.

Dr. Morley gave him his first dose, and Delphine prayed it would help.

"I'll be back first thing in the morning," he said, standing to go.

Delphine jumped up, disturbing the quiet baby, and he let out a whimper. "But you can't leave. I don't know what to do."

Dr. Morley smiled kindly at her. "You'll know. Trust your maternal instinct. If you need me, call me during the night."

"I don't have a phone," she cried.

"I'm sure any of your neighbors would be more than happy to help," he said.

The Marthas at the corner entered her mind. But she was hesitant to bother them. When was Wayne coming home? Where was he?

"And I'll give you a hand," the tall man said in the doorway.

She looked at him, unsure. "But I don't even know you!"

He stepped forward out of the background and extended his hand. His arm was long and his handshake firm and strong. "Gus Lime of Lime's Five-and-Dime."

"Oh."

Concluding that the subject was decided, Dr. Morley headed to the front of the house. Delphine trailed after him, still not feeling confident enough to be left alone overnight with a sick baby.

"What time will you be here in the morning?" she asked.

"First thing," he said. He stepped through the door and descended the porch steps.

He'd just hit the sidewalk in front of the house when she realized she hadn't thanked him. She stood on the porch and called out in a shaky voice, "Thank you!"

He nodded and put his hand up in a wave and kept walking.

The screen door creaked open behind her, and Gus Lime stepped out onto the porch.

"Is there anything else I can do before I go?" he asked.

"Thank you for your help, but that won't be necessary," she said, flashing him a quick smile. If only Wayne would get home.

"Have you eaten, Mrs. Brandt?" he asked.

She shook her head. "No. I don't know." Had she had lunch? That event seemed a long time ago. How she wished her nerves would settle. She looked at Jean-Paul, his beautiful curls plastered against his sweaty face. He slept soundly against her, one little fist resting against her breast.

"I'll get you something to eat. I'll be right back. I'll go up to the grocery store."

"It isn't necessary." It really wasn't. She couldn't ask him to feed her. Though his kindness shored her up in her husband's absence. She thanked him and walked him out.

She went upstairs and laid the baby in the crib. Her poor sweet baby was so sick and so tired, he never stirred while she set him down. She stood by the side of the crib and watched him for a while to make sure he was okay. She stifled a yawn but then a second one came, and it was futile. The events of the day had ganged up on her, and she felt sleepy herself.

She sat on the edge of the bed, kicked off her shoes, and stretched out on her back, clasping her hands over her belly.

She didn't sleep for long. Something woke her out of a deep reverie, and it took a moment to recollect where she was and what time it was: early evening. She bounced out of bed and checked on Jean-Paul. He still slept soundly, and she reached out and pressed her cool hand against his head. It was still quite warm, and she took the compress that hung over the crib rail and carried it to the bathroom, where she rinsed it with cool water, squeezing out all the excess.

Carefully, she placed it on his forehead, hoping he wouldn't wake. He frowned but continued to sleep. She stood in the window, staring at the beach and the lake beyond it. The house was so quiet.

She made her way softly down the creaking stairs, trying not to make too much noise so the baby wouldn't wake. The idea of a cup of tea sounded appealing. On the front porch, leaning against the screen door was a basket of groceries. Delphine carried it into the kitchen and set it on the table. She removed everything: a loaf of bread, some coldcuts, some tomatoes, a glass bottle of milk, and a box of cookies. There was a note and Delphine picked it up, unfolded it and read,

Just a few items in case you can't leave the house. Gus.

How thoughtful! It made her feel not so alone.

Hungry, she made herself a sandwich and a cup of tea. She'd just finished the last bite when there was a cry from the baby upstairs. Delphine dashed up the stairs and found Jean-Paul in the crib, sweaty and crying. Quickly, she ran the washcloth under the bathroom tap and wiped him down. Once she changed his diaper, she settled on the bed with him, hopeful that he'd take the bottle. He settled in next to her and drank for a while, and then was no longer interested. Although he didn't start crying, he fussed for a bit against her side. She pulled a toy rattle off the bedside table and showed it to him: a white lamb with a blue ribbon around its neck. The baby took it, inspected it, waved it around, and then threw it aside. After a bit, when his fussing increased, she wiped him down again, but he kept turning his head back and forth. She made a game of it, playing peek-a-boo with the cool compress on his forehead, covering his eyes. This got a half smile and then he grew tired of that too.

She carried him downstairs and when she entered the kitchen, she was surprised to see that all the dishes had been washed and put away and the table and the counters wiped down. She rocked the baby as she held him. She walked through to the front of the house and stepped out onto the porch, sitting on the old kitchen chair that was there, holding the baby on her lap. He leaned against her and was quiet, putting his fist into his mouth. She remained silent, content to let him be.

Martha Hahn from the corner house appeared, walking along the sidewalk. Delphine put up her hand in a wave.

Martha stepped up onto the porch. She was a pretty woman.

"Gus Lime told me the baby was sick."

"The doctor was out and gave me some medicine for him."

"Oh, the poor little thing," Martha said. "Is Wayne home?"

"No, he's out of town," Delphine said, swallowing hard.

Martha nodded. "Don't worry. If you have any trouble in the middle of the night, come down to our house and ring the bell."

Delphine shook her head. "I couldn't."

"Yes, you can," Martha said firmly. "And you will."

Delphine found herself nodding along.

"It's scary when your baby is sick. It's even scarier when you're alone."

Delphine nodded. Tears stung at the back of her eyes at the woman's kindness.

"Anyway, my mother is baking a pie for you as we speak, and we'll drop it off later."

Delphine nodded. They'd been recipients of a few of the Marthas' pies, and they were delectable. They'd had lemon meringue, blueberry, and pecan. She hadn't been too sure about the pecan pie, but it turned out to be her favorite.

"That's very kind of you," Delphine managed to get out. She was on the verge of tears.

Martha smiled warmly at her. "That's all right. That's what we do in Hideaway Bay. We take care of each other."

She didn't stay long, five more minutes, talking about the weather before she departed.

Delphine watched her go, thinking she was lucky. She hadn't been in Hideaway Bay long and she'd already made a few friends: the Marthas and Gus.

Looking at the beach, she thought she might just grow to love this town in spite of herself.

Chapter Twenty-Nine

W HEN WAYNE RETURNED FOUR days later, he received a cool reception from Delphine. As promised, the doctor had returned the day after his initial visit, assuring Delphine that not only did babies go down quickly but they bounced back up just as quickly. As he predicted, the baby improved each day.

Delphine was sitting on the porch, leafing through her mother's recipe book when Wayne pulled into the driveway. She looked up and then resumed reading. He stepped up onto the porch, his suit wrinkled, and said, "Hello, beautiful."

He leaned down to kiss her, but she pulled away.

"What's this?" he asked, frowning.

"Where have you been?" she demanded. Over the last few days her anger and resentment had grown within her.

"I told you. I went up to Buffalo," he said. "You knew that."

"I had no way to get in contact with you. No way to find you or call you," she said. Anger laced her tone.

He went pale. "Why? What happened?"

"Jean-Paul was very sick," she said. "I had to get the doctor out."

Wayne's eyes grew wide. "Is he all right?" he asked, his voice panic-stricken.

"Yes, but he's still on medicine, and he has to go back to see Dr. Morley next week. I had no way of calling you to let you know." Her voice rose with every sentence. "The charity and goodwill of our neighbors has seen me through these past few days."

Sheepishly, he said, "I'm really sorry, Delphine."

She ignored him and looked over at the lake.

"I'm going up to bed," he said, yawning.

She stood up. "No, you're not. You haven't been home in almost a week! I'm going to the beach for a little while. I need a break. You can watch the baby. He's sleeping right now, but there's a bottle in the fridge that needs to be warmed up for when he wakes."

Before she left, she went inside, grabbed her bag, and stuffed a blanket, her journal, and a pen inside of it. She stepped off the porch and looked back at him. "And don't touch the medicine."

The sound of the surf and the warmth of the sun began to relax her, and she stayed stretched out on the sand for over an hour. As she relaxed, her anger began to dissipate.

When she made her way home, she spotted Wayne sitting on the porch, bouncing Jean-Paul on his knee and singing him a nursery rhyme.

She walked up the porch steps and was relieved to see that the baby didn't look as pale as he had. Finally, he had some color in his cheeks other than that feverish flush he had in the beginning.

Wayne looked up at her, expectant, but said nothing.

Jean-Paul smiled at her, and she returned his smile in kind. He resumed playing with his father's chin.

"Before you go on your next trip, I want a phone installed here in the house. And if you can't give me a number where I can reach you, you call me at least once a day," she instructed her husband.

Now it was time for a piece of the pecan pie Martha had dropped off the previous evening and a cup of tea.

Before Delphine entered the house, she turned to Wayne and said, "And I'll give you a list of supplies that I need to start making chocolate again. I'll need those right away."

And she left him sitting on the porch, holding the baby.

By the end of the week, she had a brand-new telephone line and soon after that, Wayne had delivered all the supplies she needed to start making her chocolate. Contrite, he had made a trip to Buffalo to sort candy boxes and returned the same day.

A week later, she had her first batches done.

The first two boxes were gifts for the Marthas and Gus Lime. She pulled out the stroller, tucked the baby in it with his rattle and bottle, and tucked a light baby blanket around him.

First, she walked to the house on the corner. Both Marthas were seated on the porch, and young Martha played on the front lawn with her friend Cal. They were trying to use a jump rope but so far, their attempts had been unsuccessful. When Delphine appeared, they stopped, the jump rope hanging from young Martha's hand. Delphine smiled at them and waved.

"Hello, Delphine!" Martha Hahn called out from the porch.

"Come and sit down and have something to drink," said Mrs. Dorschel.

"I can't stay." Delphine left the stroller parked next to the bottom step, took the box of candy, and climbed up the porch stairs, aware that Jean-Paul's eyes were fastened on her. Martha and Cal abandoned the jump rope and made a beeline for the baby.

"I wanted to thank you for your kindness while Jean-Paul was ill," she said.

She was grateful to these two Marthas, some of the loveliest women she'd ever met.

"That's what neighbors are for," Martha Hahn said.

"Are you sure you won't have something to drink? Maybe a slice of pie? We've got one fresh out of the oven," Mrs. Dorschel said with an enticing smile.

Delphine laughed but resisted. There was nothing she'd love more than to sit on their porch and eat a slice of warm pie. But she had things to do.

She handed Mrs. Hahn the box of chocolate.

"Thank you for your help."

Both women looked up at her. "You didn't have to do this."

"Don't waste your money on us," Mrs. Dorschel said.

"I didn't buy them, I made them," Delphine explained.

The two Marthas exchanged a glance.

Mrs. Hahn lifted the lid off the box and showed her mother, holding the box out for her. Mrs. Dorschel inspected the contents, chose one of the chocolates, and put it in her mouth.

Her eyes widened and she exclaimed, "Oh my!" She nodded toward her daughter. "Martha, you really must try one. It's heavenly."

Mrs. Hahn chose a piece and nodded her head vigorously in agreement with her mother's assessment.

"Those are beautiful, Delphine," Mrs. Hahn said.

"Oh my, Delphine!" Mrs. Dorschel gushed.

"And you learned this in France?" Mrs. Hahn asked.

"Yes. My mother and grandmother were chocolatiers," Delphine said proudly.

The Marthas helped themselves to another piece.

"Wait until Grandfather sees these," Mrs. Dorschel said. As an aside, she said to Delphine, "he has an incredible sweet tooth."

Delphine smiled at the women and bade them goodbye.

She tousled the hair of the young children as she stepped off the porch and wheeled the stroller toward Main Street.

She lifted her face toward the sun, narrowing her eyes against the brightness and loving the feel of the heat on her skin. As they walked, the baby pointed out things, his chubby hand flying out of the stroller. He was currently fascinated by seagulls, which were everywhere in Hideaway Bay.

There were no customers in the five-and-dime when Delphine arrived.

Gus broke into a smile as she wheeled the stroller into his shop.

"Delphine! How are you?" he asked.

She smiled, thinking how much better she felt since he'd last seen her.

"Much better."

Gus bent down and brushed his finger beneath Jean-Paul's chin. "And how's the young man?"

"He's much better, thank you," Delphine said.

"I'm so glad to hear it. You must be so relieved."

"I am." She pulled out the box of candy and handed it to him. Suddenly and unaccountably, she felt shy. She hadn't felt that way with the Marthas. "I wanted to thank you for your help that day. And for the basket of food."

"The folks of Hideaway Bay look after one another."

Gus Lime looked down at the box in his hand. "What do we have here?"

"Homemade chocolate."

His eyes widened. "Did you make them yourself?"

"I did."

"Then I shall enjoy them all the more."

A moment passed between them, and Delphine felt the heat creep up her neck and blossom out into her cheeks. Fortunately, the baby in the stroller squealed, breaking the silence. He pointed to the wall behind Gus. On the wall was a clock shaped like a black cat whose tail and eyes moved back and forth.

Gus smiled. "Do you like, Jean-Paul? That's a Kit-Cat Klock."

The baby laughed and clapped his hands.

"I guess he likes cats," Delphine said.

It was time to leave; she didn't want to take up too much of Gus's time. She thanked him again, and he held the door for her as she pushed the stroller out of the five-and-dime. As she walked home, she tried to shake off the uncomfortable feeling she had when she was in Gus's presence. That feeling had nothing to do with Gus and everything to do with the fact that he was a man she found attractive, a man who wasn't her husband.

The following day, there was a wrapped package on the front porch addressed to Jean-Paul. Excited, Delphine ripped the paper off to discover a Kit-Cat Klock.

Smiling, she removed it from its package and hung it on the kitchen wall.

Wayne frowned at it. "Where did you get that from?"

"The man from the five-and-dime sent it over. For Jean-Paul," Delphine explained. When Wayne didn't say anything, she said, "Wasn't that thoughtful?"

"Hmm. I'll say."

Over the next two years, Delphine continued to make chocolate out of her kitchen, her love for Hideaway Bay growing. She ran into Gus on the odd occasion. Sometimes when she was visiting with the Marthas on the corner, he'd wave as he walked by or stand on the top step and chat for a few minutes. And sometimes, Delphine would stop in at the five-and-dime. Jean-Paul was still intrigued with the Kit-Cat Klock.

Wayne continued to be gone a lot. Sometimes for weeks at a time. And although Delphine grumbled about it, freezing him out when he returned, nothing changed. He didn't seem to care. He had taken up with two guys from Buffalo Delphine did not feel comfortable with. They'd drive down, pick Wayne up, and head off to Cleveland.

Starkey and Legs. If they weren't so sinister, they'd be comical. Starkey was the smarter of the two, Delphine thought. He was short and as wide as he was round. He never stopped talking. If there was a pause in the conversation, he made sure to fill it. Words, words, words, endless words. Legs was appropriately named because he was a tall man, much taller than Wayne, and was long and lean and all legs. He made Delphine uncomfortable. Sometimes, she'd look up and catch him staring at her through the haze of his cigarette smoke. And more than once, when he brushed past her, his arm made contact with her arm or the side of her breast. Starkey got on her nerves because he never shut up, but when Legs was around, her skin crawled.

CHAPTER THIRTY

1955

DELPHINE SPOONED A DAB of melted chocolate from the pot onto her bottom lip, decided it was the perfect temperature, and continued to seed the rest of the chocolate. Wayne sat at the kitchen table while Delphine bustled around him. He smoked, tapping his ash into the glass ashtray, watching her work.

She was in a good mood. Wayne had been home for three weeks, and they'd made plans to drive up to Niagara Falls for the weekend with Jean-Paul. She hurried to get this last batch of chocolate done, as they planned to leave first thing in the morning and there was a lot to do. Earlier in the week, she'd pulled out the suitcase from beneath the bed, where it had been sitting since they left Queens five years ago. It smelled musty, and the blue satin lining had turned pink in some places, but she brushed it off and left it on the porch to air out.

She'd never been away on a proper vacation. Granted they were only going for the weekend, but she was excited and couldn't wait. It would help her and Wayne to spend some time away.

A car pulled up outside, but she was in too much of a hurry to notice. Wayne cocked his head to one side, listening.

Delphine had the rest of her day planned out. Once she boxed up the chocolate and washed down the kitchen, she needed to pack and to remember some toys for Jean-Paul to occupy him in the car ride up. Then she was going to soak in the tub, then—

"Knock knock, anyone home?" a voice called out from the front door.

"Yo!"

Starkey and Legs.

Delphine's shoulders sagged.

"Whatever they want, you're not going with them," she hissed, poking Wayne's shoulder.

"Hmm," he said. It concerned her that he was being non-committal.

Starkey appeared in the kitchen first, followed by Legs. Starkey barely reached Legs's chest. Starkey's eyes darted around the room, but Legs's gaze locked on Delphine and stayed there. An unpleasant tingle went down her spine as she avoided any kind of eye contact with him.

Wayne looked at her, and she shook her head but said nothing.

"What brings you fellas here?" Wayne asked as he lit up another cigarette.

Starkey pulled out one of the kitchen chairs, the metal legs scraping against the linoleum. He pushed aside one of the racks of chocolate truffles, and Delphine narrowed her eyes at him.

"Funny you should ask," Starkey said. He patted the breast pockets of his suitcoat with both hands but came up empty. Wayne pushed his pack of Camel cigarettes toward him.

"Thanks," Starkey said, helping himself and tapping one out.

Legs remained standing, leaning against one of the counters, his gaze following Delphine around the kitchen, never removing his eyes from her.

"Legs and I are on our way to Cleveland," Starkey said. "Got word of something going down there and thought you might like to come along for the ride." He drew in a lungful and tilted his head back, blowing blue smoke rings out of his mouth.

Delphine froze. This was what she'd been afraid of. That these two clowns would come in and take Wayne away from her and Jean-Paul.

Wayne hesitated. "I can't. Not this weekend. I have plans."

She relaxed slightly, although she wouldn't be convinced until the two of them were out of the house and on their way.

"Come on, Wayne. You can change them," Starkey pushed.

Wayne did not look at either Starkey or Delphine, choosing to stare at the table. "Not this time, Starkey. Next time."

"There might not be a next time," Starkey said.

"We've got plans," Delphine said, her voice sounding louder than she'd expected. When Starkey looked over to her, he looked as if he'd only just noticed her for the first time or had forgotten she was there. She lifted her chin and added, "We're going to Niagara Falls for the weekend."

Starkey observed her for a moment, as if he was taking a full account of her. "Niagara Falls, is that so?" he asked.

"Yes."

He turned away from Delphine and pulled his chair closer to Wayne, leaning forward. "See the thing is, Wayne, Niagara Falls will always be there." Starkey's tone was matter of fact. He lowered his voice to a whisper so Delphine couldn't hear him.

He sat back with a smug grin on his face.

Wayne appeared conflicted. He sighed and rubbed the back of his neck with his hand. Finally, he looked up at Delphine. She knew by his expression they were not going to go to Niagara Falls that weekend. Or probably any weekend.

"Starkey's right, Delphine. Niagara Falls will always be there."

"Wayne . . ."

But there was no point. In that one moment, whatever Starkey had said to him, her husband had changed his mind. And she knew from experience that no matter how much cajoling or pleading she did, Wayne would not be budged. It was almost like a drug for him. The next big thing was always on his horizon. Starkey knew this about Wayne too.

She turned her back to him and busied herself at the sink, fully aware that Legs's eyes were on her.

Wayne and Starkey stood from the table, and Delphine did not turn around.

"Give me a few minutes to get my things," Wayne said.

When they made no effort to move, he added, "I'll meet you outside."

She heard the retreating footsteps of Starkey and Legs and was glad they were out of her house, even if they were taking Wayne away from her and Jean-Paul.

She was so angry that tears filled her eyes.

Wayne placed a hand on her shoulder, and she roughly shrugged it off.

"Don't touch me."

"Don't be like that, Delphine," Wayne whispered. "Look, when I come back, I'll take you to that restaurant up on the highway. The one you like so much."

She turned and faced him. He took a step back.

"I don't want to go to that restaurant on the highway! I want the three of us to go to Niagara Falls. You promised."

"I can't help that something has come up."

"You can never help it."

"Delphine—"

She pushed past him. "Go. Go. But I want to know when you're coming home."

"I'll be home by Monday. I promise."

She snorted. "Wayne, don't make promises. Because you can never keep them."

<center>~~~</center>

The following morning, Delphine woke still angry. She'd hoped to be up in Niagara Falls, staying at a motel and getting ready for the day. But instead, Wayne had managed to go away and here she was, still in Hideaway Bay. Alone.

Still fuming after breakfast, she stepped out onto the porch to watch Jean-Paul as he rode his bike up and down the driveway. Their car, a black 1952 Ford Customline, stood parked at the back of their driveway.

If only I could drive, I'd take Jean-Paul to Niagara Falls myself. And Wayne could go jump in the lake, she thought bitterly.

She sat up straighter. Why couldn't she drive? She'd sat in the front seat with Wayne a thousand times and had a general idea of how it worked. How hard could it be?

No, this was a crazy idea. She'd never driven before. Niagara Falls was far away. At least a couple of hours. Outside of Hideaway Bay, she had no idea how to get there.

It angered her that she was so dependent on Wayne to get around. It was one thing to live in Hideaway Bay where you could walk everywhere, but quite another if you wanted to go places.

As Jean-Paul rode his bike up and down the driveway, making all sorts of *vroom-vroom* noises, Delphine looked around, bored.

It was absolutely ridiculous that she should have access to a car and not be able to drive it.

Thwarted in her efforts to go away for a few days, she felt anxious and restless.

"Come on, Jean-Paul, let's go visit the Marthas," she said.

"Can I ride my bike, Maman?"

"Yes, of course."

Both Marthas were seated on the porch, and the younger, Mrs. Hahn, threw her hand up in a wave. Delphine hoped the distraction of company would prevent her mood from souring any further.

She stepped up onto the porch and told Jean-Paul, "Stay right out front where I can see you. I'm just going to visit for a bit."

He nodded and rode to the corner before turning around.

"Sit down, Delphine," Mrs. Dorschel said.

She sat, grateful to get off her feet. It wasn't that she was tired in the physical sense, but she was weary of the disappointments Wayne handed her on a continual basis.

"There's a brand-new pie," Martha Hahn said. "How about a nice slice?"

Delphine put her hand up and shook her head. "No thank you."

It was a little early in the morning for pie.

"I thought you were going to Niagara Falls this weekend," Mrs. Dorschel said.

Delphine pursed her lips. "I thought so too. But Wayne was called away." The Marthas were not only lovely, they were intelligent. They must have figured out that her husband did not work a stable, routine job. Out of the corner of her eye, she spotted Gus approaching. Jean-Paul continued his circuit from the corner to their driveway and then back again.

Gus lifted his hand in a wave, and Mrs. Dorschel called out to him, "Gus, who's minding the shop if you're out for a stroll?"

"No one." He laughed, changing his direction and heading up onto the porch. He leaned against the railing and nodded to them in acknowledgement. "Ladies."

They stared at him, waiting for further enlightenment.

"I needed a breath of fresh air," he explained. "I left a note on the door saying I'd be back in fifteen minutes."

Mrs. Dorschel started to laugh.

"It's good to go for a walk. It clears the head," Mrs. Hahn said.

"Going for a drive would do that too," Delphine said.

"Do you go for drives to clear your head, Delphine?" Gus asked.

Embarrassed, she shook her head. "No. I don't know how to drive."

"You must learn," Gus said.

"I'd love to learn, but I'd need someone to teach me," she said. Although she'd asked Wayne several times to teach her how to drive, especially with him being away so much and their car sitting idle in the driveway, he always put it off and never got around to it.

"I'll teach you how to drive," Gus offered.

Delphine felt her face redden. She hadn't meant to imply that.

"I couldn't ask that of you," she said.

"You didn't ask, I offered," he pointed out.

"Go on, Delphine, here's your chance," Mrs. Hahn said. "Once you can drive, you'll have more independence."

"I'd love that."

"I'll walk down after I close the shop and give you a lesson," Gus said.

"You can leave Jean-Paul with us. We'll mind him," Mrs. Dorschel said.

"I don't want to impose."

"Don't you want to learn how to drive?"

"I do."

"Then it's all settled," Mrs. Hahn said. "Gus, come on down after you close the five-and-dime."

"Terrific, see you then, Delphine," he said, stepping off the porch. "My fifteen minutes is up. I better get back to work."

Later that evening, she waited for him on the porch, spotting him as he crossed Erie Street over to Star Shine Drive. She took Jean-Paul by the hand and walked him down to the house at the corner, intercepting Gus at the foot of the Marthas' driveway.

"Go on up there and be a good boy for the Marthas," Delphine instructed.

"Come on, Jean-Paul, we've got lemonade and cookies," Mrs. Dorschel said.

Jean-Paul bolted up the porch steps. Delphine laughed.

"Are you ready for your first lesson?" Gus asked.

Delphine held up the car keys. "Yes!"

They returned to her driveway and Gus said, "Let me pull it out and turn it around. You don't need to learn how to back out on your first lesson." She handed him the keys and waited while he pulled out and then reversed into the driveway. The front of the car now faced the lake across the street.

When he got out, he held the door open for Delphine and she slid in on the driver's side. He then went around to the passenger side and got in.

"Have you ever driven a car before, Delphine?"

She shook her head. "But I've seen Wayne do it a thousand times."

Gus grinned. "Seeing and doing are two different things."

He pointed things out on the dashboard and the gearshift. Delphine tried to hide her impatience at his tutorial, but the truth was she was anxious to get on the road.

"All right, I can see you're in a hurry to drive," he said with a laugh.

"I am."

"All right. Now turn the key in the ignition and put your foot on the brake, and using the gearshift, put it into drive."

She reached for the gearshift jutting out of the right side of the steering column, but Gus held up his hand. She looked at him. "But first, look around. See who's on the sidewalk or in the street. Not only other cars but people too. Especially little children. Be mindful."

She looked at him, expectant.

"Okay," he said with a nod and a smile. "Let's go."

Delphine turned the key in the ignition, shifted into drive, and moved her foot from the brake to the gas pedal. The car lurched forward violently, and she went to slam her foot on the brake pedal but hit the gas instead. The car flew out of the driveway and landed up the curb on the grassy verge across the street.

For a moment, neither said a thing. Delphine stared straight ahead, figuring this was the end of the lesson. Finally, she turned her head toward Gus and was surprised to see that he was grinning.

"For a little lady, you sure have a heavy foot!"

She laid her head on the steering wheel and breathed out.

"Hey, take it easy, it's your first lesson," he said. "No one was hurt, and I'll bet you never make that mistake again. Now, let's switch seats so I can get the car off the grass."

They met first thing Sunday morning and then again Sunday afternoon, as traffic was light throughout town. They met Monday morning, and Delphine was starting to get the hang of it. She loved how she felt when she was driving, especially with the window rolled down and the warm breeze blowing in. Gus praised her, saying she was a quick learner. He was a great teacher.

By the time Wayne returned Tuesday afternoon, Delphine had four straight days of driving under her belt and felt slightly more confident. She was so excited about learning a new skill that she was no longer angry about Niagara Falls.

"Come on, I want to show you something," she said, laughing, pulling Wayne by the hand out through the front door.

Wayne laughed. "What's this?"

"Sit right there," she instructed, pushing him gently down onto one of the porch chairs. "Stay there."

She ran through the house, grabbed the keys off the hook, and went out the back door. Once she started up the car, she backed out, looking over her shoulder as Gus had taught her, and slowly reversed out of the driveway and pulled onto Star Shine Drive. When she pulled out and stopped, she looked up to see Wayne agog, and she waved and smiled. She did a quick run down to the Marthas' house on the corner, pulled into their driveway, and returned, pulling into the driveway slowly and grinning at Wayne. Even from where she sat, she did not miss the astonishment on his face.

Once she parked the car, she bounced out of it and ran back around to the front porch.

"I've only been gone a few days, Delphine," Wayne said with a big grin. "Where did you learn how to drive?"

"Gus Lime taught me," she said.

The smile disappeared from Wayne's face, and there was a grim set to his lips. "Did he now? I'll take over the driving lessons from now on."

"Okay, Wayne, whatever you say," she said with a shrug.

And from there on, Wayne took Delphine out driving every day when he was home until she took her test, passed it, and obtained her driver's license along with a newfound sense of freedom.

CHAPTER THIRTY-ONE

1957

WAYNE APPEARED IN THE doorway of the kitchen, wearing shorts and a short-sleeved shirt.

"I'm going to take Jean-Paul down to the playground."

Delphine looked up from her task and nodded. She was taking small scoops of ganache and rolling them between her palms, then placing the balls of chocolate on her dipping fork and setting them into the bowl of tempered chocolate to coat them.

There was a knock at the front door.

"I'll get it," Wayne said.

She nodded and went back to work, coating her truffles.

Male voices floated out to her in the kitchen. She paused, a ball of ganache still in her hands as she tried to make out the other voice.

Gus?

Wayne reappeared with Gus Lime in tow.

Delphine smiled. "Oh hello, Gus."

"Delphine. I wanted to order a box of candy," Gus said.

Wayne hesitated in the doorway. "Will I write the order down for you?" he asked Delphine, nodding toward her sticky hands.

"Please," she said. With an indicative nod, she said, "The order forms are there on the counter, in the corner."

Wayne took a pencil from the cup, found an order form, and wrote Gus's name at the top. "Did you want a one- or two-pound box?" he asked.

Gus looked at Delphine. "I'm not sure. It's for my date."

Delphine widened her eyes in surprise. She'd never known Gus to date. But then how would she know. She supposed he would date; he was an attractive, kind man, and she liked the idea that he might find someone worthy of his good qualities.

"Is it a first date?" she asked.

Gus nodded. "Yes. She's from the next town over."

"Then I'd go with the one-pound box," Delphine suggested. With a smile, she added, "Since it's the first date."

"That's what I'll do."

"Do you want all one flavor or do you want a variety?" Wayne asked.

"I suppose a variety would be best," Gus said.

"Yes, that's what I would suggest," Delphine said. "What flavors would you like?"

"I don't know. I'll leave it up to you, Delphine," Gus said. "I trust your judgement. After all, you're the chocolatier."

"All right then. You can pick it up tomorrow," she said.

"Or I can drop it off to you," Wayne offered.

"That would be great," Gus said. "Then I won't have to leave the shop. Thanks."

He turned to leave, and Wayne called out after him, "Good luck on your date, Gus. Every man needs a good woman at his side." He glanced at Delphine, grinned, and winked.

Once Gus was gone, Wayne called for Jean-Paul, who came thundering down the stairs.

"Why does he always sound like he's wearing army boots?" Delphine muttered.

"Gets that from his old man," Wayne said.

Jean-Paul arrived in the kitchen. "Are we going to the playground now, Dad?"

Wayne tousled his son's hair. "Yes, let's go." He wrapped an arm around Delphine, giving her a gentle squeeze and kissing her on the temple. "Be back soon."

Delphine looked at him. It had been a while since he'd done something like that.

September 1957

Delphine pulled on her coat and buttoned it up. Her destination was the parish hall. The Marthas at the corner had informed her that the parish hall committee had decided to set up a Christmas bazaar this year and were looking for vendors for their stalls. Both Marthas had encouraged Delphine to apply. She'd been hesitant, but they'd been enthusiastic on her behalf. Martha Hahn's husband was on the committee, so she was able to give Delphine an idea of the price for the stall. When Delphine mentioned it to Wayne, he too was enthusiastic, telling her it would grow her customer base and the extra money would be a nice addition at Christmas.

It was a blustery late-September day, but despite the chill the wind brought with it, she had the windows open in the living room, enjoying the sound of the boisterous surf across the street.

"I won't be long," she said to Wayne.

"Take your time. Do you need money?" he asked.

She shook her head. "Nope. I'm all set."

He nodded and turned his attention back to the new television set. He had brought it back with him when he returned from his last trip to Buffalo. Jean-Paul sat next to him, and they were glued to the screen, currently watching a new Western, *Maverick*. Their program of choice was usually *Gunsmoke*, and Wayne always took Jean-Paul to the movie house in town whenever there was a cowboy movie playing. Delphine, for her part, couldn't be bothered, and didn't understand their love of Westerns.

Wayne glanced out the window. "Maybe we could close this window now," he said. "Jean-Paul and I are going to have to get our winter coats."

Delphine marched over and shut the sash.

"Why don't you take the car?" Wayne suggested.

She shook her head. "No, I'd prefer to walk." She'd been stuck in the kitchen for so long that she thought the walk and fresh air might do her good.

Halfway up Erie Street, she had to bend forward, walking headfirst into the wind. Now she was sorry she hadn't taken the car. She consoled herself with the fact that on the way home, the wind would be at her back.

By the time she arrived at the parish hall, she was breathless, and the pins in her hair were barely hanging on. Stepping inside, she pulled her handkerchief from her purse and dabbed at her eyes, as the stinging wind had made them water. Then she smoothed her hair back as much as possible without a mirror and readjusted the bobby pins.

She was glad for the coat because the room had a chill in it. The four men that made up the parish hall committee sat at a table at one end of the room. Gus was one of them, and Delphine immediately recognized Dr. Morley, the rector of the parish, and Mr. Hahn, Martha's husband.

As she approached them, all four men pushed their chairs back and stood up.

"Please don't get up," she said.

They greeted her warmly. "Let me get you a chair," Gus said.

Delphine shook her head. "Not necessary. I won't be long. I'd like to sign up for a stall for the Christmas bazaar in December," she said, clutching her purse.

"Then you've come to the right place," Mr. Hahn said, and the committee members returned to their seats. Turning to the doctor, he said, "Fred, I think you have the forms there."

The doctor slid the form toward her and handed her a pencil. As she bent and filled it out, there came the unmistakable sound of rain pounding against the roof. Delphine paused and looked up at the ceiling. She'd be drenched by the time she got home.

They made small talk with her as she continued to fill out the form, hoping at the same time the torrent of rain would quit before she left. She didn't treasure the thought of getting soaking wet.

Once she paid her fee, the rector gave her a receipt and she tucked it into her purse. She lingered, waiting for the rain to abate.

"Did you drive up?" Gus asked.

"No, I walked. I wanted to get some fresh air," she explained.

He jumped up from his seat. "Come on, I'll give you a ride home."

"I don't want to impose," she said. She certainly didn't want to disturb him. But then again, the thought of walking home in this weather held no appeal.

"You can't walk home in this," Mr. Hahn reasoned.

"If you're sure it's not too much trouble."

"None whatsoever," Mr. Hahn said.

Gus pulled his jacket off the back of his chair and pulled it on. As they walked to the outer vestibule, Delphine asked, "How's Doris?"

Over the past year, Gus had stopped by multiple times to order candy for his current lady love. It had been a while since he'd been over, but Delphine assumed the two were still an item. She hoped so. Gus was so kind, he deserved to find love. He should settle down with a wife and children.

"We kind of went our separate ways," he said, his voice low.

She reached out and placed her hand on his arm. "I'm sorry to hear that. She seemed like a nice person."

Gus looked down at the ground. "She is. Was. But she wasn't for me in the long run."

"Gus, you'll find someone," Delphine said reassuringly.

He looked at her but said nothing. His expression was odd, and she didn't know what to make of it.

A car pulled into the parking lot, and Delphine saw that it was Wayne.

"Oh, look, Wayne's here. It will save you the trouble of driving me home," she said with a smile.

"It wouldn't have been any trouble, Delphine," Gus said softly.

"I'll see you around, Gus. You can pop by for another box of chocolate as soon as you start dating someone else."

She made a mad dash for the car. Wayne waited, the car idling and the windshield wipers making a squeaky sound as they tried to keep up with the rain.

CHAPTER THIRTY-TWO

1959

Jean-Paul was off at the playground a few streets over with some of his friends. The bright mid-afternoon sun was high in the sky. The lake was still and flat, like a mirror. Sun shimmered along it, sparkling.

Delphine sat on her porch, sipping a tall glass of tart lemonade, having given up on chocolate making for the day. It was too hot, the temperature in the nineties.

Her face broke into a smile when she spotted Gus heading toward her home. She leaned forward in her chair. He stopped at the corner and spoke to the Marthas, his hands in his trouser pockets, probably jingling his change like he always did.

Delphine held her breath as Gus made his way down to her. She supposed it was wrong to be attracted to a man that wasn't her husband. But it was more than that. He'd been such a good friend to her down through the years; she could depend on him.

His smile broadened when he turned up the short path to her front porch. Delphine sat at the top step. It was his lunch hour and with Wayne gone more and more these days, she was glad of the company. She spent time down on the porch of the Marthas, and that helped, but it was nice to have another adult to talk to. She knew the tongues around town wagged about their friendship, but she didn't care. Her conscience was clear, and she slept well at night.

"Delphine," he said with a slight nod like he always did.

"Gus."

"How's the chocolate making going today?" he asked. He climbed up the steps and sat down next to her.

"It's too hot to make chocolate," she said. "The air conditioner is out again, and I had no luck this morning with the batches."

Gus frowned. "Do you want me to take a look at it?"

She shook her head. "No, I've called Wayne, and he'll bring a new one home tomorrow."

Gus's shoulders stiffened beneath his short-sleeved shirt. He was no fan of Wayne's and vice versa.

"How's the five-and-dime?" she asked.

"Good," he said. He was on his lunch hour. As he was a one-man show, he had to close up the store for the forty-five minutes he allowed for his lunch. Most days, he ambled down and sat on her porch with her, shooting the breeze. This had been going on for years.

The sun blazed, and Delphine felt beads of perspiration break out on her brow.

"I'll get us some lemonade," she said. She stood from the porch step and noticed the youngest Martha running toward them from her house on the corner.

Martha had just turned thirteen, still at that gangly phase where she was all legs and arms and knobby knees. She arrived at the edge of the driveway, breathless.

"Mrs. Brandt, can I take your photo? I've got a new camera!" The girl waved the camera around in the air.

"Of course."

Gus stood to step off the porch, but Martha protested, saying, "No, Mr. Lime, stay where you are."

Gus stood on the top step and Delphine stood behind him on the porch and crossed her arms over her chest, leaning against the pillar.

Martha stood in the center of the walkway, lined up the lens, hid her face behind the camera, and a huge flash went off.

"Thanks, Mrs. Brandt! Thanks, Mr. Lime!" she said, and before they could say anything else, she was off, heading in the direction of town.

Weeks later, young Martha Hahn stopped by to drop the black and white photo off to Delphine. She thanked her and when the girl refused any money for the photo, Delphine gave her a box of candy to which she replied, "Gee, thanks, Mrs. Brandt!"

After she'd gone, Delphine studied the photo with a smile and tucked it safely away into her journal.

Chapter Thirty-Three

1960

"Wayne, I'm not leaving Hideaway Bay." Delphine stamped her foot on the kitchen floor in frustration. *Not this again.* Not packing up everything and leaving the home and place she'd grown to love. Not again.

"You don't understand," Wayne said. "We don't have a choice. We have to leave." His words were articulate and firm.

She looked around the kitchen, every available space covered in chocolate candy, a stack of orders piled high at the corner of the counter next to the phone and stacks of boxes of chocolates ready to be delivered.

"I can't. Look at all these orders I have," she said, sweeping her arm around the room.

"Delphine, stop! We have to go."

"I don't want to," she said again. "What about Jean-Paul? He's happy here."

"He'll be happy wherever we land, as long as we stay together." He looked around, his eyes wild. "Take only what you need." He glanced at his wristwatch. "One hour."

"You want to leave now?" she asked in disbelief.

"I have no choice."

"What did you do?" she groaned.

"Come on, Delphine, get a move on." He snapped his fingers repeatedly as if to emphasize the urgency.

But Delphine leaned against the counter and folded her arms across her chest. "I'm not moving one inch until you tell me the truth. Why do we have to leave?"

"Come on, Delphine!"

She shook her head. "No."

He rushed her, grabbing her by the forearms and shaking her. "Don't you understand? I'm in big trouble. I have to get out of here."

Wayne had never been physical with her before. It just wasn't his way. But now, him manhandling her, coupled with that look in his eyes of a trapped animal, frightened her.

"You're scaring me."

"Good." He drove his hand through his hair, disheveling it.

"Tell me," she said quietly. She'd lost count of how many times she'd bailed him out, giving him the money to pay off his debts. Wilma had been right. Once he could count on her to rescue him, there'd been no end to it.

He regarded her, the muscle ticking along his jaw.

"Wayne . . ."

He drew in a deep breath. "I borrowed some money."

"Pay it back."

"I can't. The horse I bet on lost." As if it would make any difference, he wailed, "He was a sure bet! He couldn't lose! He was the odds-on favorite! But he stumbled out of the gate."

"And you lost the money?"

"It wasn't my money to lose."

Delphine drew in a sharp breath.

"I was supposed to deliver that money to someone else, but I placed a bet on it instead."

Nausea gripped her stomach. "How much?"

When he told her the amount, she blanched. Her voice shook as she spoke. "Where are we going to get that kind of money?"

"We can't. That's what I'm trying to tell you. By now, they probably know what I've done and are on their way here."

She looked toward the backyard, where Jean-Paul played outside.

"Jean-Paul . . ." she whispered.

"Can you be ready in an hour?" Wayne asked.

"Do I have a choice?"

He bit his lip. "I'll get the suitcases out."

"I've got some things to do around town," she said.

"Forget it. There's no time."

Delphine stomped her foot. "No. This is important."

All right, but be back here in twenty minutes," he instructed.

Jean-Paul ran in at that moment, seeking his father to show him something in the backyard. As Wayne went out the back door, he said again, "Twenty minutes, Delphine."

"Okay," she promised. As soon as he disappeared out the back door with Jean-Paul tugging at his hand, she picked up her recipe book from the counter and walked to the front of the house.

For a moment, she stared at the living room floor. Beneath the small area rug under the coffee table was a loose floorboard she'd discovered when her brand-new throw rug had snagged on it. It had become a secret hiding place for her. No one knew about it. Not even Wayne. It was where she kept her finished journals.

She was torn. Did she get out the hammer and retrieve her journals or did she go see the Marthas and Gus? It was important for her to say goodbye to her friends. There wasn't time to do both. She had to choose.

Within seconds, she was flying through the front door, recipe book in hand, heading south along Star Shine Drive. The journals would have to remain where they were.

Black clouds rolled in off the lake, the low rumble of thunder sounding in the background. The water appeared dark and churlish. By the time she reached the corner of Star Shine Drive and Erie Street, the thunder had increased in frequency and volume. She landed on the front porch of Martha Hahn's house and rang the doorbell, keeping her eye on the threatening black sky over the lake. When no one answered, she banged on the door. She didn't want to leave without saying goodbye to the Marthas. They'd been good friends to her since she'd arrived in Hideaway Bay.

When no answer was forthcoming, Delphine went to the window and peered in. She scanned the front parlor through the filter of the sheer curtain but saw no movement. With her hope dimming, she rang the bell one more time.

Finally, she gave up. From the porch, she spotted the funnel of a waterspout out on the lake. Hurriedly, she left the porch and headed toward Main Street. The heavy black clouds picked up speed and rolled in from the lake, casting dark shadows over the town. Arriving at the five-and-dime, she leaned against the brick post of the store. She shivered despite the humidity. Her hand went to her side, where a painful stitch had developed.

Breathless from her run, she waited a minute. Gus was going to think she was out of her mind. As the thunder increased, pedestrians cleared the street, seeking shelter in the various shops, except for Milchmann's grocery store. Elvira Milchmann had made it clear she didn't care for loitering.

Delphine's heart ached at the thought of leaving Hideaway Bay. Tears stung her eyes.

Her breathing settled down, and she smoothed down her hair and made her way to the five-and-dime. Through the window, she spotted Gus behind the counter, his tall, slim form bent over something, his focus serious. It brought a smile to her face.

Oh, Gus.

When she opened the door, he looked up and his eyes widened in surprise.

"Delphine!" He came out from behind the counter. "What are you doing out in weather like this?"

Before she could respond, there was a bright flash of lightning outside the window followed by a loud boom of thunder that shook the building.

His eyes narrowed and he stepped away from her, walked briskly to the front door, turned the "open" sign around until it read "closed," and locked the door.

"Come to the back office and sit down," he said quietly.

She shook her head. She couldn't.

"I'm leaving," she managed to sputter out.

"What?" Confusion clouded his features. "What do you mean you're leaving?"

She nodded. "Wayne came home a few minutes ago and said we had to go."

"Right now?" he asked. There was a flash of anger in his eyes. "Is he in trouble again?"

There was another flash of lightning and a clap of thunder, this time closer.

She nodded again, her teeth chattering, almost regretting ever confiding in Gus about her husband. It wasn't fair to Wayne. It was disloyal. "Yes."

The features of Gus's face softened, and he took her hands in his. "Delphine, do you want to leave?"

The tears flowed. "No, of course not. Hideaway Bay is my home. But I don't have any choice."

"You have options." His gaze locked with hers.

Her breath caught, and her heart missed a beat.

Don't say anything, Gus. Don't ruin our friendship.

He squeezed his clasped hands over hers. He leaned in until there were only inches between them, every line and mark and feature on his face up close and personal. Her eyes flicked back and forth around his face, memorizing every detail and nuance of it. How she loved his Roman nose!

A simultaneous boom of thunder and lightning shook the building, and the power went out, shrouding the five-and-dime in shadows and dim, dull daylight.

"Don't leave," he said. "Stay here with me. You and Jean-Paul."

His idea, now spoken out loud, was so preposterous that she stared and blinked at him, uncomprehending. "Gus?" she finally stammered out.

"I realize what I'm asking is big. It means leaving Wayne and breaking up your marriage, but I think by now you know how I feel about you."

With a quivering chin, she could only nod. She hadn't been blind. From the time she'd arrived in Hideaway Bay, he'd been solicitous of her. Always kind, always willing to help out. And Wayne had never been a big fan of Gus Lime's. There was always a snide remark. Had it been that obvious? Or had she made the conscious choice not to see it? To remain blind. She'd been desperate for a friend.

Gus let go of her hands and squeezed her shoulders. "I love you, Delphine. I'll take good care of you. You'd never have to worry about a thing again."

"Oh, Gus," she murmured. "Don't say those things. I'm not in a position to accept." She thought about his standing in town and Mrs. Milchmann right next door and added, "And neither are you."

Everything came at her all at once.

Life with Gus would certainly be easier in some ways, there was no doubt about that. No more picking up and leaving a place in the middle of the night. No more being afraid of putting roots down in a place because you might not be staying long term.

But then there was Jean-Paul. How would it affect him if she left his father and took up with Gus? That was something that didn't bear thinking about. That alone was enough to quash any desire. It would be scandalous for the tame town of Hideaway Bay. They'd have to move anyway, and Gus would have to forfeit his family business.

Most importantly, she didn't love Gus. Not the way she'd once loved Wayne, back when she'd met him during the liberation. Not the way Gus deserved to be loved. What she did love was the friendship she had with him.

"Say yes, Delphine," Gus whispered. His smile was warm and generous. "Say you love me too."

Suddenly, she hated herself for letting this friendship of theirs get to this point where Gus had to expose his vulnerability, her knowing full well that she couldn't give him the one thing he wanted: herself.

Before she could respond, he wrapped his arms around her, pulling her closer. He bent his head, pressing his lips to hers. Delphine's eyes widened, then they closed as she melted, briefly, into the warmth and insistence of his kiss. But at the back of her mind, a little voice whispered, *You're a married woman*. Placing her hands on his chest, she gently pushed him away.

"I'm sorry," she mumbled.

Gus's arms fell to his sides, and he looked at her, waiting. Expectant. Hopeful.

She hated herself for what she was about to do to him. "I'm sorry, Gus. But I can't . . . He's my husband."

The expression on his face crumpled, but he nodded in wordless understanding. He took a sudden step back as if burned and placed his hand on the counter as if to brace himself.

"Please forgive me," she said. The last thing she wanted was to hurt him. Not him of all people. It killed her, but Wayne was her husband, and she could never forget that he'd done two very important things for her: he'd given her a new life in America, and he'd given her Jean-Paul. She would never forget that, no matter how much her heart wanted to stay. It was enough to see her through all the ups and downs of her marriage, even if there seemed to be more downs than ups.

"It's all right, Delphine." Gus was quiet, as if the spark had gone out of him. He stared at the old scuffed wooden floor.

His hurt was palpable.

Swallowing hard, she handed the recipe book to him.

Taking it from her, he frowned and said, "This is yours, Delphine."

"Yes. I want you to have it," she said. Her voice was tremulous. "As a gift."

"I can't take this," he protested. "This is a family heirloom. It's your most prized possession."

Her eyes filled with tears. "Yes, it is, and that's why I want you to have it."

"I think you should take it with you. This book is so important to you."

She smiled and tapped her temple. "I have the whole thing memorized up here."

He went to hand it back, but she placed her hand gently over his and pushed it away. "Please, accept this gift from me."

Although she couldn't give herself to him, she could give him a part of herself. An important part.

"I will treasure it," he said quietly, opening it and leafing through it.

"Thank you," she whispered.

A silence settled between them.

"Goodbye, Gus," she said. She stepped forward, clutched his elbow, and kissed him on the cheek.

"So long, Delphine," he whispered.

Without another word, she turned and briskly strode out of the five-and-dime. With tears streaming down her face, she ran all the way home, jumping with every crack of thunder.

She pulled herself together before opening the screen door of her own home.

Two old, battered suitcases stood next to the front door. Next to them were brown paper bags filled with items, mainly from the kitchen, and there was a large cardboard box filled with her chocolate-making equipment.

Wayne appeared from the kitchen. "Where have you been?"

She was on the verge of tears and her emotions were raw. With a trembling voice, she mumbled, "Saying goodbye to someone."

For a moment, he regarded her, his eyes narrowing. He had to know where she'd gone, but he chose to not remark on it. He tapped his wristwatch. "We need to get out of here."

"I'm doing the best I can on such short notice," she said wearily.

Delphine dragged herself up the stairs and landed in their bedroom. She rifled through drawers, removing clothes and throwing them into an open suitcase on the bed.

"Is that ready to go down?" Wayne asked behind her, startling her.

"Yes."

"Okay, let's go."

"I'll be down in a minute."

"One minute, Delphine," he said.

She nodded and as soon as she heard his footsteps on the stairs, she pulled the chair over to the front window and climbed up on it. With a quick glance toward the doorway, she unhooked the drapes from the curtain rod and poked around in the pleated seams, loosening the stitches to remove her billfold of money. It was one of the few hiding places Wayne hadn't discovered yet. She knew he'd looked; she could tell by the way he never put her things back the way she had them.

Once she tucked her cash into her brassiere, she put the chair back and ran down the stairs.

She did one last run through to the kitchen, making sure there was nothing more she wanted to bring. In the front room, Jean-Paul was kicking up a storm and barraging Wayne.

"But I don't want to go. I don't want to leave Hideaway Bay. What about my friends? What about my bike? And where am I going to go swimming? Please, Dad!"

"Get in the car, son," Wayne said tightly.

Jean-Paul intercepted Delphine on the way from the kitchen. "Maman, I don't want to leave. I don't want to live anywhere else."

She wrapped an arm around his shoulders and gave him a gentle squeeze. "It's going to be all right."

"Maman, please—" His voice was frantic, and that just about killed her. Over his head, she glared at Wayne.

"Shh, everything is going to be all right," she said. "I promise. Now be a good boy and get in the car."

Ten was such a tough age. Not quite a teenager and really no longer a child. And he'd been happy here in Hideaway Bay.

"Come on, let's go," she said. She took his hand, and they ran to the car. "How would you like to sit in the front seat?"

Sullen, he nodded. The car door creaked as she pulled it open, its hinges needing a shot of oil. Jean-Paul climbed into the front seat and Delphine got into the back. She wanted to be alone, and this was the best she could do. This way she could cry in private as they left Hideaway Bay.

As the car made its way down Star Shine Drive, she twisted in her seat to watch the house through the rear windshield. Thinking of Gus, she thought it was perhaps best that she leave. At that moment, the sky opened up and rain slammed down around them.

Once Wayne turned onto Erie Street, the house disappeared from sight, and she turned around to face forward and never looked back.

Chapter Thirty-Four

1974

Delphine worked around her kitchen with a smile on her face. She couldn't quite believe the news Jean-Paul and his wife, Marjorie, had delivered the previous night over dinner. A baby was on the way. She was going to be a grandmother. She couldn't remember the last time she'd heard such wonderful news. It was so exciting it had kept her up half the night, fantasizing and making plans for her future grandchild.

On a kitchen chair stood a large cardboard box ready to be filled with smaller boxes of her candy. Over the years, her long-ago dream of owning her own shop had faded, and she'd continued to work as a chocolatier out of her own kitchen. Wherever they'd lived. Currently, they were in Colorado, where they'd been the longest—almost eleven years, one more year than their time spent in Hideaway Bay. Jean-Paul had graduated from high school here, gone to college, and met and married his wife. He appeared happy, and that made Delphine happy. Of all the places they'd lived, Hideaway Bay had been her favorite, but as the years went on, the memories faded, and her wish to return faded too as she put down roots in Colorado, raised her son, grew her business, and made friends. From time to time, she thought of the Marthas on the corner and all the other lovely people who'd stopped into her kitchen over the years. And also, she thought of Gus. She hoped he'd married and settled down. He deserved that. As for the recipe book and her journals, she figured they were long gone by now.

As she filled smaller individual boxes with her homemade chocolate, her mind was on her new grandchild. Her life was already full, and this was going to be a bonus.

Wayne appeared in the doorway. Time, his lifestyle, and his late nights had ravaged his handsomeness. She barely recognized the man she'd met as the war was coming to a close. His once solid frame was now thin to the point of being gaunt.

"You were up all night," he said by way of greeting.

"The news kept me awake."

He laughed. "I can't believe I'm old enough to be a grandfather." He reached into a cabinet and removed a milk glass tiger mug he'd picked up from their nearby Esso station. He filled the kettle at the kitchen sink and asked over his shoulder, "Do you want tea?"

"No thanks."

His whistling filled the air as he made himself a cup of coffee, pulling down a jar of Tasters Choice and spooning it into the mug. When he sat, he crossed his legs and pulled out a packet of Camels from his shirt pocket. He tapped a cigarette out, lit it, and then snapped his lighter shut.

"Would you put lighter fluid on your grocery list?"

She nodded, counting out pieces of chocolate and filling a box. When finished, she stacked it on the counter with the other boxes.

"I was thinking it might be time we moved on," he said casually as if remarking on the weather.

Stunned, Delphine gathered herself. "Move on from what?"

He waved his hand around, the bluish smoke trailing from his cigarette leaving a circular arc in front of his face.

"From here. I'm getting itchy to try out a new place."

She stared at him for a moment, her mouth hanging open.

"Are you in trouble?" she asked.

"No."

She believed him. Once they'd left Hideaway Bay, she'd told him she'd never bail him out again, and he'd taken her seriously. From there, he'd drifted from one low-paying job to the next. But they'd managed to make ends meet and put Jean-Paul through college. And although he still liked horse racing and gambling in general, there were no more dodgy deals or questionable characters.

"I thought a change of scenery might be nice," he said. "I was thinking of going out west."

Delphine responded to this with a snort. "We are out west. How much further west could we go? The ocean?" Sick and tired of this kind of nonsense that had dominated the twenty-five plus years of their marriage, she wasn't going to just get up and start packing. She piled some of the smaller boxes of candy into the cardboard box; it was easier to deliver that way.

She had no intention of leaving. She liked her church and the priest. There was pinochle on Monday nights with her group of friends and the various classes the community college offered that she liked to pursue. She'd learned how to paint, how to keep her books, and how to change a flat tire. They had a magnificent view, and she loved all the fresh mountain air. And Jean-Paul and Marjorie came over every Sunday for dinner.

"I heard California is nice." Wayne rubbed the back of his neck and sipped his coffee.

"Listen to me." Delphine straightened up and turned to face him. "My family is here. My friends are here. It's the longest we've stayed in one place. I don't want to move."

"Well, I do. I'm bored. There's nothing here anymore," he said, taking a long drag on his cigarette, the ash lengthening.

"Nothing here?" she repeated. "Jean-Paul and Marjorie? That's enough for me. And now a grandchild."

"I don't want to stay here," he said quietly.

Not caring, Delphine shrugged. She didn't know what to tell him. All she knew was she wasn't bored. She was happy and content, life made more joyous by the impending arrival of a grandchild.

"Delphine, come on, it'll be fun," he said with that lazy grin of his that had convinced her so many times in the past.

She leaned forward, pressing her palms against the edge of the table. "Wayne, we have a grandchild on the way!"

"I know. I was there when Jean-Paul told us the news last night." Irritation laced his voice. When she didn't respond, he added, "We can come back and visit."

"Like we did with your mother after we moved to Hideaway Bay?" It still stuck in her craw. That whole affair still bothered her. After the move to Hideaway Bay, they'd only seen Wilma a handful of times until her death when Jean-Paul was five.

"How long are you going to throw that in my face?"

Probably for the rest of our lives.

He sighed. "Well, I'm leaving. I'm going to California." He announced it with intent and firmness.

"Go ahead. I'll be right here." She resumed stacking the candy boxes into the bigger cardboard box.

"You'd let me leave without you?" he asked, aghast.

"Yes, I would. I'm done with moving around and now that I have a grandchild on the way, I won't leave Colorado. I'm staying put."

"You can't live your life around your grandchildren."

"Oh yes I can, and I will," she said. She folded the flaps inward on the cardboard box. "You do what you want, Wayne, I won't stop you. I'll still be here in this house if you decide to return or if you ever finish doing what you want to do. But make no mistake, I'm not leaving. My life is here now."

With a grim set to his jaw, he pushed back his chair, scraping the metal legs against the linoleum. Without a word, he left the house, slamming the door behind him.

1980

"That's right, you're doing a great job!" Delphine told six-year-old Valerie as she sat at the kitchen table using a pipette bag to put filling in the chocolate candy. The table was one great big glorious mess. There were smears of chocolate everywhere. Strawberry cream filling—which was Valerie's favorite—was all over the place: along the edge of the table, beneath the little girl's fingernails, and even in her hair. As Delphine walked by behind her, she couldn't resist the urge to reach out and embrace the girl, kissing the top of her head.

"You're the best little girl I know," she told her.

Valerie rewarded her with a gap-toothed smile.

"When I grow up, I'm going to make candy just like you," Valerie said, and went back to her task.

"I hope so." Delphine looked heavenward and muttered, "From her lips to your ears, Lord."

When she turned around, Valerie was chewing.

Delphine put her hands on her hips in mock outrage. "You're not eating all the chocolate, I hope! What about our customers?"

Valerie shrugged and giggled, putting her hands out, palms facing Delphine. They were covered in chocolate.

"Now, it's time to learn some French," Delphine said with authority.

"Bonjour," Valerie chanted. "Bonjour, bonjour, bonjour."

"Very good."

And on and on it went.

"Bonjour!" called Wayne from the doorway.

"Poppy!" Valerie said excitedly.

"How's my girl?" he asked, lifting her up into his arms.

Wayne never left for California. Once he realized he'd have to do so without his wife, that urge died within him. But to his and Delphine's great surprise, he took to heart the role of being a grandfather to Valerie and Chuck.

"Making chocolate and speaking French," Valerie said.

"Aren't you lucky?"

As they sat together and admired Valerie's handiwork, Delphine announced, "When you grow up, I'm going to teach you everything you need to know about chocolate. And then someday, you'll be a chocolatier like the women in your family before you. And who knows, you might one day open a little shop." That statement was so full of promise for Delphine that it made her smile. Valerie laughed and ate another piece of chocolate, her legs swinging beneath the kitchen chair.

Chapter Thirty-Five

1995

DELPHINE LEFT THE STORE and stepped out into the bright sunshine and cool air of spring, a shopping bag full of supplies on her arm. She had two more stops to make. It was going to be a busy week. And she couldn't be more excited.

Valerie was coming home from college for a mini break. She had made the dean's list every single semester, and had one more year to go until she'd graduate. Another college graduate in the family, just like her father, Jean-Paul. Pride swelled in Delphine. Her celebratory mood was justified.

Her granddaughter had called her last week, saying she was looking forward to coming home and taking a break from her studies. Said she wanted to spend the week making chocolate with her grandmother. As soon as she hung up the phone, Delphine began making lists of things she would need. Easter was coming up, and she thought they could make some chocolate truffle eggs. That might be fun.

She missed the years when Valerie was young. As soon as she hit her teenage years, her interest in chocolate making was put on the back burner in favor of music and boys. Understandable. Delphine had been young once herself. Even if it was a lifetime ago and under less-than-desirable circumstances.

Last night, she'd lain awake in bed, thinking she really needed to write down the family recipes for her granddaughter. These recipes were important. Even if Valerie never pursued chocolate making, someone down the line might.

And that was her next stop, the stationery store. Her plan was to purchase a fancy journal. You couldn't put the family recipes in any old notebook.

Her mind was on a million things as she stepped off the curb, the stationery store in sight across the street, but there was a smile on her face.

She never saw the car coming. Hadn't even looked both ways as she'd taught her son and grandchildren to do. There was a horn and a deafening squeal of brakes and a loud thud when the vehicle made contact with her body. Her face crumpled in stunned disbelief on impact. The last thing she was aware of was sailing through the air.

PART THREE

Valerie

CHAPTER THIRTY-SIX

VALERIE WALKED UP ERIE Street and crossed over to Main Street and headed toward the five-and-dime. In her hand, she carried the black-and-white photo of Nana and Mr. Lime on the front porch of the house on Star Shine Drive.

Although curiosity filled her as to why Mr. Lime had been so evasive about knowing Nana, she decided she had to respect his privacy and would leave it alone. The journals had given her more than enough insight into her grandmother's life. Probably more than she had a right to.

Mr. Lime lifted his head from the ledger he was studying when Valerie entered the store. Two women rifled through the bins, looked up briefly at Valerie, and resumed their task.

He regarded her warily. "I have no information for you."

Ignoring his pronouncement, she marched purposefully up to the counter and laid the black-and-white photo on the countertop in front of him.

He picked it up, peered at it through his bifocals, and staggered back for a moment, setting it down.

"Where did you get this?" he demanded.

It was difficult to reconcile this surly present-day version of Mr. Lime with the one six decades ago in the photo, where he appeared relaxed and congenial, or the Gus Lime of Nana's journals, who always had a kind word and was always ready to lend a hand.

"It was in one of my grandmother's journals. You know, Delphine Giroud Brandt, who lived on Star Shine Drive. That's the two of you on her front porch, there." She thumped her finger on the photo on the counter.

"I can see that," he said. His tone was spiky.

"It was a long time ago," Valerie said.

His voice was wistful when he spoke. "Yes, it was."

After a moment, he looked at her and asked sharply, "Why are you showing me this?"

"I thought you might like to have it," she said.

His expression softened, and he picked up the photo to study it. "Thank you, young lady. I would like that very much."

"Take care, Mr. Lime," she said, and she exited the shop.

Jeff had been unreachable for three nights in a row. Valerie couldn't understand why he wasn't answering the phone or responding to her texts. Finally, she sent him another text, angry that he was doing this to her:

Fine if you don't want to talk to me. But please let me know you're all right.

Twenty minutes went by. With the time difference, it was too late to call Renee to see if she'd heard from her father. Maybe she'd call Jeremy. Now she was worried that something had happened to Jeff and he was in the hospital. Just because they were going through some difficulties didn't mean she didn't care about him. It wasn't a switch that flipped off after almost thirty years of marriage.

Her phone pinged and relief filled her when she saw Jeff's name flash across the screen.

I'm fine. I need some space right now.

She nodded even though he wasn't there to see it. She had to respect his wishes. After all, she'd needed space too. With a sigh, she tossed the phone on the bed and decided to run a bath. She'd picked up some scented candles and bath salts in town and was looking forward to soaking in the tub.

CHAPTER THIRTY-SEVEN

I N AN EFFORT TO get out of the house and get some fresh air and exercise, Val took a walk right before lunch.

Her walk took her all the way to the end of Erie Street and instead of crossing over the boardwalk to the beach, she turned onto Main Street and decided to go and sit in the gazebo. She liked the view from the green and at this part of town, it was much quieter.

Seated on the bench in the gazebo, she stared out at the lake, thinking it was time to start making some fillings for her chocolate candy and deciding what flavors she'd like to test. Strawberry cream was definitely one of them. Out of the corner of her eye, she spotted the crooked figure of Mr. Lime approaching her.

He was dressed in a crinkled short-sleeved shirt of white, yellow, and orange plaid, and he wore bright yellow pants and white shoes with a gold buckle. He looked like a throwback to the 1970s. A glasses case and pen were visible in his shirt pocket.

She waited, expectant and curious. For a brief moment, she wondered if he was going to return the photograph.

As he stepped up onto the gazebo, he nodded to her in acknowledgement. "I saw you pass by my window."

In his hands he carried a small, battered brown book. When he sat down on the bench next to her, he placed it in his lap.

He opened up with: "Your grandmother and I were good friends when she lived here."

His gaze wandered out over the lake. "But for me, that friendship grew into something else. Delphine Brandt was the only woman I ever loved."

Of all the things he could have said, Val hadn't expected this. Not knowing what to say, she said nothing.

"I met her when she first moved here," he continued. "I'd been back from the war for a few years and had taken over the five-and-dime after my father's death. One day, she literally ran into me running out of her house. Her little boy, Jean-Paul, was sick, and she needed help. He needed a doctor."

He paused and his rheumy eyes clouded over as if he were no longer in the present. "My God, she was beautiful. With that hair and those eyes and her accent." He shook his head, his chin jutting out. "The Marthas on the corner took her under their wing. I think they felt connected to her because of their French lineage. But soon she was well thought of by everyone in Hideaway Bay."

He paused again, either lost in thought or collecting them.

"It broke her heart to leave Hideaway Bay. But she felt her place was beside her husband."

"I've read my grandmother's journals," Val said. "She speaks of your friendship, but she never mentioned love."

"Sadly, it was one-sided. She viewed me as a friend." He grimaced as if the thought still brought him pain.

Valerie winced, remembering a time before Renee had taken off to France, when she'd been put in the friend zone by a crush of hers and how devastated she'd been.

Wanting to soften the blow, she said quietly, "I'm sure my grandmother treasured your friendship."

"Your grandmother used to come into the five-and-dime from time to time." With a laugh, he added, "And Jean-Paul loved the banana-flavored saltwater taffy." He smiled at the memory of it. "Over the years, we became very good friends."

Valerie tried to imagine Nana wheeling a stroller around the town with her father as a young boy in it. It brought a smile to her face.

"Your grandfather was gone a lot, doing whatever it is he used to do." His tone indicated dislike or at the very least, disapproval. "Although I've never been married, I imagine all marriages go through rough patches."

Her own marriage came to mind, and she wondered if it was only a rough patch. Hard to tell if it was something transient, something that was salvageable or a lost cause. There was time later for reflection on that.

"She'd been unhappy," Mr. Lime continued. "Wayne was gone a lot, either to Buffalo or Cleveland, and the source of his income was always questionable." His voice was neutral. And that was good because Valerie was ready to jump in and defend her grandfather if need be. He wasn't perfect and he hadn't been a good provider, but he was a kind man in his later years, and he had adored his wife.

"I think Delphine would have preferred a more stable husband," Mr. Lime said. "I'm not saying that Wayne didn't have good characteristics, I'm sure he did, but his unpredictability jobwise and the constant moving was distressing for your grandmother."

He stared off into the distance. The sun was just past its highest point in the sky, but between the wooden roof and the giant oak trees scattered across the green, the shady interior of the gazebo had to be five degrees cooler than the outside temperature.

Gulls cried in the distance, and there was the constant rhythm of the surf rolling in, hitting the shore, and receding. The contrast of colors on the beach was appealing with the dark brown sand against the navy-colored lake and the light blue sky. In the distance, a mother set up her beach umbrella as a baby watched from its stroller, and two children under the age of five stood there holding beach pails, one blue and one orange. The mother's voice as she spoke to her children carried over to them, though somewhat muffled.

"Do you know why they had to leave?" Delphine asked. There had been nothing in the journals about their departure.

There was a grim set to his lips. He stared at the floor of the gazebo and then lifted his chin, looking at her. "Delphine came to see me the day they left. Said they had to leave town in a hurry because of Wayne." His voice held distaste as if he'd tasted something bitter.

Valerie swallowed. This validated what her grandmother had written about her grandfather in her journals. It had been easy to read between the lines of Delphine's growing frustration with Wayne.

"Anyway, he had to get out of town again—"

A shiver ran down Val's spine.

"Before she left, she gave me this," Mr. Lime said, and handed the small leather book to Valerie. "I think you should have it."

With trembling hands, Valerie took the book from him. It was a hardcover, small, maybe five inches by seven or less, and there was a water stain on the bottom left-hand corner. Carefully, she flipped open the cover to the first page, and her heart beat faster as she recognized her great-grandmother's name handwritten in ink: Marguerite Giroud, and the date, March 1939. Beneath that were more words written in French, possibly an address. Mesmerized, she flipped through the pages.

"It's your grandmother's family recipes for chocolate making," Mr. Lime said. With a nod toward the book, he added, "That was written by your great-grandmother before the occupation."

Overwhelmed and speechless, Val turned the pages slowly, the French words written neatly in a striking script, with notes along the margins of some of the pages jumping out at her.

"I don't know what to say, except thank you."

"You're welcome."

Turning his head, he gave her a rueful smile. "I guess at heart, I'm a hopeless romantic. That book has been in my safe for many decades."

A smile spread across her face. Clutching the book to her chest, she said, "I can't thank you enough for this. For keeping it all these years . . ."

"I was hopeful your grandmother would come back for it someday." Sadness laced his voice. Valerie felt great compassion for him.

"Did you ever hear from her?" she asked.

He shook his head. "No. I often wondered what happened to her. For years after she left, I thought about her every day. But then as time went on, I thought about her less and less."

His heartbreak was palpable.

"Where did she end up?" he asked.

"In the end, Colorado," Valerie said. "She did finally put her foot down and told my grandfather she wasn't moving anymore. It was around the time I was born. She said she wanted to be near her grandchildren. And she never did move again."

He chuckled. "I can't picture her in Colorado. I can only see her in Hideaway Bay."

The more time Valerie spent in the lakeside town, the more she could also easily picture her grandmother living there, walking along Main Street or along the beach.

"Has she been gone long?"

Valerie sucked in a breath. "I was twenty-one when she died." It was a long time ago, but then it also seemed like yesterday.

She explained to him the circumstances of her grandmother's death. His expression crumpled, and he appeared shaken for a moment.

Finally, with some difficulty, he managed to stand, patting his shirt pocket as if making sure his glasses and pen were still there. "I must get back to the shop. When you're in business for yourself, you can't take a lot of time off."

Valerie also stood, her mind racing. With her grandmother's recipe book in hand—a book she didn't even know existed until a few minutes ago—her thoughts about her brand-new business took off in another direction.

Mr. Lime navigated the three steps down to level ground carefully, holding on to the rail as he went.

"Thanks again, Mr. Lime," she said, stepping off the last step of the gazebo.

The sun was high in the sky, its heat warm on her face. Her mood hadn't been this buoyant in a long time.

He regarded her thoughtfully before pronouncing, "You know, I can see Delphine in you. Especially around the eyes."

Valerie beamed. "Thank you."

He nodded. "Stop in the shop anytime."

"I will," she promised. With a wave, he set off.

The war memorial caught her eye, and she ambled over to it. It was a black granite affair that shimmered in the sun. Etched into the granite were the names of those lost in the wars, going back as far as the First World War. Under WWII, there were eleven names. She immediately recognized the name Hahn and wondered if it was a relation to Martha Cotter. She'd been a Hahn.

The world had been a different place back then.

Poppy and Mr. Lime had survived the Second World War as had her grandmother. Regret filled her at all the questions she did not ask or the stories Nana had told her whose details she'd forgotten. But she supposed that was the way it was.

Once home, she made another appointment with the translation service company up in Buffalo to translate the recipe book. And then when that was squared away, she got down to the business of experimenting with different chocolate flavors.

CHAPTER THIRTY-EIGHT

July 20th

V AL SAT IN THE third row of chairs set up in the parish hall as Della Rossi called the meeting of the Hideaway Bay social club to order. Beside her sat Thelma, and on the other side of her sat Isabelle Monroe.

The social club met regularly, and Valerie liked to attend from time to time if only to get involved with the community and meet other townspeople.

A wave of hot, humid weather had gripped the Northeast for most of the month. The old parish hall did not have central air conditioning, but it did have two noisy window air conditioners, which were currently on full power, rattling loudly and doing nothing to relieve the heat and discomfort inside the hall.

Valerie sat ensconced between Thelma and Isabelle, her face and body damp, wishing she'd taken a seat in the back row or on the end of the aisle. Hopefully, Della would keep the announcements brief.

"I'm excited to announce that we're setting up a badminton tournament for the month of August. Then starting in September, we'll have a Ping-Pong league," Della said excitedly.

Next to Valerie, Thelma raised her hand. "May I make a suggestion?"

"Of course, Thelma," Della said with a nod.

"What about lawn darts? I love that game," she said.

The room went quiet, and Sue Ann Marchek said, "Thelma, lawn darts are banned."

Thelma looked genuinely shocked. "They are? When did that happen?"

"Years ago," Jack Stirling replied. "Back in the eighties or nineties."

"Huh. I still use mine," Thelma said. She looked around quickly, folded her arms across her chest, and muttered, "I guess I better get rid of them. It's a shame though, it's a great game."

With an indulgent smile, Della continued. "Anyway, the sign-up forms for the badminton tournament and the Ping-Pong league will be on a table at the back of the hall. Sue Ann has them. What I'm most excited about is that we have a professional genealogist coming in to talk to us about researching our family trees."

Della continued to list the different events that were planned right up until Christmas. As much as Val wanted to do all of them, she only had so much time. Right now, the chocolate making was consuming most, if not all of her time. If she were serious about starting a business—which she was—she'd have to put the time and effort in.

But still she forced herself to get out and mingle, if only to socialize and meet people. And everyone in town was so nice.

After the meeting broke up, townspeople lingered and spoke to one another while helping themselves to lemonade and iced tea that had been set up at the back of the hall. But Val headed for the exit, nodding to people she'd begun to recognize from town, anxious to get home. The next meeting was for the monthly birthdays, and she was glad her own birthday had only recently passed. Being a new arrival in town, she wasn't keen for the spotlight.

The recipe book had been translated and she'd been poring over it for the last week. Her great-grandmother, Marguerite Giroud, had written out her recipes meticulously, sometimes changing a measurement with the explanation for the reason of the change. There were notes scattered here and there about triumphs and failures; chocolate not setting properly seemed to be a big one as was tempering, and the one that apparently irritated Marguerite Giroud the most was fingerprints on the chocolate. She'd ended one note about this with the word *Delphine!* Val had chuckled over this.

Jeff's anger had dissipated to the point where they could carry on a civil conversation, albeit a brief one, almost every night. Sometimes he was available to talk and sometimes he wasn't. It wouldn't have been fair for her to take his distance personally. So she didn't, choosing instead to concentrate on getting her chocolate business off the ground. She was able to source some items from the five-and-dime, and she was going to make do without the rest. But she did splurge on a professional candy thermometer she thought would be better than the one she had at home.

Once home, she donned her apron and got down to work. She went about tempering some chocolate and once it was ready, she set the bowl aside. From the spare bedroom, which was the coolest room in the house and where she had set up makeshift tables, she removed a pan of caramel she'd made earlier in the day. With her finger, she pressed the edge of it, testing for firmness. Satisfied, she took the pan of caramel, gently turned it upside down, and let the slab land on her workspace. She set the pan aside in the sink and pulled the parchment off the caramel. Then she bottom-coated it with chocolate by spreading a thin layer over the caramel slab. She had to temper her impatience as she waited for it to set properly. Once she was satisfied, she took a ruler and a knife and began cutting one-inch squares of the candy. With her fork, she dipped the squares in the bowl of tempered chocolate, scraping any excess off the fork using the side of the bowl.

When that was finished, she stepped back, satisfied with the neat rows of chocolate caramel. After she cleaned up, she looked at the pints of fresh raspberries she'd picked up at the fruit-and-veg stand. The next day, she planned to make raspberry puree then make a chocolate raspberry ganache. She couldn't wait.

August 20th

A month later, Valerie had her first prototype completed of a box of candy. Grinning, she stared at her finished box, and pride swelled within her. Inside, it contained four different types: chocolate raspberry truffle, strawberry cream, cherry amaretto, and caramel.

It felt momentous. It called for champagne. It called for a celebration. But here she was, alone in her rented home in Hideaway Bay. Her children were scattered over the world and her husband was back home in Colorado. It was such a meaningful moment that she wanted to share it with someone. But it was too late to call Renee in France; she'd already be in bed. And Jeremy didn't always answer his phone. That left Jeff. Would he be happy for her? Or would he drag her down and ruin it?

With a sigh, she caved into the urge to share her news and called her husband. She sat at the kitchen table with one leg crossed over the other. She sat up straighter. These types of phone calls where you didn't know what kind of reception you might receive made her terribly anxious.

"Hey," he said, answering the phone.

"Hi, Jeff," she said. Her voice sounded higher than normal.

"Everything all right?" he asked. "We usually don't speak until later."

"I know. I wanted to share something with you."

He waited and for a moment, Valerie wondered if she'd made a mistake in calling him. Finally, she said, "I made my first box of chocolate today. It's all boxed up."

"Congratulations," he said.

Immediately, her shoulders sagged and her posture relaxed in relief. She let go of the breath she'd been holding.

"Thank you." She'd been keeping him abreast of her progress, the mistakes and the successes. And although it was difficult to gauge over the phone, he appeared to be interested.

"Did you go with the strawberry cream or the cherry amaretto?" he asked.

So he has been paying attention.

"I did both," she told him.

"And what are your plans for your first box?"

"Actually, I'm going to gift it to the Monroe sisters."

"The ones who found your grandmother's journals."

"That's right," she said with a smile.

"You won't eat it yourself?" he teased.

"I'd love to. But I can't put on any more weight," she said with a sigh.

"You know that never bothered me, Valerie. I'm not that type of man," he said seriously.

"I know," she said, thinking of how he'd never made her feel ashamed of her recent weight gain. It was true; he wasn't that type of man.

They spoke for a few more minutes and when they hung up, she was smiling. For the first time since she'd left, she missed him. She really missed him. And she kind of wished he were there to celebrate with her.

The following day, a dozen long-stemmed roses arrived, surprising her. She pulled the card out of the florist's envelope.

"Congratulations. I'm proud of you. Love, Jeff."

Ohhh.

She put the roses in a vase full of water and set them down on a table where she could look at them all the time.

She picked up her phone to text him and then thought better of it. If he could go to all that trouble to send her flowers, then at the very least, he deserved a phone call. He picked up on the second ring.

"Hey."

"Your beautiful flowers have arrived, and I wanted to call you right away and thank you," she gushed. "They made my day." It was amazing what a thoughtful gesture could do to improve your mood.

"Good. I know how important this is to you. I'm trying to be supportive."

"That's wonderful. I appreciate it. But can I ask what brought this on?"

He hesitated and sighed. "After you were gone, I started thinking about what you said to me and why you left. I've been seeing a marriage counselor by myself for the last several months."

This floored Valerie. She stood there with her mouth hanging open for a moment. Recovering, she asked, "You have?"

"Yeah."

"Wow. I don't know what to say."

"You don't have to say anything. But know that I'm willing to try again."

"All right." She felt buoyed by this recent development. They spoke for a few more minutes and before they hung up, she promised to call him the following day.

As she moved from room to room in the house, she brought the vase of flowers with her, setting them on a table or dresser so they were always in view. It was such an unexpected gesture from her husband that she couldn't help basking in the glow of it.

Eventually, she settled down, fixed her hair, applied some light makeup, and walked over to the Monroe house. She hoped she'd find the sisters at home or at least one of them.

The air was heavy: warm and oppressive. The ten-minute walk to the Monroes' left her feeling clammy. Lily and Alice sat on the front porch, dressed in summer dresses. Alice's went to her thighs and had cap sleeves, while Lily's fell to her ankles and had spaghetti straps. As she walked up the driveway to the front porch, Lily and Alice waved at her. As Val stepped up onto the porch, the dog, Charlie, jumped up so fast he frightened himself. Lily reached out to pet him and reassure him.

"Come and take a seat," Alice invited.

"Thank you."

She handed the box over to Lily, who regarded it with a raised eyebrow and then broke into a smile. "Is this what I think it is?" She showed the glossy white box to Alice.

"It is. It's my first batch and I wanted you to have it. I hope it meets with your approval."

It would be a lie to say she wasn't in possession of some anxiety that they might not like her chocolate. But even if they didn't, she knew they'd be kind about it.

"I see you've named your business after your grandmother," Alice said, referring to the embossed logo that read "Delphine's Chocolates."

"It seemed . . . fitting."

Lily removed the top of the box and surveyed the perfect little candies inside. She looked up at Valerie. "Are they different flavors?"

"Right now, I only have four: caramel, strawberry cream, raspberry truffle, and cherry amaretto truffle."

Alice's eyes widened. "Lucky us."

Lily chose first and handed the box to Alice. Both chewed thoughtfully as Valerie waited, biting her lip. She held her breath. When both women closed their eyes and sighed, she relaxed.

"Wow," Lily said softly, helping herself to another one. Alice followed suit.

"These are amazing, Valerie," Alice said.

After finishing their second piece, they each took a third. Lily promptly put the lid on the box and set it aside.

"We better save some for Isabelle."

"But if we eat the whole box before she gets home, she'll never know it was here." There was a sparkle of mischief in Alice's eyes.

Lily's grin was also roguish. "Alice Monroe, you are strictly devious."

Valerie left their house, her head a little higher and her mind a little clearer. The sisters' show of enthusiasm had boosted her spirits, and she headed home to her kitchen to do more experimenting. The next flavor she wanted to play around with was chai. A spark of inspiration had hit her as she sipped her chai tea the previous night, loving the combination of cardamom, ginger, cloves, and cinnamon. Immediately, she'd opened her notebook and begun making notes on how to make a chai flavored chocolate truffle. This one excited her because it was not one from the recipe book, it was one she would create herself. It didn't bother her that she might come up with the perfect flavor in one day or in a month, it was all about the process.

As she walked home, she thought that was one of the prime directives of family business, to keep going on, staying true to its heritage but also evolving at the same time. When she worked in her kitchen, she felt as if her grandmother's spirit was hovering, pushing her along, encouraging her. Just as she had done when she was alive, and Valerie was a little girl.

Valerie had spent three days experimenting with perfecting a chai flavored chocolate candy. The kitchen was a mess, and measuring cups and bowls were scattered across the countertops and piled high in the sink. There were three different batches of chai chocolate on the table, and the results were encouraging. It wasn't quite where she wanted it, but she was getting close. She was debating whether it needed more cardamon or maybe a tiny hint of nutmeg. Or maybe both. That would be three more separate batches.

A knock at the front door startled her.

Her hair was clipped up haphazardly. Her apron was stained with smears of chocolate, and she looked around the state of her kitchen and groaned. Hopefully, whoever it was could remain outside.

Her heart sank a tiny little bit when she spotted Alice and her fiancé, Jack, standing on her porch. There was no way she couldn't invite them in.

"Hey," she said, opening the door.

"Is this a bad time?" Alice asked.

"Because we can come back another time," Jack chimed in.

Valerie held the door open wide and waved them in. "No, not at all. I was in the middle of a break."

They followed her in.

"We should have called," Alice said as she and Jack looked around the disaster that was Val's kitchen.

Valerie was profuse with her apologies. Her cheeks went hot as she realized it looked even worse than she'd thought, if the expressions on their faces were anything to go by.

"I was doing some experimenting."

"Don't apologize," Alice insisted.

Jack looked at Alice and teased, "It looks exactly like your kitchen when you're baking."

Playfully, she nudged him in the ribs with her elbow. It reminded Valerie of how she and Jeff used to be when they were first married: that playful, teasing, flirty banter. She missed that. Hopefully, it would last forever with Alice and Jack. They were such a lovely couple.

Both their gazes landed on the table full of chocolates.

"I'm trying to make a chai flavored chocolate," Val explained.

"Ooh," Alice said. "That sounds yummy."

Jack looked at Alice and laughed.

"Would you like to try one?" Valerie asked tentatively. "Maybe you could give me your opinion."

Alice did not hesitate. "I would love to."

The three of them stood at the table. Valerie pointed to one of the batches. "This is the best of the bunch by far. Try one."

Alice and Jack picked a chocolate off the rack and popped it into their mouths.

"That's nice chocolate," Jack announced. Since she'd spent more time in Hideaway Bay meeting people, Val had learned that Jack was often referred to as "the Colonel" in recognition of his service to the armed forces and his rank when he'd retired after more than twenty years.

"I'm still trying to find the right mix of spices, particularly the cardamon and the nutmeg," Val said. Maybe she needed another opinion.

"Let me try one more to get a better sense," Alice said, helping herself to a second piece. As she let it melt on her tongue, she looked up to the side, appearing thoughtful. Finally, she put up her hand, her thumb and forefinger almost touching. Narrowing her eyes, she said, "Just a pinch more of cardamom and maybe a little tiny bit of nutmeg."

"Ah, thank you. That helps." Valerie's smile was profuse.

Alice eyed the chocolate as she spoke, and Valerie wondered if she'd go for a third piece. Finally, she dragged her eyes away from the table and Jack grinned, bemused.

"You're probably wondering why we've stopped," Alice said.

"There is a reason for our visit," Jack added.

"But boy, were we happily sidetracked." Alice glanced toward the chocolate again. She looked up at Valerie. "We were wondering if you could make the favors for our wedding."

"Really?" Valerie was unable to hide her surprise. That was quickly replaced by excitement. "What were you thinking of?"

"A small box of chocolates, say maybe four or six," Alice explained. "In a neat little box and tied up with ribbon that matches the theme color of the wedding."

"Okay." Valerie's mind went into overdrive. "What is the color?"

Alice grimaced. "I can't decide between sage and lavender."

"Either color would suit your hair coloring," Valerie said with a nod toward Alice's abundant mane of vibrant red curly hair.

"No one ever says if sage or lavender would suit me," Jack teased.

Alice looked up at him and laughed. "Oh you! Any color would suit you."

"When is the wedding?"

"Next September. I wanted to have it in the summer, but it's too hot and I don't want to be sweating."

"Nobody wants to look at a sweaty bride," Jack joked.

"Stop!" Alice said with a laugh.

"September's usually a beautiful month. At least it is in Colorado."

"It is here as well."

"How many guests?"

Here they looked at each other and laughed. "Almost three hundred. We keep trying to pare it down, but there are some people we can't not invite." Alice's brow furrowed.

Valerie's mind started doing some math, and she wished she had commercial premises to do this kind of project. It was one of her goals for the future, but it was not in the immediate future. There were thirteen months until their wedding, so she had time. She'd have to wade through all the rules and regulations of starting up a food business in New York State.

It also dawned on her that she was almost halfway through her six-month lease, and she hadn't even thought of leaving Hideaway Bay. Now, if she took this project for their wedding, it committed her to staying.

"Do you know how much you'd charge?" Jack asked.

"I couldn't give you a figure right now, I'd need to work it out."

"That's not a problem. Let us know. But would you be interested?" Alice asked.

"Yes, definitely. Thank you for thinking of me."

When they left, Valerie threw a fist pump in the air and shouted, "Yes!"

CHAPTER THIRTY-NINE

AFTER ANOTHER WEEK OF experimenting, she'd perfected the chai chocolate combo. At present, she was going through the family recipe book, deciding on the next flavor. It was a toss-up between almond and buttercream. As it was, she was leaning toward the almond to balance out the flavors she already had. It wouldn't serve her to rush, she was going to take her time perfecting each one.

She'd filled out a registration form for the New York State Agriculture and Markets about selling her chocolate. She was currently looking for premises as she had to have a separate kitchen. And she had an appointment with the local Department of Health to see what the rules and regulations were.

Quickly she developed her routine. First thing when she woke up, whether it be at the crack of dawn or later in the morning if she'd been up all night, she'd go for a walk on the beach. Gradually, she was increasing her steps, her goal being a mile. She found if she pushed herself and walked farther, she tended to sleep better that night. Once that was done, she returned home and got straight to work, stopping only for a break of tea and a sandwich, doing any errands that needed to be done, and then getting right back to it in the evening.

Mondays were her day off. Taking a page from someone she'd spied on the beach during her early days in Hideaway Bay, she'd bought a beach chair on Amazon and liked to prop it up at the shore, stretching her legs out in front of her and letting the water wash over them. Weekdays tended to be less crowded than the weekends, which was why she chose to work straight through them.

Every evening, she spoke to Jeff, and at least once a week, she spoke on the phone to Jeremy and Renee. But she did text them every day. Renee had insisted on seeing pictures of her creations, sending texts of support and encouragement. Jeremy responded all the time with "Looks good." No matter what happened between her and Jeff, their children had turned out to be good people. She was proud of that.

She'd formed a nice friendship with Della and Sue Ann as they were around her age. And every so often, she met up with them for lunch or dinner.

She supposed she missed Jeff and what could have been. But she reminded herself that her marriage hadn't been so great when she left. It was easy to golden-plate the past, being so far away and with time as a buffer, but she needed to be real about it.

By this time, she knew she'd never return to Colorado. Maybe to visit friends and family, but not to live there full time. But before she made any decisions about settling permanently in Hideaway Bay, she wanted to get through one winter there. She expected it to be bleak, but she hoped the community remained vibrant through the colder months.

The sun was getting too hot, and Valerie stood from her chair, removing her wide-brimmed hat and pushing her hair back. Her hair was damp with sweat, and she slapped the hat back on her head. Once she gathered all her belongings, she walked off in the direction of home, with the chair tucked neatly beneath her arm. It wasn't more than a fifteen-minute walk, and she thought she'd shower and figure out what to do with the rest of her day. She planned on going up to the fruit-and-veg stand to get some fresh produce and then maybe over to Cabana Sally's for a late lunch. They had a nice deck that overlooked the lake, and she thought she might want to sit outside. It sounded like a good plan for her day off.

As she rounded the corner of her street, she spotted someone sitting on her front porch. She was too far yet to make out if it was someone familiar. Had she forgotten an appointment? If she didn't write things down, she tended to forget. The problem was remembering to write things down. As she neared the house, she immediately recognized the car.

Jeff.

She stopped in her tracks, the beach chair still under her arm, and stared at him, gape-jawed.

What was he doing here? And how long was he here for?

It dawned on her that her carefully constructed life here in Hideaway Bay was not dependent on her husband or his presence. She didn't know what to make of that.

He'd spotted her and put up his hand in a wave.

When she saw him standing there, after so many months away, there was an initial surge of joy to see him again, mixed with a sense of uncertainty.

"Hello, stranger," she said.

"Valerie."

He looked good. He had some color and didn't look as pasty as when she'd last seen him.

She set the beach chair down so that it leaned against her leg. He stepped forward to hug her as she leaned in to hug him, and they bumped heads. The hug was awkward. They were out of practice.

"It's good to see you," he said, giving her an extra squeeze.

"And you," she said lightly.

When they pulled apart, she asked, "Were you waiting long?"

He shrugged. "About half an hour."

"I'm so sorry. If I had known . . ."

"I wanted to surprise you."

"Consider me surprised," she said with a laugh.

"I tried calling."

"I was down at the beach and sometimes with all the noise, I can't hear it ringing in my purse." She held up her straw beach bag to show him.

He nodded.

"Come on in. Let me get you something to drink," she said. She picked up the beach chair and immediately Jeff reached out for it.

"I can carry that."

She'd forgotten about that. How he always jumped in to pick things up for her or carry stuff for her. In the months since she'd last seen him, she'd gotten used to doing things by herself.

As she unlocked her side door, she said over her shoulder, "You look good. You've got some color."

"I've taken up golf."

The door swung open, but Valerie didn't move forward. She stopped and turned and looked at her husband. "Really?" She was unable to hide her surprise.

He laughed when he saw her expression. "Yes, really."

"Why?" This was not the Jeff she knew.

With a chuckle, he scratched the back of his head. "It's a long story."

"Can't wait to hear it." She stepped into her house, followed by her husband.

Once inside, she gave him a quick tour. "It's not that big, but for right now it's perfect."

He nodded, keeping any comments to himself.

They ended up in the kitchen. "And this is where I make all the chocolate."

"Where the magic happens," he said, his gaze sweeping the room.

She liked that comment and tucked it away for future reference. She pulled two tall glasses from the cabinet and filled them with ice and iced tea, handing one to Jeff.

They sat at the kitchen table and Valerie removed her hat, setting it on the table but out of the way.

"How long are you here for?" She wanted to ask where he was staying, but she couldn't. Did he expect to stay with her? She felt nervous, like it was a first date or something.

"I don't know. I guess that depends on you and us. I think it's time we sat down and talked. We can't keep our marriage in limbo like this."

"I agree," she said. She supposed this conversation had to happen sooner or later. And it could only be done in person. Something as important and serious as this could not be done over the phone.

As a gesture, she said, "You can stay here. I have a spare room."

"I appreciate that, but I've booked a room at the Highway Hotel." He hesitated before adding, "I didn't want to pressure you."

She tilted her head to the side. "I appreciate that."

They were silent for a beat. "I've stayed there," she said. "It's a little dated, but it is clean."

"I saw that when I checked in." His smile was full of mirth.

"This town could really use a B & B," she said.

"Definitely. There were a few Airbnb's and a couple of summer rentals, but they were all booked."

"That time of year," she said.

Jeff nodded, looking around the place. Val wondered how it looked through his eyes. Was he comparing it to their home in Colorado? She knew her rented accommodation wasn't much and it certainly was dated, but it had suited her.

"Why don't we go out for lunch," Valerie suggested. "And we can discuss things. But I need to take a shower first."

"That sounds great. I can't wait to hear all about your business and how it's going."

"It will probably take me a half an hour to get ready."

With a grin, he said, "You mean forty-five minutes."

She smiled and nodded. "I guess I do mean that."

"I've boxed up all your candy-making supplies that were on the top shelf of the pantry. I'll bring them in for you."

She was touched by the gesture. "Thank you, I appreciate it."

"Look, take your time getting ready. I thought I might take a walk into town and check the place out."

"That's a great idea. Go to the end of the street and make a right onto Erie and take it to the end. You'll see the beach ahead and the town to your left."

"That's what I'll do then."

"Why don't I pick you up when I'm ready? I'll find you," she said.

"That's great. I'll move my car out of your driveway and park on the street."

Before he left, he carried in a large cardboard box full of supplies and set it on one of the kitchen chairs. She'd look through that later. It impressed her that he'd had the presence of mind to gather them up and bring them with him.

After he'd gone, Valerie stood there for a moment, examining how she felt. How did she feel? She was relieved that she wasn't annoyed or irritated at his surprise visit. In fact, she was looking forward to going to lunch with him and sitting out on the deck of Cabana Sally's in the sunshine. It kind of felt like a date.

And maybe it was a step in the right direction.

Jeff had been right. It did take Val forty-five minutes to get ready. She washed and did her hair and applied some light day coverage and some mascara and lipstick. It really was starting to feel like a date, even if it was with her husband.

She drove slowly through town, trying to spot Jeff. There he was, coming out of the Hideaway Bay Olive Oil Shop. He took a step back and looked up at the awning and then stepped closer to read some kind of flyer posted in the window. There was a vacant space in front of the five-and-dime, and she pulled in. When he spotted her, he waved.

Val got out of the car, clicked the fob until she heard the familiar beep that told her it was locked, and said over the roof of the car, "We're going right over there. Cabana Sally's." She half turned and pointed toward the two-story building on the other side, almost at the end of Main Street.

His glance followed her finger and he nodded. "Looks good."

He joined her on her side of the car and together they crossed the street.

"It's a really nice little town," he said as they strolled side by side along Main Street. As they went, he peeked into the shop windows.

"Who knew you could make a living selling olive oil." He shook his head.

"That's a busy little shop."

When they arrived at Cabana Sally's, the hostess informed them that all the tables outside were full.

"How long is the wait?" Valerie asked.

"Twenty minutes."

Val looked at Jeff. He shrugged and said, "I don't mind waiting. It's not like we have anywhere to be."

"All right, we'll wait," Val said.

The hostess handed her a pager and smiled. "You know the drill."

"I do."

"There are benches outside on the beach if you'd like to wait there," the hostess informed Jeff.

"Sounds good." Jeff turned to Val. "How about we get a drink at the bar and go sit outside."

"Perfect."

At the bar, Jeff turned and asked her what she'd like to drink. He pulled out his wallet from his back pocket and ordered a piña colada for Valerie and a bottle of beer for himself.

He currently sported a sage-green polo shirt and a pair of navy shorts with topsiders. She couldn't believe how tan he was. It was almost like a transformation. She couldn't wait to hear all about it.

They carried their drinks outside, walked through the occupied tables, and took the small set of stairs at the other end of the patio down onto the beach. There was a small grouping of benches that faced the lake. Currently two were unoccupied. Valerie chose the one closest to the patio.

She set the pager between them on the bench. Her glass was sweating profusely in her hands. Jeff crossed his ankle over his knee and leaned back, his left arm draped over the back of the bench.

"Wow, that's some scenery," he said with a glance toward the lake.

"I know, right?" Even though she'd only been there a few months, she never grew tired of looking at it or listening to it.

They sat in silence for a few moments. Valerie sipped her drink slowly, enjoying the taste of coconut and rum.

Curious, she asked, "So tell me. What's been going on since I left?"

Jeff didn't answer right away. He continued to stare at the lake. "After you left, I was really angry at you. Enraged is a better word."

Valerie went to say something, but he held up his hand. "Let me finish."

"Sorry."

He turned to her and grinned. "I'm used to it. You've been interrupting me for almost thirty years."

Valerie couldn't help but wince. She hadn't realized that.

"Anyway, like I said, I was furious when you left. For a few days, I practically saw red. I couldn't understand how you could abandon me, us, our marriage."

She flinched at his use of the word "abandon."

"Once I settled down and got over my initial shock and anger, I realized you must have been deeply unhappy to make such a bold move like that."

This admission by Jeff and the truth behind it made Val's chin quiver, her emotions skating just below the surface.

"I began to take a long, hard look at my life, at our marriage." His voice was quiet as he spoke. With a sigh, he said, "And I saw that you were right."

Valerie remained silent, waiting for him to continue.

"You were right," he said again. "I was in a rut. Our marriage was in a rut, and you were in a rut."

"The rut was pretty crowded," Valerie teased.

Jeff let out a bark of laughter. "Yeah, I guess it was. Anyway, I realized that all I did was work and then come home and sit around watching TV. I didn't even like myself. I can understand why you left."

Valerie sighed. "I didn't leave because of you personally."

"I know that."

The pager vibrated noisily to life between them.

"That's us. Hold your next thought until we get to our table."

"Will do."

Once the server seated them, she handed them menus and asked if they'd like another round of drinks. As she was driving, Valerie opted for water, and Jeff ordered a Diet Coke.

They decided to scan the menu and order before they picked up the trail of their conversation. The sunshine was bright, and they kept their sunglasses on.

Within five minutes, they'd made their choices. Valerie pretty much knew the menu by heart and had no trouble deciding. Neither did Jeff.

The server brought their drinks and took their orders, and they resumed their conversation.

"Once I got over my disbelief and rage that you'd actually left, I was angry at myself," Jeff started. "Angry that I was wasting my life working and watching television. Angry that I had no life." He looked over at Valerie and said, "And if I was honest with myself, I'd agree that our marriage was suffering. That we were merely co-existing under one roof."

"We're both to blame for that. You weren't alone in that rut. Neither one of us wants to simply co-exist."

"No."

"After Jeremy and Renee left, it was like our main roles of parenting were over, and we had identified so much as parents that I no longer knew who we were as a couple," she said.

"Maybe we didn't take care of our marriage as we should have," he said.

This was a surprising comment from Jeff, and Valerie said so.

"So that's why I went to marriage counseling." He appeared sheepish and cleared his throat.

"I can't believe it." Her shock must have registered on her face, because he laughed.

He sighed. "I figured if I wanted you back and wanted to save our marriage, then it would require counseling. It wasn't something I could do without outside help."

"That's encouraging," she said.

"I've learned a lot." He folded his hands on the table. "It's been eye-opening to say the least."

"Is that why you started golfing?"

He shrugged, tilting his head one way and then another. "I was encouraged to explore outside interests. So I thought I'd give golf a try. I wanted to see what the big deal was."

"And?"

"It's a big deal. It's highly addictive. I golf one afternoon a week and one day on the weekend." He launched into a tale of golfing, his handicap, and the courses he'd played on back home. Valerie listened with interest, happy to see her husband finding an outside interest that he was passionate about and that didn't involve a television.

"Anyway, I came out to Hideaway Bay to see if you would give our marriage a second chance."

She opened her mouth and then closed it. When she'd first arrived, she'd been angry with Jeff. But then she got busy making chocolate and the anger evaporated, to be replaced with a sense that she might have to go on without him. But now, here he was, sitting in front of her, making an effort. Was it too late? Even though they had a lot of time invested, almost thirty years, she no longer felt that fact alone necessitated staying. It was possible that two people could grow apart and in different ways along the course of a lengthy marriage. Did she want to give their marriage a second chance? And most importantly, did she still love Jeff?

Before she could respond, the server appeared with their orders.

Jeff had ordered the steak sandwich and it was placed before him, fine strips of steak on a hoagie roll with melted provolone, grilled onions, and red and green peppers. Valerie had ordered a chicken Caesar salad. A dish they were sharing, a blooming onion, was placed in the center between them.

"Everything looks good," Jeff said, scanning the plates on the table.

He inspected his sandwich, approaching it from all angles and finally picking it up gingerly before taking a bite of it.

"I'm impressed that you're going to marriage counseling," Valerie said. "But I can't go back to the way it was before."

He looked up from his sandwich, swallowed his mouthful, and said, "Neither can I."

She nodded and cut up some salad, spearing it with a piece of chicken before popping it into her mouth. She chewed thoughtfully for a moment before going on. Did she share her dream with him, or would he stomp all over it? She didn't want or need any negative energy around her when she was trying to establish herself. How she wanted to share it with someone. She didn't want to keep it all to herself. She wanted it out in the world.

"I'm serious about the chocolate. About turning it into a business. It's not a hobby, Jeff. It's going to be my new career."

"I know you're serious. I can hear it in your voice when you talk about it over the phone."

"I need to know that you would be supportive in that endeavor."

"Sure. It's a big undertaking. Are you going to continue out of your kitchen?"

She shook her head. "I can't. I'm currently looking for commercial premises. Rules and regulations and all that."

"I can help you look for something suitable."

"You'd do that?" she asked, unable to hide her surprise.

"Of course. I'd like to help."

"I was hoping to get something here in Hideaway Bay."

"It's a nice little town. It would be perfect for that."

Did he not understand? Feeling a bit uneasy, she said, "It means, Jeff, that I won't be returning to Colorado."

"I know. But is there room for me here?" He looked deliberately at her, his gaze never wavering.

"You want to come to Hideaway Bay? Move here?" she asked, incredulous.

"Yes," he said firmly. "What are you not getting, Val? I don't want a divorce. I love you and I want to make our marriage better. Stronger. I will support you in this business."

Doubts still niggled at her. "What about your job? Our house?"

"Valerie, I've been at that job a long time. I've learned a lot. And I think I can work anywhere. I'm nearing retirement." He took a sip of his Coke and said, "And who knows, maybe you could find a place for me in your business."

Valerie blinked. "You'd want to do that? Work with me?"

"Yeah, sure, why not? I'm no chocolatier but I could do other things. Anything involving IT, like setting up a website. I could do the books." He shrugged and said, "Maybe sourcing the best supplies. Helping you pack boxes. Handing out flyers—"

She put up her hand and laughed. "All right, I get it. But what about the house? Our friends and family?"

"I'll go back, put the house on the market, and pack up. We can't worry about our family and friends. Our parents are gone, and Jeremy and Renee have left, so we're free to go anywhere we want." He paused and added with a chuckle, "Although I wish you had picked Florida."

"Sorry," she said with a wince.

"People move all the time." He pushed his plate away and leaned back in the chair. "But the question is, do you want me to move to Hideaway Bay. Since I've arrived you haven't given me any indication that you want the marriage to go on."

"I know. Your arrival caught me off guard."

"I wanted to surprise you."

"I like everything you've said: moving here, helping with the business, but I think we should go to marriage counseling together."

"I'm already a veteran of it, but I agree that going together as a couple is a good idea."

Her smile was shaky, but she said a little breathlessly, "It's a deal. Let's do this."

He surprised her by standing up and coming around to her, wrapping an arm around her shoulder and kissing her on the lips. "I love you, Val," he whispered.

Overcome, she nodded, tears filling her eyes, and patted his hand on her shoulder. "I love you too, Jeff."

As they departed Cabana Sally's, he asked, "Is there a golf course around here?"

Valerie nodded and pointed south along the shore. "There is one over there, up along the cliffs." It was also where the million-dollar houses were.

"I'll have to check it out."

She hoped he would. "Does this mean I'm going to be a golf widow?" she teased.

He winked at her. "I'll try to work it around you." He wrapped his arm around her shoulders and gave her a squeeze. "Come on, Val, why don't you show me around town."

CHAPTER FORTY

JEFF WAS STAYING IN town for another week. In the first few days, they searched around for a marriage counselor, found one, and set up an appointment. Jeff played a round of golf up at the Hideaway Bay Golf Club over on the cliffs and was impressed, commenting that he could get used to playing there regularly. By day three, Valerie invited him to come and stay at the house with her, so he checked out of the Highway Hotel and brought over his things. And there was no sense in him sleeping in the spare bedroom if they were going to try and work on their marriage. How would they do that from different bedrooms?

Valerie got ready for bed on their first night together, her anxiety climbing. She washed her face and brushed her teeth and pulled on a light cotton nightgown. Jeff was down to his boxers and a T-shirt, his usual night wear.

Once he climbed into bed on his usual side, the right side, Valerie flipped off the switch at the wall, and the room was blanketed in darkness. She made it to the bed and sat on the edge, the mattress sinking beneath her.

Jeff reached over and caressed her arm.

"I'm not ready for that," she said over her shoulder. "To resume things, I mean."

"Okay," was his whispered response. But then with a joking laugh, he asked, "Do you know when you will be?"

"I don't know," she said honestly. "I'd like it to happen naturally."

"Okay."

Relieved, she spun around and lifted her legs up onto the bed, pulling the sheet over her. It was too hot for a blanket. When her head hit the pillow, she sighed.

Jeff spoke in the darkness. "I suppose you're going to need a lot of help making all the chocolates for that wedding."

"I will. I'm nervous about that. It's my first big order."

"I'm not nervous for you at all," he said.

"You're not?"

"No, that chocolate is out of this world."

"Thank you, but I've got to whip up three hundred favor boxes."

"Valerie, let me remind you that at the age of forty-nine, you packed up your bags, drove clear across the country, and started a new life in Hideaway Bay." He paused and added, "If you can do that, you can do anything."

They spoke for a few more minutes, their hushed tones making her drowsy.

She'd forgotten that: the whispered conversation at bedtime as they fell asleep. She hadn't realized how much she'd missed it, the intimacy of it.

"Can I hold your hand?" he asked.

Valerie did not miss the hesitancy in his voice. "Yes, you can," she said. She pulled her hand out from beneath the sheet and laid it on top. Jeff reached over for her hand and laced his fingers through hers.

She smiled in the dark.

Jeff returned to Colorado, hired a moving company, and packed up their things and put their house on the market. He'd given his company a month's notice, and they'd turned around and counter-offered, proposing that he work remotely at reduced hours. This was preferable to Jeff. He still had his job but would also have extra time to help Valerie with her business.

When he returned, they began to look in earnest for a house. They knew they definitely wanted something right in Hideaway Bay. Valerie needed to be within walking distance of the beach.

Jeff devoted his free time to looking for suitable commercial premises for the chocolate shop, always reassuring Val that something would come up. It was nice for her to let someone else worry about those things while she focused on the actual chocolate making. She practiced, creating a lot of chocolate and boxing it up. She gave it away to the Monroes, Gus, Thelma, Della, Sue Ann, Viv at the hotel and Lottie Prescott and anyone else who crossed her path since she'd arrived in Hideaway Bay. And the feedback had been unanimous: her chocolate candy was a hit.

Valerie sat at the kitchen table, piping strawberry cream into chocolate candy. She knew Mrs. Cotter to be fond of these and had planned on giving her a box later.

Jeff arrived in the kitchen and looked at all the chocolate. "Do you have an extra box? Assorted?"

Valerie joked, "I've got more chocolate than I know what to do with. Why?"

"I've got an idea."

"Care to share it with me?"

He grinned, leaned in and kissed her cheek. "Not yet. Let me see if it pans out first."

She smiled at him. "Okay. There's two boxes of assorted in the spare room. They're labeled."

He grabbed a box and headed out. "I won't be long."

She nodded and went back to piping.

Jeff was right. He wasn't gone long. Val had finished the chocolates and was currently in the process of cleaning up. Her husband was all smiles when he stepped into the kitchen.

She paused from loading the dishwasher and tilted her head. "What's up with you?"

"I've got you commercial premises," he said.

"What?"

"And it's right on Main Street."

"Stop it!" Excited, she went over all the shops on Main Street in her mind, wondering where it could be.

He laughed.

"Come on, Jeff, tell me. Don't keep me in suspense."

"I went to talk to Thelma Schumacher. And I asked her if we could lease or buy the Old Red Top."

Valerie blinked. Stunned. "And she said yes?"

"The box of candy helped," he teased. "No, but seriously, when I approached her about it, told her that you—"

Valerie interrupted him. "We."

"That we were looking around for a commercial location, she thought about it for a minute, and—"

"And she said yes?" Val was still shocked.

"She did. She said it was time to let it go. That it's what her husband, Stanley, would have wanted. To see a new business in there."

"Wow, now what?"

"She's going to meet with her attorney and then come back to us with more details next week. But in the meantime, she'll meet us there tomorrow to give us a tour of the place."

"That's wonderful." She paused. "But can we afford it?"

"I've thought about that too. We'll have the proceeds from the sale of the house and if we have to, we can dip into our savings."

"Plus, I still have some of my severance pay."

Val abandoned the dishwasher, moved closer to Jeff, and wrapped her arms around him. "Thank-you so much."

"You're welcome." He held her close, and they stayed like that for a moment.

She couldn't believe it. Things were happening and moving in the right direction.

She looked at Jeff with gratitude. He'd really gone above and beyond.

The counseling was going well, and she was excited about this new phase in their marriage. Without the constant demands of parenting, they were able to laser focus their concentration on their relationship and each other. They were going away for the weekend, driving up to Toronto for a little getaway, and she didn't know if she was more excited about the actual trip and taking a break from work or the fact that it had been Jeff's idea. Either way, she was looking forward to it.

She closed the door to the dishwasher and turned it on. Without looking at him, she said, "It looks like a nice day for golf."

He glanced out the window. "It does."

"There won't be too many days left before winter sets in."

"I know."

What he didn't know was that she'd already purchased a golf vacation for him for January in Florida. She couldn't wait for him to open it on Christmas Day.

He made no moves to leave. She set the bag down and said, "Will you go out and go golfing? You've got the whole afternoon."

"But don't you need me here?" he asked, clearly torn.

"I do, but there's nothing that can't wait until tomorrow."

"Are you sure?" There was hesitancy in his voice.

"I am, now go," she said with a laugh, making a shooing motion with her hand.

"Okay, I will. Dinner later? At Cabana Sally's?"

She nodded. "That sounds wonderful." He knew how much she hated cooking.

He laid his hand on her shoulder and kissed her goodbye. She was smiling as he kissed her.

"Okay, then, I'll see you later."

"Enjoy."

"It's golf. Of course I will."

EPILOGUE

9 months later . . .

"ARE YOU READY?" JEFF asked with a grin.

Val clasped her hands against her lips as if in prayer and nodded, closed her eyes, and thought about Nana.

A small crowd had gathered on the sidewalk in front of the building formerly known as the Old Red Top. For the past six months, renovations had been taking place turning it into a purpose-fit building, and today was the official opening.

Val couldn't quite believe it was happening.

She stepped forward and stood next to Jeff, facing the small crowd that had gathered around them. He reached over, took her hand, gave it a gentle squeeze, and winked.

A year ago, these faces would have been strangers, but now she counted them as friends. The Monroe sisters were front and center. Next to them was Thelma. They'd taken her on a private tour two days ago and she'd shed a tear or two, saying how wonderful it looked and how happy Stan would have been. On the other side of the sisters stood Della Rossi and Sue Ann Marchek. She spotted Martha Cotter and her granddaughter, Mimi. And standing tall out in the back was Baddie Moore. Ben and Tom Anderson were there, and so was Jackie Arnold with her daughter and her parents. The sea of faces was smiling, and her heart felt ready to burst with gratitude.

But there were two people she wanted up front with her and Jeff for the big grand opening.

She waved Jeremy and Renee over to join them. Both were full of smiles.

Then she beckoned for Lola Duquesne, her very first employee. Someone who was trying to rebuild her life after her divorce. Alice Monroe had recommended her when Valerie mentioned she was looking to hire one employee. For now.

"Okay, Val, it's time," Jeff prompted.

She nodded.

"Speech," "Speech," came a resounding chorus.

"Oh, right," she said, her voice shaking. She hadn't prepared a speech, but she supposed she should say something.

"First of all, thank you all for joining us today at our grand opening. In a short period of time, Jeff and I have grown to love Hideaway Bay and our neighbors. I know I speak for both of us when I say we feel this town is a hidden gem. Thank you for opening your arms and hearts to us. And a special thank-you to Thelma Schumacher, who agreed to lease us the Old Red Top, which is right where we want our chocolate shop to be: in the heart of town. So, without further ado, I give you Delphine's Chocolates!"

With a flourish, she pulled the cord attached to the cream-colored drape above them, sliding it back to reveal the sign. Renee had created a modernized version of the logo on the old candy box Martha Cotter had given her when she'd first arrived in Hideaway Bay looking for information on her grandmother.

She looked up proudly at it. She wished Nana were there to see it. It felt like all her dreams had come true. And Renee's and Jeremy's presence, a surprise arranged by Jeff, was the icing on the cake.

"And one more thing," Jeff called out.

She smiled and nodded at him.

He cranked the brand-new awning down, revealing a striped canvas in cream and pale turquoise with the logo of Delphine's Chocolates centered over it.

It was beautiful.

There was more clapping and cheers.

Jeff handed Val the ceremonial scissors, and she used them to cut the large turquoise ribbon that was placed across the front door. The ribbon fell away, and she handed the scissors back to him. She opened the door and she, Jeff, and the kids stepped back to let the townspeople in first.

Her heart was in her throat, beating and drumming along with excitement.

Inside, surfaces gleamed, and chrome shone. There were display tables set up around the interior and a glass case that ran the length of the shop. They had preserved the shop's distinctive round domed ceiling, and it had been painted cream to match their color scheme.

Lola wore her brand-new apron over her clothes, in stripes to match the awning outside. Immediately, she stepped behind the counter and was joined by Renee, who also donned an apron.

Jeremy came up to Valerie and broke into a huge smile. As he engulfed her in a hug, towering over her, she thought back to when he was a toddler and used to wrap his arms so tightly around her neck. She smiled at the memory of it.

"Mom, I'm so proud of you," he said.

"Thanks, honey."

She and Jeff stood there, watching the store, which was now full of people, with pride. Together, they had realized a dream.

With tears in her eyes, she looked at Jeff. "Thank you for everything. I couldn't have done it without you."

He shrugged, sheepish. "I believe in you, Val."

She nodded quickly and wiped away an escaped tear. "I know."

He leaned into her and kissed her on her cheek. "Besides, we make a great team."

"That we do," she agreed heartily.

*****

To stay up to date and receive exclusive bonus material including a Hideaway Bay novella, you can sign up for my newsletter at www.michelebrouder.com

AFTERWORD

What a book this has been to write! In a rare instance, I had the entire book mapped out in my head before I even sat down to write it. That doesn't usually happen. The process is more a gradual discovery of both the character and the story. As it turns out, it's my longest book to date. And I probably could have written so much more.

Going in, I knew nothing about living in France during the Occupation and making chocolate (although I love chocolate in any form!) But there were a few books that I would highly recommend if you're interested in reading further. *Life Under Nazi Occupation: The Struggle to Survive During World War II* by Paul Roland, *The Unfree French: Life Under Occupation* by Richard Vinen. For the chocolate lovers there were *Chocolate for Beginners: Techniques and Recipes for Making Chocolate Candy, Confections, Cakes and More* by Kate Shaffer and *Encyclopedia of Chocolate: Essential Recipes and Techniques* by Frédéric Bau & Ecole du Grand Chocolate Valrhona

Any mistakes are solely mine.

ALSO BY MICHELE BROUDER

Hideaway Bay
Coming Home to Hideaway Bay
Meet Me at Sunrise
Moonlight and Promises
When We Were Young
One Last Thing Before I Go
The Chocolatier of Hideaway Bay
Now and Forever

The Lavender Bay Chronicles
The Inn at Lavender Bay
Lost and Found in Lavender Bay
Second Chances in Lavender Bay (Coming in September 2024)

Escape to Ireland
A Match Made in Ireland
Her Fake Irish Husband
Her Irish Inheritance
A Match for the Matchmaker
Home, Sweet Irish Home
An Irish Christmas

Happy Holidays
A Whyte Christmas
This Christmas
A Wish for Christmas
One Kiss for Christmas
A Wedding for Christmas
Audiobooks
Coming Home to Hideaway Bay
***All books available in ebook, paperback, and large print
paperback. Audiobooks coming soon.***